PENGUIN BOOKS

Juniper Lemon's
HAPPINESS INDEX

D0336135

ABOUT THE AUTHOR

Julie Israel did a lot of telling stories before she ever figured out how to write them: around the campfire, in grade-school parodies, at meals when she had to account for the peas that mysteriously vanished from her plate but did not end up in her stomach.

She didn't try writing a book until high school, and didn't finish one until after she had graduated college, taught English in Japan, tutored, written freelance, begun volunteering, and completed her first secret mission as a spy. Okay, she was never a spy. She's still telling tales. It's one of her favourite things to do from her native Portland, Oregon, where she really does enjoy making art, learning, and sometimes vegetables.

Juniper Lemon's Happiness Index is her first novel.

Follow Julie
@thatjulieisrael
www.julieisrael.wordpress.com
#JuniperLemon

Juniper Lemon's

HAPPINESS

INDEX

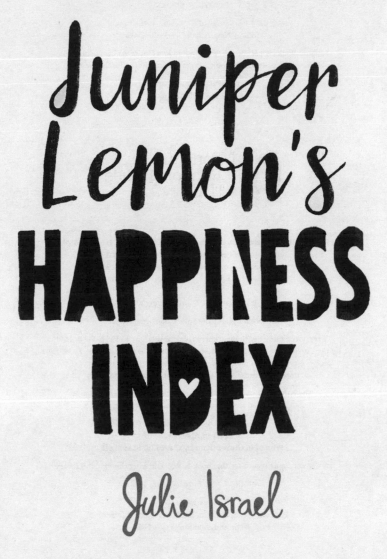

Julie Israel

PENGUIN BOOKS

PENGUIN BOOKS

UK | USA | Canada | Ireland | Australia
India | New Zealand | South Africa

Penguin Books is part of the Penguin Random House group of companies
whose addresses can be found at global.penguinrandomhouse.com.

www.penguin.co.uk
www.puffin.co.uk
www.ladybird.co.uk

First published in the United States of America by Kathy Dawson Books,
an imprint of Penguin Random House LLC, 2017
Published in Great Britain by Penguin Books 2017

001

Design by Jasmin Rubero
Text set in Apollo MT Pro
Printed in Great Britain by Clays Ltd, St Ives plc

A CIP catalogue record for this book is available from the British Library

ISBN: 978–0–141–37642–4

All correspondence to:
Penguin Books, Penguin Random House Children's
80 Strand, London WC2R 0RL

www.greenpenguin.co.uk

"and this is the wonder that's keeping the stars apart
i carry your heart(i carry it in my heart)"

—e.e. cummings

DAYS WITHOUT HER:

The girl in the picture doesn't look any different.

Things you see: brown eyes. Honey hair to the shoulders. Natural eyeliner.

Things you don't: stitches. A neck brace.

The sleep rings hidden beneath her makeup.

I lower my new student ID card. My throat is tight with all the changes I carry, but don't find there. Still, I'm grateful not to wear them like a flag on my forehead: *Ask me about my tragedy!*

There's talk enough without advertising.

Even as I stow the card and cross the cafeteria, I catch two girls sneaking glances at me from a nearby table.

Girl #1: "Do you think she saw it happen?"

Girl #2: "Uh, yeah? She was there."

Girl #1: "No, I mean—" (She lowers her voice.) "The *mo*ment when Camil—"

That's when Girl #2 knocks 1 in the ribs and 1 sees me watching, and both shut up and look quickly away, in opposite directions.

I scrunch Camilla's bag closer. It still smells faintly of her dark vanilla rose spray. I haven't used it all summer because I've wanted to preserve it, to keep its last little proofs of her intact, but today I had a feeling I would need it.

It's hard to keep close a person everyone keeps telling you is gone.

Whispers follow until I duck into an alcove beside the stairs. Alone at last at a tucked-away table, I cross "ID Card" off my Back-to-School Orientation List and resume doodling at the edges. Normally I'd have bounced from this fun house by now, but alas—today Dad had Plans. These involve me "hanging out" with my peers before class starts tomorrow, which is why he left me here to ~~die~~ socialize while he ran errands.

Great Plan, Dad.

I finish a garden of curls and accents around my name, and have just paused to add tallies to

PEOPLE CAUGHT STARING

|||| |||| |||| |||| |||

when a backpack crashes down into the chair across from me.

"Oh!" The redhead it belongs to startles when she sees me. "I—I didn't think anyone else would be here. Sorry." Fumbling, she yanks it up again to leave.

Is there someone here more flustered than I am?

"Wait! You don't have to—*Kody*?"

There are only so many people at this school with long red waves.

Called by name, she freezes and turns to face me. "Hi, Juniper."

Kody Hotchkiss. Now there's a girl who looks different. "Kody, you look—wow."

Kody smiles—modest, but clearly pleased. "Thanks. I . . . switched to contacts and started running this summer."

"It shows. I mean, not that you didn't look awesome before; you're lovely, you've always been—"

I stop before I can embarrass myself. Kody grins at my ineptness.

Maybe Dad had a point about that social practice.

"Seat's open if you want it." I gesture at the chair and Kody, still smiling, indulges me. I can't get over the change in her. Forget glasses or contacts; this Kody carries herself.

Confident.

"So," I prompt when she looks comfortable, "what brings you to my hiding place?"

Her smile falters. "Morgan."

I don't have to ask if she means Morgan Malloy: the school bus bully who turned "Hotchkiss" into "Hershey's Kiss" in middle school. There's no way she'd miss her old mark's transformation.

My eyes widen. "Did she . . . ?"

"No, it's just—" Kody closes a fist. "She was ahead of me in the picture line. I thought, if I hung out for a while—"

"Less chance of running into her at IDs?"

Kody nods.

"Well, you're welcome to lie low here with me."

A sigh. "Thanks."

Then: "Who're *you* hiding from?"

"What?"

"You said 'hiding place.' Who're you hiding from?"

Everyone. But mostly—

"Lauren." Lauren is my real fear today: that the one person I actually want to talk to doesn't want to talk to me. Maybe what I'm really hiding from is finding out. "You haven't seen her, have you?"

I shouldn't hold my breath; Lauren has a history of avoiding awkward situations. The last time she was dodging someone—a guy she only dated for a month because she didn't know how to break up with him—we spent weeks taking long ways at school and carrying scarves and sunglasses around for snap disguises.

It had actually been kind of fun then.

"No. But I'll help keep an eye out for her."

"Thanks."

This time, our smiles are sly. Conspiratorial.

Hiders in crime.

"So how long does it take our IDs to print, anyway?" She leans back, but her eyes flick to the table. "You look like you've been here a while."

"Hm?"

I follow her gaze to the doodles on my Orientation List.

"Oh—not that long. I already got mine. I've just been killing time until my ride gets here."

"Cool designs." She leans closer, inspecting something. "What are all these little notes in between?"

The tallies.

"Nothing," I say too quickly. I pull back the sheet before she can read *Number of times I've heard Camilla's name*: 21. *Number of times I've heard mine*: 17.

People who have offered condolences:

0.

"Oh," I cover, gathering my things, "I think I just felt my phone buzz. That's probably my dad. Do you mind?"

"Sure. I mean—" Kody composes herself. "I'll be fine. Don't let me keep you."

"I'll see you around. You really do look great," I add.

Even as I pass her, I feel terrible. Kody did nothing wrong.

I walk toward a row of vending machines, for once today not counting the stares. Would Camilla coming up be such a bad thing? Surely *every*one won't just shut down on me like Lauren has.

When I reach the Diet Coke machine, the least popular in the strip, I have no interest in actually buying a bottle—but I figure I should *look* like I'm considering something, so I get out my wallet and some bills.

"Could I trade you some change for—"

The voice beside me breaks off. I know before I turn that it belongs to—

"Lauren."

We both go cardboard. Lauren sees Camilla's purse on my shoulder and I see that she's holding her phone: not about to answer the text I sent her this morning, or one of the dozens I sent all summer for that matter, but playing Candy Crush.

Even Lauren—the friend who held my hand when I got my ears pierced, who took the fall for me when I dropped her sister's snow globe, who's surprised me with Juniper- and Lemon-flavored candies ever since Morgan called me Cough Drop in fourth grade—doesn't know how to talk to me anymore.

For several long, terrible moments nothing happens; we both just stand there looking at each other. Then a *really* weird thing happens.

"Heeey." Lauren shuffles the last two steps over and hugs me hello.

Oh god. This is worse than I imagined.

"How's it going, Juniper?"

How's it going?

How's it *GOING*?

"Good," I answer automatically. "You?"

A breathless nod. "Good."

We stare at each other. Time stretches painfully between us, a gulf of the dozen things we must both be thinking, but leave unsaid. Once it looks as though Lauren might say something, but then she presses her lips together so hard, I think she's cut off her air supply. Oh my god, is she actually turning blue?

WARNING WARNING

AWKWARDNESS AT CRITICAL LEVELS

Employ emergency exit strategies

I open my mouth to say something—"Better grab a free lanyard," "I have to use the bathroom," "YOU KNOW WHAT I THINK I LEFT THE STOVE ON"—but before I can fake a fire or an aneurysm, an actual miracle occurs:

My phone rings.

"That'll be my dad," I gush, gratefully pawing through my bag. "I should—"

Lauren nods. "Of course."

We stare a moment longer.

"I guess I'll . . . see you tomorrow," I finish lamely.

An overwarm smile. "Tomorrow."

I lift a hand goodbye. Lauren does the same, and after more impossibly long fake smiles I turn in mortification. Conversations ended gracefully today: two for two.

When I find my phone, I see the dollars I'm still holding and wince before answering.

"Hey Dad."

"There you are," says his voice in my ear. "I was beginning to think you might actually be having fun in there."

"Ha."

"I'm right out front, Juni. Can't miss me."

"Okay. See you in a minute."

I stash my phone in my jeans and put the money away. But this time, when I drop my wallet back, something crackles in the bottom of the bag. I pry it open to see what.

An envelope.

Curious, I pull it out. Then I nearly drop it, too, because when I turn it over, there are three things that I know in a heartbeat:

1) I didn't put this in the bag.
2) I am holding a letter.
3) I recognize the writing on the front, but not because it's mine.

Because it's hers.

The drive home is quiet. At first Dad asks me questions, but after having to repeat himself and receiving only grunted answers, he eases off, and the strip malls, front yards, and fir trees blur by in silence. Or what would be silence, if it didn't somehow magnify the ringing in my ears.

Once home, I make a beeline for the stairs. Not that Mom is stopping us to chat—even when she isn't "resting" these days, she's not particularly awake—but if I don't open that letter now, I'm gonna burst.

On the way to my room, I pass Camilla's. The door is shut. I don't know who shut it or when exactly. Is it easier this way? The closed door sort of gives the illusion that she is in there: on the phone, sleeping, playing guitar. That she'll be out in a few minutes for dinner, come downstairs to watch a movie, or barge unannounced into my room, plop down on my bed, and make me watch the latest bad lip-reading or stupid cat video.

Part of me likes that.

Part of me hates it.

Part of me is afraid of what I'd see if her door was open.

I hurry past and shut my own door behind me.

When it's closed, I rip the envelope from my purse.

You

it says, in Camie's buoyant, cursive bubbles.

Goose bumps.

I turn it over. It isn't sealed.

With shaking hands I remove a single, folded page and open it. At the top—

July 4

My throat closes.

The day it happened.

I sink onto my bed and read:

Dear You,

Brevity is the only way to deliver a sting, so here goes—

I've been thinking about what you said and I've decided that you're right: It would be better for both of us this way. I know I could handle the distance, but part of college, like you said, is opening yourself up to new experiences—and I'd be sealing myself off to those if I kept my heart in a jar for someone I left in high school.

Still, I hate, <u>hate</u> to think of this as a breakup letter, because I hate to think of this as an ending. It isn't an ending; it's the start of another chapter. I don't know what the future holds, but I do know that it doesn't change the past. It doesn't change what we've shared. Your life has touched mine: I'm a better person for having known you, loved you, and been loved by you—and wherever I am in the unknown ahead, you (in the pocket of my heart) will also be.

So call it an end, if you must, but I love you—today, yesterday, and always.

Yours,
Me

I lower the page. Cam was *seeing someone*. Is this what she couldn't tell me that night?

Is this what came between us at the end?

I read it again. And again, and again, and again. Clearly the letter was meant for someone else—but even so, I see "You" at the top and feel like parts of it are talking to me. *The future doesn't change the past. It doesn't change what we've shared. Your life has touched mine—*

I look up to quell the wave I feel rising in my chest. I can't keep doing this. *School* starts tomorrow. I can't just gallop off and bawl for an hour every time I remember Camilla: the way she piled her hair on top of her head to do her makeup, how she hummed when she did the dishes, or that she always ate cookie dough by the spoonful even after we'd added the eggs.

Suck it up.

I fall back against my bed and stare. It's just been in her bag this whole time. Waiting. I mean, I never thought to *look*; even this morning, when I swapped out Camie's wallet for mine, I just assumed that was all that was in there.

I hold the letter between me and the ceiling. She couldn't have meant to mail it; the envelope was open and unaddressed, much less stamped. There's barely even a recipient—just "You."

But who on earth is that?

The last guy Camie dated (well, clearly not, but the last guy I know about) was Shawn Parker, and they broke up more than a year ago. They'd remained friends—good enough for her to go to his big Fourth of July party—but nothing more. At least, not to my knowledge. Besides, they both graduated in June; she wouldn't have "left" Shawn in high school. Couldn't have. He, like the boy before him, was the same year as her.

So who else was there?

I grab the envelope again and study it. *You,* it says, a lone word in the blank. *Who are you?* I want to ask it. *How did you know my sister? Why don't I know you?*

What did you mean to each other?

Did you love her?

I trace the letters of YOU's name. If he loved her before . . . Could he still?

I wake the next morning with a start. I know it's morning because the light has changed, and there's drool on my pillow, and someone's pounding on my door like the fire department.

"Juniper!" Dad calls from the other side. "Five minutes! You awake in there?"

I groan and twist away from him. Something crinkles and floats off my chest. I open my eyes enough to glimpse my own handwriting and recognize the list I scrawled early this morning:

PEOPLE WHO MIGHT KNOW SOMETHING
1. Melissa
2. Heather
3. Shawn?

Melissa, one of Camie's closest friends, already told me what she knew when I asked her about Camie's weirdness back in June. But Heather—Lauren's older sister and Camilla's *best* friend—said nothing when I asked her the same questions.

Which makes me think that she might actually know something.

"Juni?" *Poundpoundpound.*

"Yeah! I'm *awake*!"

"There's my annoyed ray of sunshine. Four minutes now. Hop to."

"Unnnngh."

Rubbing my eyes, I retrieve the list and stumble out of bed. I spent the better part of last night racking my brain, replaying endless memories for signs of YOU or his identity. How long had he and Cam been dating? Where and when had they met, spent time together?

Why was their relationship secret?

I leave the names on my desk with Camie's letter—and then dress, shove my hair into a choppy ponytail, and grab a jacket.

It's only as I'm lacing up my shoes in the doorway that it hits me: I forgot to do my Index card last night.

Of all the things to space on—

I turn back for it. If I have few physical things to remember Camie by, I have even fewer rituals with which to honor her. Recording positives in my Happiness Index each day is one of my only ways of keeping her alive.

"Juniper, let's go!"

"Coming!"

In a moment I have the whole collection out from under my bed: a slim black shoebox, closed, originally for ballet flats, now for my daily practice. I lift the lid and skip past the Before cards for the numbered After ones. Sixty-three, sixty-four . . .

Sixty-five!

I snatch the offender out. It may be a hole, but at least it's one that I can fix by the end of the day.

"Juniper!"

With a last glance at the letter, I grab my bag, shut the card inside one of my books, and hurry out.

The school year has barely begun when the next hole appears. First bell rings and the trig teacher, Ms. Jacobson, takes roll.

Then it goes like this:

"Juniper Lemon?"

I raise my hand.

"You must be—ah." Her smile falters.

I had thought myself prepared for this. I really had. I mean, some teacher *always* sees "Lemon" on the roster and asks if I'm Camilla's sister. But this year, I figured, anyone that knew Camilla would also have heard what had happened to her. Evidently Ms. Jacobson *had* heard; it just took her a moment too long to remember.

The look in her eyes says everything "ah" does not: I'm sorry.

I'm sorry I brought it up.

I'm sorry for your loss.

I'm sorry nothing I do or say can change what is and has been.

My eyes sting and I feel a sharpness under my ribs. I spend the rest of class hating the way Ms. Jacobson, after that briefest moment's silence, just picks up and goes to the next kid on the list—"Darrin Mills?"—as if that tiny hesitation hadn't been there.

As if *she* had never been there.

Another Camilla-shaped hole.

I don't make it to choir.

A funny thing happens after trig: I stop at my locker; I

change out my books; I approach the music room with minutes to spare, but when the doors loom up in front of me, I walk past them. And keep walking.

And walk out.

And when the bell rings, I am sitting on the bleachers by the football field, half curled into my knees.

How can things that aren't there hurt so badly?

For a long time I just sit there in their grip, their collective pressure weighing me down. Then I get out a notebook.

Holes

A sister.
A lined card.
A lover in a letter.
A blank night, a blackout:
the hours I can't remember.

Inside, the bell rings, startling me from the page. Has it been a whole period already?

Sure enough, in moments students are pouring out of 3 Hall. First open campus lunch is always the most popular of the year.

Lauren and I couldn't wait to eat off campus. As freshmen, we'd met at the flagpole on our very first day and then walked over to Pippa's.

"What should we order?" she'd asked when we stood before the menu.

"Something celebratory," I'd replied. "What food can you toast the new school year with?"

The answer, of course, was something toasted. We chose bagels.

"To high school," Lauren had prompted.

"To choir and going for a solo."

"To straight A's so my mom will pitch in money for a Nikon!"

I'd laughed. "Cheers."

We'd then raised our bagels, toasted each other's intentions, and eaten. Last year, we did the same.

This year, Lauren isn't at the flagpole.

I spot her walking instead with two other girls from choir toward a sub shop. One of them shows the others something on her phone and they all laugh.

What gives?

I start to text Lauren before I can stop myself.

> A summer of silence and now—

No no; stop. This isn't how you fix things.

Delete delete delete.

> I'm OK. You know, just in case you were wondering when I didn't show up for my favorite—

Juniper.

I try a different route.

> Lauren, I could really use someone to—

Pathetic!

I hit CLEAR and start again:

> WHAT KIND OF BEST FRIEND ARE YOU???

∞

Finally, I just hold down the backspace until the screen is blank. I know better than anyone:

You never know when you won't be able to take something back again.

Instead of joining the lunch crowd, I exchange my phone for *Great Expectations* and withdraw yesterday's forgotten Index card from it: *65*.

And with the pressure in my chest redoubled, I begin to write.

By fifth period I am counting down the days that remain in the school year.

At least nothing can feel worse than what I wrote on my Index card.

Fortunately, when Mr. Bodily strides into his classroom, he squanders no time on roll call or introducing AP English. Instead he distributes a list of discussion questions and tells us to pair off and start talking.

"Hey . . . Juniper, isn't it?"

I turn in my seat. A boy I don't recognize in flannel and jeans regards me with olive eyes and brows that rise into his front flip.

I pull myself together. "Uh . . . yeah?" *65* peeks out from my book and I nudge it away.

And you are?

"Nate." The stranger sticks out a hand, smiling. "Savage. Resident new kid."

Nate Savage? Call American Eagle. I think this boy fell out of their catalog.

"If you're new here, Nate," I propound as we shake, "how exactly is it that you know me?"

Nate turns his head and squints a little, a sidelong smile like he can't quite decide whether or not I am joking. "I sit next to you in trig."

Oh.

"Oh," I say, unable to think of anything better. "Uh . . . yeah. Sorry. My head was kind of somewhere else this morning."

Nate nods, thoughtful. He reaches into his backpack and drops his own copy of *Great Expectations* on the desk with a thud. "And here I thought you were just ignoring me."

"Ignoring you?" Oh god. How out of it *was* I first period?

"Yeah. I spent two minutes trying to offer you a Tic Tac before I figured you were morally opposed to wintergreen."

"Oh my god, I am *so*—"

Wait. Morally oppos—?

A joke, Juniper. A joke.

Nate's smile winds into a grin. In spite of everything that's happened today, I feel myself starting to laugh. And not a graceful laugh, either: several flatulent bursts that drag into a snort so ridiculous it makes Nate laugh, which makes me laugh even harder in turn.

Both of us are holding our stomachs when Mr. Bodily approaches.

"What's so funny over here?"

Nate and I look at each other.

"Are you *kidding*?" Nate wheezes, stepping in and slapping his knee when I am helpless to reply. "Pip's crash course in table manners. Herbert is like . . . a passive-aggressive Queen of Genovia!"

"Queen of Genovia?" Mr. Bodily raises his brows.

"You know—*The Princess Diaries*? Julie Andrews ties

Anne Hathaway to her dinner chair with a scarf?" Nate mimics her stretch for the salt and I cover my mouth. "This Dickens guy should've done stand-up."

"A modern comparison." Mr. Bodily nods appreciatively, then circles around and slides into a neighboring desk. "It is *refreshing*, Mr. Savage, to hear this classic framed in pop culture references. An idea for your first paper, perhaps?"

"Uh," Nate laughs, but his mirth shrinks back a little.

Bodily smiles. "Kidding! Who talks papers on the first day of class? I may not grade on a curve, but I'm not *that* evil."

I'm not sure which is greater: Nate's relief, or Bodily's amusement at it as he gets up and jaunts to the next table. Camilla mentioned a zany student teacher once; I wonder briefly if this is him. The thought warms me. Sharing things my sister once experienced makes me feel closer to her now.

For once, I realize, I don't mind the idea of living in her shadow.

After school is the Club and Activity Fair, a lunchroom maze of balloons and poster boards rigged up by Fairfield's clubs and sports teams to recruit new members. I don't normally go because I already have musicals and choir, but I don't know if I'll ever feel like singing again, let alone for a year and a grade. I need a new activity, and besides that, a new cause to fill my free time: Dad cut me off from volunteering last week, saying that now that summer's over, I'd need to focus on school. No more picking up whatever open shifts I could grab at the animal shelter.

At least *they* didn't mind my enthusiasm.

At the head of the stairs from 2 Hall, I stop to survey the

scene before me. I don't scan for long before I spy a row of flags: International Club. Last year it would've been Camie sitting behind them, handing out tickets to the latest foreign film downtown and chatting and laughing with people. This year, it's Lawrence Torres, a computer geek with turquoise frames and a gift for picking up languages—among other things.

"Excuse me, are you just gonna stand there all day? *Some* of us have lives to get on with."

I step aside, speechless, for Morgan Malloy. Camie always stood up to Morgan when she saw her bullying someone, especially on the bus we all once rode together—once turning her insult around so fast that the whole bus laughed at her for three stops, and again when Morgan got off.

The bully got her license after that.

She's also hated Camie since.

"Thanks," Morgan sneers as she passes.

I scowl after her. Ironically, it's only because I'm grumbling at her back that I see her take a box to the yearbook table—across from which I discover what may be the only unmanned, unattended display in the cafeteria.

General Student Booster Club.

A hole.

I cross over to it, immediately drawn to the sparse display board. On it are pictures from different cause-supporting events: students making cookies for the bake sale, posing with scavenger hunt clues around town, decorating the gym for the annual Shaker. Half the photos look like they're from the eighties, which makes sense considering Booster is about as popular today as pickled beets or Monday pop quizzes. I wonder how long it's been since they've even had someone to run the table.

Booster, an oversized font declares. *We put the "fun" in fund-raising!*

The only other text, apart from a few scribbled captions, is to say that officers will be elected in Mr. Garcia's room, A-23, at 2:45 this Thursday.

And to help yourself to a *Lucy Killman* bookmark ↓.

I follow the arrow down to the table. A spread of shirtless boy in skintight pants greets me, obscuring the few shots actually of Lucy. Gah! Staff has even resorted to ab-tastic movie swag. If they need the six-pack and smoky eyes of actor Rush Hollister to sell Booster, they must really be desperate.

But the bigger the ruin, the bigger the fix-up.

This could be a real chance to make something better.

I swing my backpack off a shoulder, shuffle out some books for my planner and a pen, and mark down *A-23, 2:45* on my calendar.

I'm about to put it all away when a loud series of *POP!*s makes me jump and spin around. At a distant table, box cutter poised where three balloons used to be—

Brand Sayers.

Brand Sayers: a senior everyone at Fairfield knows by name, if not acquaintance. Hobbies include arson, destruction, detention, and his band. There are only two things in the world Brand Sayers cares about: his electric guitar and his haircut, short sides with messy bangs across his forehead like a bird's wing. Everything else is kindling and knife-fodder.

Exhibit A: the spent balloon skins he's now plucking from his jacket.

As if he senses me watching, Brand looks up just then and catches my eye.

Then he tosses his tawny hair and smirks at me.

Smirks.

At *me*.

I'm so thrown, for a moment I lose sight of what I'm doing. I walk straight into another kid, and both our books and papers go scattering across the floor.

"Oh my gosh—"

I stoop to help the stranger pick up his things. First I see the copy of *Great Expectations,* and then, as I reach for it, "wintergreen" on a box of breath mints.

"You change your mind about those Tic Tacs?"

My gaze hits a familiar smiling face.

"Yes," I answer, the apology dropping from mine, "because the only way to improve a flavor as hopelessly offensive as wintergreen is to drop it on the floor of a high school cafeteria."

"Oh-ho!" Nate takes his dictionary-sized novel from me, clutching it with raised brows. "Watch out, Charles—a fellow comedian!"

I catch his eye and grin.

"Hey lovebirds."

We look up. Brand Sayers, apparently finished with his work on the far side of the cafeteria, now leers over us from the GSBC table, a cluster of balloons in one hand, box cutter poised to puncture them in the other. He looks from Nate to me, lips curled.

"Get a room."

And then one, two, three; the trio he is holding is a bouquet of wilted plastic.

"What is *that* guy's problem?" Nate asks when Brand takes up a tune I recognize—something by Queen—and moves away.

I shrug.

"Hey," a new voice prompts behind us. "Are you okay?"

I turn, expecting a teacher—someone following Brand's trail of destruction.

But the hand that extends to Nate belongs to somebody else.

"Let me help you up," she insists.

With a side glance at me, Nate takes it.

"I'm Morgan, by the way."

"Nate." He collects the last of his books and offers me a hand up in turn. Morgan frowns as I accept.

"Are you looking for a club, Nate?"

"Think I might've found one, actually." He nods at the barren Booster board.

Morgan scoffs. "Booster?"

"*You're* applying for something, right?" Nate turns to me, ignoring her question. Morgan's face goes crimson.

"'Apply' might be a generous word for it . . ." I chew back a smile as I indicate the sign and lack of forms to fill out.

"Is this the application?" Nate lifts one of the bookmarks and tilts it from side to side as though Rush's abs are holographic. "If so, count me *in*."

Beside us, Morgan glances darkly at me and mutters something like "Lost cause," and then returns to the yearbook table.

Nate looks relieved. "Geez, I thought she'd never leave. Did you get all your books?" He nods at the haphazard stack in my arms.

"Think so."

"Good."

Nate's thousand-watt grin returns, lighting up the room.

It's hard to bask in that brightness and not be affected.

Beyond us, Brand Sayers still floats from table to table, dispatching balloons in time with the melody of "Don't Stop Me Now."

I swear he looks at me right where the song should say *you*.

Despite my best efforts to be quiet, I have barely locked the front door and started up the stairs when Dad sticks his head out of his office to greet me.

"What's the score?" he calls up at my back.

The score. Like "the weather," "the verdict," and "the report," this is one of Dad's many euphemisms for asking how I'm doing these days. I'd only started rating "Happiness" on my daily cards sarcastically, but now that Cam is gone, that 1–10 number makes it easy for Dad to check in on me without upsetting anyone.

I reflect on the day's events. "Three."

"Three," he repeats. Even though I haven't turned around, I can hear the rise, the note of interest in his brows.

Then, perhaps deciding not to push his luck, Dad says, "Welcome home," and retreats into the study.

I follow his lead, returning to my room and my list from this morning.

From: Juniper Lemon
To: Heather Han
Subject: favor

Dear Heather,

How is Oregon State? I hope you're liking college so far!

I, uh . . . found something that suggests Camie was
in a relationship with someone. For a while. This may
be what I was asking you about in June, when I thought
something was up with Cam, but do you know anything
about that? I think she would've wanted whoever she was
seeing to have what I found, but I can't give it to him (or
her—assuming "him" based on her dating history) if I
don't know who they are.

Please, Heather. If I could just know enough to pass it
on to the guy (girl)—or maybe give it to you to deliver?—
you wouldn't even have to tell me who it was. This might
be the last thing I can do for Cam. You don't know what
that would mean to me.
Thanks,
Juniper

I spend an hour debating whether or not to ask about
Lauren in the message. In the end, I decide against it. This
is about my sister, not Heather's; I don't want any weirdness
with Lauren to be a reason for Heather not to answer me.

I suck it up and hit SEND.

When I lean back in my chair, it's already dark out. Guess
I'd better do today's Index card before I forget like yesterday's.

Sliding out the box from under my bed, I tick back to
66, pull it, and begin my list of highs and lows for the day:

```
                            66

    Happiness: 3
    Wintergreen (+).
    Dickens humor (+).
    Ms. Jacobson (−).
    Heather: possible You lead? (+).
```

Then I hold the card out to review.

66. It's been *sixty-six days* since I stopped dating my Index cards, and started numbering them. Or rather— since I numbered them all. I used to date them as I went, but after the accident, "July 5" didn't feel right for a heading; it suggested that nothing had changed. So I started counting, and labeled every last card in the box to remind myself what had.

Cam would not be pleased that I'm using the cards to mark the days since her death. She'd see it as the ultimate negative, a kind of counter to what the Index was supposed to even be. Then again, she knew I was no Ms. Optimism; I've included negatives in my entries almost as long as I've been keeping them. If Camie was queen of the bright side, I'm the un-sugared plum fairy: champion of reality, dosing bad with good. Sometimes unsweetened means raw, but isn't it more truthful that way?

I could be counting just negatives.

All at once I feel worn through—like all the things that

don't show on my face have been gnawing at my bones from inside.

Returning to the box, I sort back through the cards to put 66 away—only to realize at 64 that I still haven't filed yesterday's.

For the love of—

I unzip my school bag, heft out the Dickens tome I put it in, and open to the very back.

Except, when I get to the space between the final pages and the hardback cover, the card I took to school this morning isn't there.

It.

Isn't.

There.

Okay; no problem. I probably just tucked it in somewhere else.

But a page-by-page inspection, and then a rapid flip-through, and then a shakedown by the spine reveals that not only is 65 nowhere within chapters 58 or 59; it is nowhere inside the book.

I check my backpack. One by one I fly through my other books, panic clawing up my throat. Nothing. Not in my binders. Planner. Notebooks. When there are no books left I wrench my backpack open wide and plunge my hands into the bottom, groping, and finally lift it by the straps and dump it onto the bed. Pens, pencils, makeup, keys, and a pouch with change tumble out in a heap.

But no index card.

I drop the bag with the rest of the mess, reeling.

Suddenly I'm not very tired anymore.

Falling

Once there was a girl who made a wish in anger. She
didn't mean it, but that didn't matter, because at that
very moment a star was falling and heard her and
listened.

When her wish came true, the girl wanted nothing more
than to pick up the pieces of that star and glue them
together, put it back in the sky. I didn't want this, she
pleaded—first silently, then aloud, and then to any force
that might be listening. Take it back.

But a star could only fall.

The girl couldn't unsay the wish, so she tried to make up
for it. She did as many good things as she could find to,
stacked and piled them high together, tried to climb them
like a ladder to the moon. But even on tiptoe, she could
never quite reach the place where the star had been.
Not that it mattered; even if she replaced it, what was
to keep it there?

A star could only fall.

She began to dream of falling: not of falling herself, but
of holding in hand that which was precious to her and
then watching it slip through her fingers. She saw it fall

from a cliff edge, down a canyon, off slippery boat rails into the sea. Down, down, down it always plunged into darkness.

Every time she tried to hold tighter, to dig her nails into the other girl's hands for purchase—

But gravity was always stronger.

A star could only fall.

67

I can't look for my card the next morning; the cafeteria, where I last took out *Great Expectations* and I'm certain I must've dropped 65, is busy before school and there'd be too many eyes. But when possibilities make me sweat through first period—*What if someone like Morgan found it? What if she held it over me, or worse, gabbed, and it got back to Mom somehow? What if Mom blamed me?*—I know I have to do *some*thing. My name may not appear on the card, but how many have lost a sister lately? It wouldn't take a genius to trace it back to me. And people talk.

I can't let that secret get out.

Although I don't get to search for it that morning, between classes I manage to track down Fairfield's greatest resource.

"Hello, Juniper."

He doesn't even look up from his laptop when I approach his corner in the cafeteria.

"Sponge."

Lawrence "Sponge" Torres is a local legend. A fellow junior, this formerly home-schooled, neon-spectacled loner has an eagle eye and an inhuman capacity for detail. His talents were discovered when, on Fairfield's opening night of *A Midsummer Night's Dream* two years back, the kid playing Oberon ran offstage and lost his lunch. That was when Sponge, then just Lawrence, had left his place at the control booth, climbed up on stage, and surprised everyone by filling in and finishing out the show for him.

"I thought you'd never read the play?" the drama teacher famously asked him after closing curtain.

"I haven't," then-Lawrence answered.

But he *had* done sound and lights for several dress rehearsals, and for his absorbent mind, that had been enough.

"That kid is a sponge," the same teacher commented when later interviewed about the incident.

The nickname fit—and stuck.

Nowadays, Sponge is known for a wider range of abilities: memorization, reading people, seeing everything in a room or a crowded scene at once. He's a radar for trivia: who is wearing what, what is in whose locker, where people go during lunch and what they most often buy, the number of people or cars in a parking lot. He can place quotes in an instant, tell you your crush's phone number, or even say whether or not you are lying.

For these and other reasons, many avoid Lawrence Torres. Like maybe he'll take in who they're with or what they're doing one Wednesday and someday use that to incriminate them. But Sponge doesn't side with good or evil.

Mainly, he works for Reese's Pieces.

"How'd you know it was me?" I ask.

"Footsteps," he says, typing, not lifting his eyes from the screen. "No one else is that purposeful at nine in the morning. Plus, I heard the crinkle. You always come prepared."

It isn't the first time I've visited. I once asked Sponge how to spell a hot exchange student's name on a dare from Lauren, and just last March needed Camie's locker number so I could deck out the space for her birthday.

I slide into the seat across from him. "I need to know something."

Sponge sticks out his hand. When I deposit the bag I bought on the way over he actually looks up from his screen a moment and smiles. Then he tears the package, tilts a few Pieces into his mouth, and resumes typing. "What can I do for you, Juniper?"

"I need to know when school trash and recycling are picked up."

The typing stops. Sponge blinks at me. "The trash?"

"Yes. And recycling. You *do* know when they're collected, don't you?"

"You mean, like when the janitor empties them?"

"I mean, when trucks come and empty the dumpsters out back."

Sponge narrows his eyes. I can see the analysis pistons at work.

"Tuesday," he says. "Tuesday mornings."

Finally some luck. That means I have till next week to recover my card.

I try not to look too relieved. "At what time?"

Sponge's eyes remain watchful. "Around five."

I nod my thanks, and get up to leave.

"May I ask why?"

I stop. Sponge is as good for confidentiality as any doctor or priest, but even so, the whole point of my visit is to prevent anyone from finding out. Especially someone who would remember.

"It's personal," I say.

Sponge says nothing. Then he just shrugs and throws back a few Pieces, returning to work. I adjust my backpack and turn to go, but after a few steps pivot back.

"Sponge . . ."

"Yeah?" He doesn't look up.

"You wouldn't happen to know if . . ." I let the sentence fade, then decide there is nothing to lose. "If my sister was . . . *dating* anybody, would you? This last year, I mean?" Sponge isn't infallible, but if anyone might've noticed a secret relationship at Fairfield, it's him.

"Dating anybody?"

His expression is strange. Is that a blush on his brown cheek? Oh my god—Sponge is in International Club. So was Cam. What if they hit it off, and—?

But no; Sponge's mouth pulls to the side. I decide he is just surprised, and considering.

And I'm too eager to find You.

After a long pause—so long, I adjust my backpack, check my watch, and am about to write it off:

"She had flowers in her locker on Valentine's Day."

I plant my feet again. "Flowers?"

"White ones. Lilies."

Camie's favorite.

I nod. "Thanks. Let me know if you remember anything else."

"Keep the goods coming and I will." Sponge raises the bag of Reese's Pieces to me, already half emptied.

Running late from my detour, I move a little faster through Main Hall to my next class. Still, I can't help scanning the row of lockers where Camie's used to be, imagining a white bouquet inside one of them and who might've left it.

I am trying to recall which was hers when there's a gasp behind me.

It happens so fast, I'm not even sure what comes next: the other gasps, the bang of metal on metal, or the many-grained *shhhhhhhh* that scatters forth from somewhere like poured cereal. I spin to look, and by the time the rain settles, everyone is staring at the landslide of Hershey's Kisses and sugar packets that has just spewed itself onto the floor from an open locker. A last few trickle down and roll off the heap.

The girl who stands in front of it grows as scarlet as her hair.

Kody.

Across the hall, someone snickers. I glance up in time to see Morgan Malloy's sneer before somebody else laughs, and then those closest join in, and then the whole hall explodes or pretends not to notice, which is worse. Some even applaud.

The bell rings. The crowd disperses without offering to help.

When the rest have gone, Kody kneels to pick out her books. Then she stands and squeezes them to her.

She runs without wiping her face.

I should've said something. I should've helped Kody, or told Morgan off, or at least done something about the mess while Kody was probably crying her eyes out in the bathroom. Camie would've.

Things I didn't make right today: +1.

"Okay, everyone," Ms. Gilbert calls when she's finished taking roll for Art I. "Help yourselves to an apron, then come up front."

I follow her direction and unfold a smock that looks like a handkerchief a car blew its nose in. This is supposed to *keep* me from getting messy?

Ms. Gilbert opens a block of clay. "Now." She works a string through the slab as though it were a giant stick of butter, lopping off a portion. "Our first unit this term is ceramics. Today we will be doing practice throws—and I emphasize *practice,* because it tends to take a few before you get the hang of it. But if you stick with it, a month from now I guarantee you'll have some quality pieces like the ones I pulled from storage to show you today."

She gestures at the rows of warehouse shelves behind her. An assortment of ceramic odds and ends fill the first two, a third one bare—probably for future projects.

"Okay? So let's get started. Your assignment today is four practices, so the first thing you'll want to do is divide your block into quarters. Then ball them."

She demonstrates with expert quickness, converting her block into four malleable balls before placing the first on the wheel. The wheel begins to turn, and, wetting her hands in a bowl of muddied water, Ms. Gilbert attaches the lump to its surface.

When she pulls her palms back, they are slick with brown.

"After that," she continues as the lump spins and spins, "it's just a matter of shaping and pulling the clay by guiding it with your hands. Observe." She makes a wide, angled cup with her palms and lightly braces the spinning mass. Rapidly the clay shoots up, rising through her open grip. Then, before the class can even finish marveling, she presses one wet hand into the other, closing from the top, and funnels the hill she's made back down. I forget to be grossed out by my smock.

It's like magic.

She combs the mud up and down; makes its girth blossom and shrink; opens a vortex in the middle for a bowl. Lastly, Ms. Gilbert shows us how to stretch the clay until it breaks: wobbles and folds and spins out into a sad, limp ruin.

Breaking, she tells us, is good: It is the only way to learn.

Then it's our turn.

Following Ms. Gilbert's example, I place a ball in my wheel's center and pat it down into a round. Then I wet my hands and start it spinning.

Schloop.

The clay is cold. I watch, fascinated, as at my slightest touch, the mud elongates and shrinks, widens and narrows, hollows and spreads itself into a bowl. I cup my hands and squeeze, opening my grasp so the clay will rise through it. The mass moves up, up, stretching beyond my hands into a cup, a vase, a tower—

There is a sudden sucking sound. The tower withers into flap.

And then the mud on my hands is red, and the thing slipping through my fingers is a lifeless face.

"Juniper? Are you all right?"

I realize I am standing. Ms. Gilbert and the whole class are staring, and I have the vague impression I may have just screamed.

"I . . ."

My hands are wet. The room is swimming. Red drips from my palms and fingertips.

No—brown.

Clay brown.

"I think I'd better go to the nurse's office."

The first thing I remember is a dry, cracked feeling beneath my nails. Someone had done a quick rub of my hands, wrists, and forearms, but hadn't been able to reach the deeper places under my fingernails. The edges, I remember, were red. Tulip red. When I saw the color I began to feel the cake of it on my skin, crimson and brown licking up to my elbows, and I knew, even before they told me, what had happened.

I got up and started scrubbing.

Now the water runs clear into a white sink, as it did then, and swirls down an indifferent drain. Now, as then, I am still scrubbing long after the color, tears, and soap bubbles have passed.

I attempt to withdraw from art.

"Says here you've already changed a class," says the cloying admin who answers the window during lunch. And it's true; I switched out choir for French this morning.

"Yes," I start to explain. "But—"

"One class change allowed. After that we call home for confirmation. Would you like me to call now?"

"Um," I say.

She doesn't.

But administration does, apparently, get in touch with Ms. Gilbert, because in the middle of history, I get a note from her saying that we can discuss alternatives later, but as for now I remain in her class, I should complete the day's assignment—and sooner, rather than later.

After school, she suggests.

Today.

When final bell sounds, it's a good fifteen minutes before I can drag myself back to the studio. *I can do it,* I tell myself. *I can be done in half an hour.* What is three more throws? Nothing.

Just don't think of the accident.

"Ms. Gilbert?"

The door is propped open. I find a sign-in sheet taped to it with a note: *Out at a meeting, but the studio is open! Leave throws on second shelf please.*

Guess that's my cue.

I write my name down and shuffle inside. The place is empty. It'd almost be peaceful, if not for my lost card hanging over me. I wish I could be looking for 65 now—but if I don't make an effort, Ms. Gilbert will probably call the Lemon house herself. What would Dad think if he knew I'd given up on singing *and* art?

With a steeling breath, I return to my station. This time, afraid of seeing red, I have to psych myself up to make my wet hands meet clay again. Even then, it's a few minutes more before I manage to keep them there.

Mercifully, when I finally get it, the rest comes easily: I attach my first ball to the wheel. Once it's fixed, I manipulate my hands so that the flattened round moves up, then down; widens, then narrows; shapes itself around a well I open in the middle with my fingers. On this last maneuver, however, I comb the brim out too far and the lip, already thinned, bursts and the bowl deflates.

It falls on my supporting hand like a death sheet.

I jerk back. The hanging pancake slows to a stop and I am instantly at the sink, rinsing with a vengeance. Then, absurdly, as I am scrubbing I feel the demented urge to laugh—and do. One down!

Two more to go.

More confident, I go to lop another section off the block Ms. Gilbert left out for me. But this time, as I'm lifting it, I fumble the slice and it drops.

The wedge falls to the floor.

And instead of clay, I see the fall of a lifeless hand.

I flinch backward, knocking the shelf behind me. The structure rocks, and the item closest to the edge, a fired navy bowl, goes diving to the floor and breaks into a dozen pieces.

Only, it isn't a bowl.

It's a driver's-side mirror, and the pieces are fragments of glass.

The next thing I know I am lying facedown across a wooden worktable, heart pounding. Slowly, with infinite reassurances—*It's okay, you're okay, it wasn't real*—I gather my breath and pull myself to my feet. When I work up the courage to look, the shards on the floor are blue again: nothing more than a ceramic bowl cracked from the center out.

With a sigh, I look around for the broom.

Once I've swept the shards into a dustpan, though, I'm not sure what to do with them. Throw them away? Ms. Gilbert said she'd pulled these from storage; I guess it's not like anyone will miss them.

Still . . .

I raise my eyes to the shelves. A bowl-shaped vacancy stares back at me.

Another blank space.

I am haunted by them: the pause at Camie's name. The gap in my Index. The sidesteps where she should be in conversations, but isn't. Her empty chair at dinner; her toothbrush and her shampoo; her shoes from the entryway, her keys from the kitchen hook, her tea and favorite cereal from the cupboard.

YOU.

I can't escape the holes. My life is braided through with my sister, and now that she is gone, everything is coming apart. Counting positives was her idea; her death has cast a shadow over that. Taking art was her idea; I can't touch clay without remembering she is dead. The party was her idea—

We all know how that turned out.

A terrible thought occurs to me. What if going to Shawn's party was just a way to get the letter to YOU? Cam's inviting me a means to an end? That would mean she never actually forgave me. And I'd thought things were okay, or finally starting to be, between us again, but if Cam was just playing nice to get her car keys back from Mom and Dad—

Any progress that night's null and void.

VOID

The dustpan falls from my fingers with a clatter. I stare tensely at the shards on the floor.

Then, instead of picking them up, I thrust my arms into the shelves and shove.

Whole rows of pottery shatter loudly upon the ground, but I don't stop there; I take a vase from the next shelf and hurl it across the room.

Crash.

I take another, then another, then another, flinging and

launching and smashing work against the floor and tables and walls until everything in reach is obliterated, and earthen and colored and two-tone shards make the studio a junkyard of bones.

My shoulders rise and fall. My breath is ragged, blood racing, and for once the thing raging in my chest is not a flood, but a hurricane. I do not feel like crying; I feel like ripping the world to shreds.

That's when I look up, and notice Brand Sayers in the door.

He stares at me, his pale blue eyes impenetrable. I feel the wild power that's possessed me falter. I have been seen. There will be consequences.

But Brand doesn't say anything; he only crosses the room, calmly skirting the ceramic explosions, and moves past me to the other side of the shelf. Then he hefts up an object— an ugly penguin cookie jar—and hurls it against the floor.

Crash.

He picks up another. Looks at me through the aisles.

An invitation.

In answer, I pick up another vase. I look back at him, and we're in agreement: Our selections go flying.

Then we are both destroying every finished and unfinished ware we can lay hands on: flowerpots, mugs, pitchers, bowls, plates; dishes with golden bears, trays in the shape of fish or fallen leaves, misshapen piggy and Oscar the Grouch banks; vases with two handles, heart-shaped boxes, a Georgia O'Keefe–style cow skull; a pumpkin, a book, a ceramic taco.

Crash, crash, crash.

When there is nothing left—nothing small enough to

throw—we stand in the ruins. Through the empty shelves our eyes meet. I am still breathing hard. I feel like screaming, I feel like laughing, I feel like reaching through the shelves and either shoving Brand or taking his hand—I'm not sure which. But before either of us can do anything—

"BRAND SAYERS!"

Ms. Gilbert stands in the side door, livid. Her eyes bulge like Peeps in a microwave. I realize, breath catching, that from where she is standing she can see only him—I'm obstructed by shelf frames and sacks of raw, unfired clay.

Brand's eyes hold mine through the vacant space. Then—

He takes off, toppling a birdbath and a bowling pin in his wake.

"BRAND SAYERS, GET BACK HERE!"

He makes for the opposite door, leaping broken heaps like hurdles so that Ms. Gilbert must scurry, stumbling on shattered pieces, to follow.

Then both are gone, and I am alone in the wreckage.

68

The next day Ms. Gilbert asks me in at lunch to discuss an alternate art unit. Today will mark the third in a row I haven't eaten with Lauren, and as I cut through the cafeteria on my way to the portables I can't help but wonder if that cements it. If I look for her at our old table, will she be there?

The lunchroom is split level, and when I make way across the lower floor I don't see her.

The end of our old upstairs table is empty.

My stomach sinks. I realize I'd been hoping for a chance to explain myself to Lauren—that I'd skipped out yesterday because I'd needed air, been too shaken after art—not been avoiding her.

But maybe she's avoiding me.

"Juniper!"

I whip around, hopeful. But the person who jogs over from the bank of vending machines is Nate.

"Hey," he says when he catches up to me. His grin's the size and brightness of California. "You still checking out Booster today?"

I attempt to reflect his warmth. "That's the plan. You?"

"Yep. Thinkin' treasurer has my name on it—unless you want it?"

He looks so serious asking, my lips can't help but twitch into a real smile. "All yours."

"Whew! No political tension."

"Not from me. But with Booster so popular, I don't know, you might be up against a lint ball or a tumbleweed or something . . ."

"Better bring my A game."

Geez, this kid's resting face is contagious. What does that thing run on: candy and rainbows?

Nate nods at something below eye level. "So, do all the cool kids eat off campus, or—?"

I realize he means my empty hands. "Oh—no, I'm just on my way to see the art teacher."

"Ah. Well, if you see a cool kid, will you ask them for me?"

I shove his arm. "Shut up. I'll see you at Booster."

He grins back. "See you."

Ms. Gilbert is waiting when I enter the studio.

"Juniper!" she calls when she spots me. "Come in. Have a seat."

I hug my elbows as I approach the desk, trying hard not to look too furtively at the floor. I'm astonished to find the concrete swept clean, the shards of yesterday heaped in garbage sacks in the corner. Did Brand put them there?

More importantly, did he say anything to Ms. G?

I pull up the chair and sit.

"So." Ms. Gilbert watches me carefully. A lump slides down my throat. "It seems ceramics doesn't agree with you."

My shoulders tighten. She knows.

"I—"

"I saw your throw yesterday," she explains. "Left out on the wheel. I figured you wouldn't have left it like that unless you'd had to leave in a hurry."

Oh. I guess I didn't clean that up, either.

But wait—does that mean she still thinks it was just Brand?

I nod, afraid anything more will give me away.

"Well . . ." Ms. Gilbert pushes a half-eaten sandwich aside. "I've worked with at least one other student who had a hard time handling clay before. Sensory issues. I'm not sure if that's what you're experiencing . . ."

She pauses and lowers her chin at me. When I realize she is waiting for affirmation, I stiffly bob my head again. Why not?

She really doesn't suspect me?

"But what we did in that situation," she continues, "was just to have him explore another medium. So for the rest of the unit, while the class did ceramics down here, he worked upstairs on his own projects. Like independent study. Would that be a better fit for you, maybe?"

I know a good deal when I see one.

"What do I have to do?"

After school, I finally have the chance to search the cafeteria for 65 without being watched. Of course I don't find it there; it's been two days since I lost it, so I don't really expect to. But I had to check before resorting to more drastic measures.

Measures involving rubber boots, a raincoat, and yellow dishwashing gloves.

I always pictured dumpsters to be like oozing, mold-infested treasure chests: everything heaped together, milk cartons with PB crusts with calzone goop, carrot sticks with corndog butts in slushie melt. But when I lift a lid off one of the four out back, what I see is black plastic: large sacks like the ones the broken pottery was in. Of course it's in bags.

But bags or no, the stuff is *rank*. I get a noseful of Garbáge No. 5 and immediately drop the lid, sending several fat flies whizzing off in start.

God almighty. How am I going to do this?

I check my gloves again and face the dumpster. Look around and suck in a breath.

Then I run at it, wrench up the lid, and nab the first sack I lay hold of. The lid slams shut, leaving me panting with my prize.

There—that wasn't so bad, was it? I drop the bag on the ground. I didn't even have to climb inside like I'd originally thought.

I find the knot at the top and tug it loose. The sack spills open.

"Yugh!"

Reflexively I cover my nose with my coat sleeve. The stench is like pizza and curry and black bananas. And no wonder: Judging by the bites of sesame bun and the grease-stained fry boats jutting out, I've exhumed a cafeteria special.

Bracing myself, I poke the sack open further and begin picking through it.

Ramen cup. Spork. Soda can. Four tots and a smear of mustard. Brown bag. Pretzel bag. Nacho chips fused to banana peel. Wedge of deep-fried meat; can't tell if chicken nugget or chicken fried steak, which does not actually contain chicken. Soggy lettuce. Bean slop. Remains of taco shell.

When I feel something gloppy through a glove, an unfinished pudding, I startle and drop the sack. A straw pokes through the bottom, and a sticky orange liquid begins to pool on the ground.

Rain boots, don't fail me now.

I rake the whole load without glimpsing so much as a torn sheet of wide-ruled. When I go to put it back, it occurs to me that my Index is probably closer to the bottom—in a sack from two days ago—so I pull my next bag, and the next, from deeper down.

When I finally find one whose papers date September 8, the day I lost *65*, the sacks are so deep that I'm having trouble reaching them. The only way to get to them now is . . .

Don't even think it

. . . To go in.

A shiver skitters down my back.

I ignore it.

Screwing up my face, I zip my raincoat to the chin. Pull up my gloves. Boots. Hood for good measure.

Then, with a deep, stomach-expanding breath of air I'm not convinced won't be my last, I step up and boost myself over the rim.

Squish.

Despite my rubber boots, something soft rolls beneath one of my feet and I slip, landing on my butt.

Oh god—

Flies. One crawls up my arm and another finds my glove and a third brushes my face. I yelp and thrash at them and they scatter, but their buzzing is everywhere. My eyes sting and I want to retch, as likely from the smell and their touch as the squelch of objects rotting below.

Pushing myself up—more mystery items sag, crunch, crumble, and give way—I quickly clamber back to my feet. But before I can catch my breath—

A voice.

Crap.

I drop back down.

The sound, male, is followed by footsteps and resolves into a tune, growing louder. I press low, willing that the singer won't look inside—or worse, toss something in.

But today's entertainment doesn't concern himself with the open dumpster; there is a clicking sound, and a new smell, and the song, "Another One Bites the Dust," becomes nasal as though hummed through clamped teeth.

I hold my breath. When he blows air out, cigarette smoke wafts in. He must be inches from where I cower.

When at last the song is over, there's a crunch of shoe on gravel: the rubbing out of the cigarette. Thank god. I inhale through my nose, wait for the footsteps to move away.

They don't.

Instead, a rattling sound. Then—

Kshh kshh. Kshhhhhhhhhh.

A new smell overtakes me: a pretentious musk two years of high school has equipped me to recognize anywhere. Sure enough, I see the mist rise up in jets.

I can't take it. Garbage, smoke, body spray—the three meld in a disgusting bouquet and fill my mouth like a cloth. My stomach heaves, my eyes water, my throat tickles and constricts—

Cough.

"What the—?"

The spraying stops.

There's a clunk of metal and a shadow falls over me. When I dare to look up, I find the bone-defined face of Brand Sayers looking down.

"Well, well!" Brand rocks on his feet, smirking where he stands along the rim. "If it isn't Lemon Little. Why so down in the dumps?"

I stare at him, paralyzed. Partly because I don't know what to say; partly because Brand is laughing at his own joke, and I don't know whether to laugh with him or fear for my life. Inclined toward the latter, I slowly rise to my feet against the opposite wall.

Act natural, a helpful inner voice suggests.

"Hi," I start, coolly not gagging on Axe. "I, um. Lost something."

"That so?" Brand grins, a look of dangerous amusement. I can't help noticing one diamond-edge canine in his smile: a feature that makes him look both dashing and like the very devil.

"Yes," I say, less firmly than I mean to.

He looks me over and pushes his lips together. "I don't suppose it was your way home or grasp of inclement weather."

The rain gear. My gloves.

"Or is Fisherman Yellow just 'in' right now?"

"It was . . . my lucky . . . hairpin," I say, snatching up the first loose article I spy. "Found it! Guess I can go now."

"*Lemon.*" Brand slides sideways after me with an air of aren't-we-all-friends-here—not blocking my exit, but stopping me, anyway. "I took the *fall* for you! Five days in-school suspension and a hairy old X on the permanent record. All I ask in return is the answer to a simple question. Is that so unreasonable?"

I fold my arms and face him.

"What do you want?"

"All I want to know"—Brand's blue eyes narrow as they move between mine in scrutiny—"is what you're really looking for."

What I'm "really" looking for?

"In this dumpster, or in life?"

He gives me a look.

"Fine."

I glance away from him and down at my feet. I know I could leave, just walk away and say nothing and come back to look for 65 tomorrow—but I'm arrested by his intentness. Why should he even care?

Does he care?

With a thin breath, I say matter-of-factly, "An index card."

"An index card." Brand looks skeptical.

I shrug. Let him make what he will of it.

His eyes tighten. "What's on it?"

"That . . . is for me to know."

And no one ever to find out.

I turn dismissively and stoop to return to work, figuring he'll soon lose interest and hop down, leave me be. But Brand does neither; instead he drums his fingers along the metal, weighing something.

Then he leans in over the rim on his elbows.

"Tell you what, Lemon."

"Juniper."

"I'm gonna help you find your little secret."

The bag in my hands goes limp. "What?"

The dumpster bangs as Brand jumps down from it. A

moment later he opens the one beside me.

"And when we find it," Brand continues aboard this vessel, "you're going to show me what it says."

I watch him take a sack from the top.

"But—"

My words fail me. I've no arguments.

"Why?" I blurt instead.

"Why not? It's clearly something worthwhile." He heaves the bag down and dusts his hands, squinting against the sun. "So—what kind of card we talking here? Three by five? Five by eight? Lined? Blank?"

I don't answer him.

"It isn't, like, Grandma's Secret Cookie Recipe, or some shit like that, is it?"

I hold my head with my forearm.

"Look." I inhale and straighten in a way I hope looks authoritative. "I didn't ask for your help."

Brand tosses back his bangs. "And I didn't ask your permission."

"Brand—"

"Jesus Christ! *Look,* Lemon. I'm trying to do you a favor. Why don't you just stop being an ass and let a good thing happen?"

I scoff. As if Brand Sayers "helping" were a good thing.

"Seriously—what's the big deal? You know I can keep a secret. I didn't tell anyone about all that pottery, did I?"

My mouth opens, but no retort comes. Brand cocks a brow, waiting.

". . . Yet," he adds, impish.

My stomach drops. "You wouldn't."

"Only one way to find out. Feelin' lucky, Lemon?"

I hold his gaze, challenging. Damn that mischievous smile!

"Fine," I concede again, irritated. "You want to dig through the trash with me? Be my guest."

I throw my bag down on the ground, grumbling. By the time I climb out after it, Brand's pompous smirk is gone, replaced by a dutiful grimace as he smears something thick and caramel-colored from a finger onto a napkin.

"So." I look away as his eyes shift to me again. "If you won't tell me what's on this secret card of yours, how am I supposed to know it when I see it?"

"I don't know. *You* signed up for this."

He shoots me a dirty look—or what *would* be a dirty look from a normal person, but from someone with Brand's cheekbones, mob relations, and affinity for fire is decidedly more like a death threat.

"It's only the first week of school," I add, voice rising a little. "How many index cards can there be?"

As it turns out, there can be plenty. As I comb my own bag for 65, Brand appears to have found one from the first day of Health I. He pauses frequently to read aloud anonymous questions like "Can you catch an STD from a toilet seat," "What is the functional purpose of armpit hair," and "If a guy died having sex, would he still be saluting, and how would this be dealt with at the funeral?" from the boatload he finds there. He snickers after each and asks if the card it's written on is mine. I roll my eyes.

There are cards in his next bag, too. Fortunately those turn out to be just reading responses to *Great Expectations*. Brand seems disappointed: no more ammo to annoy me with.

Just when I think he'll shut up for a while—*god*, I liked

him better as the strange and silent type—he says, "So hey, not that it's any of my business, but uh—what was all the rage about?"

I don't look up at him. "Rage?"

"The pots and shit? That wasn't just because you lost something. You were angry."

My hands stop, tightening around a fistful of quizzes.

"My sister is gone," I say quietly. "How am I supposed to feel?"

To that, Brand says nothing.

I wish he hadn't asked. Now the silence elongates, oppressive.

Out of nowhere—perhaps of a need to fill it in again—I look over my shoulder and say, "I found something."

Brand stops digging. "What?"

"Not here. I mean—of hers."

"Your sister's?"

I nod, not sure if I can trust him. How much I can share? "It was something she kept from people."

"We all have secrets, Lemon."

"Sure." I turn all the way around to face him. "But not like this."

"Like what?"

It isn't my secret. But I can't exactly talk to Camilla about it, either.

Or anyone else.

"The other day I found this . . . letter."

I don't tell him everything, but I hit on the important stuff: the use of "You" and "Me," the fact that Camie was "leaving him in high school," and oh yes, let's not forget—that she was breaking up with him.

"She had this whole . . . secret relationship with someone. Probably right here at Fairfield."

For a moment Brand and I just look at each other, and then abruptly, as if released by some spell, he shifts and returns to his bag.

"And what would you do if you found this guy?" he asks, sifting. "Guy?" he adds for verification.

"Think so. I'd give him the letter. Then . . ." I frown and lift my shoulders. Brand waits for me to complete the thought, but I just shake my head. "I don't know, maybe I'm sticking my nose where it doesn't belong. Maybe it's after the fact, and it doesn't matter. I mean, Camilla's already—" My throat walls up and I close a hand. Brand knows what she is.

I switch gears instead. "Do you think a breakup letter would just be a kick in the nuts?"

A crooked smile. "You said 'nuts.'"

I scowl.

"But no, if you want my opinion—I don't think it's after the fact. Just the opposite. *You* still miss her, don't you?"

"What kind of question is that? Of course I miss her."

"Well—dude she wrote that to probably misses her, too. If anything, I bet the letter'd give the poor sap some closure. Hell, delivering it'd probably give *you* closure."

Or make up for something terrible.

"Probably. But how am I supposed to find this 'You' guy? I've already done some asking; one of Camie's best friends knew nothing, and the other isn't talking. If I can't get any leads from them, then—"

But Brand has stopped listening. He is staring at something in front of him.

A card.

Hope and fear vie in my chest—I *knew* I'd last seen it in *Great Expectations*! I must've dropped 65 in English after all.

But when I take it from his hands, the smile falls from my face.

Brand's found a secret, all right. It just isn't my secret.

It's worse.

Below a discussion question ("Who changes most over the course of the novel? Explain.") is a paragraph that's been violently scribbled out. Under it, in tiny writing:

> FUCK IT
> I've had enough. I really thought this year was going to be different. (It is: It's WORSE.) How can people be so cruel? Tomorrow I'm cleaning out my locker. Saturday I'll end this misery *once and for all.*

"Is it just me," says Brand, "or is that last bit kind of morbid?"

I turn the card over. A name has left impressions in the paper, and I squint and make it out just before I spot the silver Kisses in Brand's trash bag.

"Kody."

If the whispers in the halls are true, her locker isn't the only place she's been finding little presents the last few days: chocolates. Sugar substitutes. Diet sodas and weight loss shakes. All part of a balanced Morgan plot against her. I heard one girl in history say that they're passed to Kody from the front of the room every time the teacher sends back handouts.

Horrifying.

"Kody Hotchkiss?"

Brand has heard, too, apparently. I suppose he learns a thing or two during all those classes he cuts.

"Yeah." I read the card again. "We have to do something."

He folds his arms. "And just what would you suggest?"

"Anything! Call her house. Tell a teacher. Talk t—"

"Hold your cape, superhero. Kody will have to live with the consequences."

"Isn't that kind of the point, though?—That she *lives*?"

"You're not hearing me, Lemon. Intervention is tricky. If it goes badly for her, Kody could end up even *more* miserable. This has gotta be handled delicately."

"Delicately?" That's rich. What would someone who goes around destroying things with a lighter and box cutters know about being delicate?

"That's what I said. Seems to me young Kody could really use a friend right now."

"So—what? We invite her to eat lunch with us or something?"

"Uh," says Brand. "*You* invite her. I can't go around befriending people. Bad for my image."

"What?" This *is* the guy who signed everyone's yearbooks "Go to hell" last June, isn't it? "I thought you didn't care what people think."

"No—I don't care what any*body* thinks. Singular."

"What's the difference?"

"What *people* think—collectively—shapes reputation. If *people* think I'm a softie, it's bad for the band."

"Well—are you?"

Brand's frown deepens. I step back, seeing the haircut,

the jeans, the cigarettes, the guitar—even the aloofness in new light. "Oh my god, you totally are!"

I grin. Brand says, "Fuck off," and starts away from me, hands shoved tight in his pockets. His defensiveness makes me grin even harder.

"You know—" He spins back without stopping. "I would've expected a little sympathy from the girl who headed straight for Ghost Town Central at the Club Fair."

That gives me pause. "What do you mean?"

"Your choice of club? Don't tell me you weren't avoiding people when you joined—"

"Oh my god—Booster!" I wrestle off a yellow glove to check my watch.

Great.

I've just officially missed the first meeting of the GSBC.

On Friday, I do it.

I brave lunch in the cafeteria.

It isn't for me, you understand; it's for a better cause. A better cause named Kody Hotchkiss.

I find her near the wall by the milk machine. She sits at a small round table, alone, poking at a Tupperware salad and reading. I squint and catch the title of the book in her hands: *Lucy Killman: Underling*. What else? And oh, look what shirtless wonder graces her lunchbox.

I walk as if toward the milk machine, then veer close like something's caught my eye.

"Is that Rush Hollister?" I ask, indicating the lunchbox in question.

Kody looks up from her salad. "Guilty."

I gesture *one sec*, buy a bottle of strawberry milk I have no intention of drinking, and return to the table.

"What're you reading?"

I slide into a seat.

Kody looks around like she's not sure she's the one I'm talking to. "Um. *Lucy Killman*. I've already read it four times, but I wanted to read it one last time before . . ."

My breath catches.

"Before I see the movie. My parents wouldn't let me do the midnight premiere, so I'm seeing it tonight."

"You are?"

Shit. What if Lucy Killman is the last thing standing between Kody and a toaster in the tub? Her card said Saturday.

"Yeah, the late show. I heard people are dressing up."

But if I got her to go later—

"Kody," I start, tentative, "I know this is kind of sudden, but I was hoping to see it this weekend, too, and—and the thing is, I haven't really been tight with my best friend lately. You know, since Camilla . . ." I pause to see if she understands. Kody nods. "And anyway . . . do you wanna maybe, go together?"

A wedge of cucumber falls from her fork. "Together?"

I smile and nod, a silent prayer the pity card will work for me.

"Uh . . ." Kody straightens and tucks a wisp of hair behind her ear. I have caught her totally off guard. "Yeah. Sure. I guess."

"Really?" I light up like a carnival. Camie used to say I could turn on the charm when I really wanted to. "Thanks, Kody, I'm so glad! But oh, minor detail. I promised the neighbors I'd babysit for them tonight, so would you mind if we waited until tomo—"

The lie dies on my lips.

Walking toward us is Lauren. She's tapping at her phone and doesn't see me, but I can't look away. Hide or say something, hide or say something?

Kody frowns at me. "Juniper?"

When she hears my name, Lauren looks up.

Say something.

"Uh—hey, Lauren," I offer.

Lauren blinks at me. "Hey."

For a moment, the exchange feels normal: eye contact. Acknowledgment. Relative ease.

But then, like our last encounter, after a few seconds, neither of us really knows what to say to each other.

"You . . . know Kody?" I venture, at last unable to withstand the silence.

"Hi." Lauren lifts an awkward hand with a smile. "Are, um. Are you . . . ?" Her eyes stray toward our former table.

Does that mean she actually *wants* to eat together?

"Kody and I were just making plans for the weekend," I volunteer, miraculously more casually than I feel right now. "Do you . . . want to sit with us?"

Hope knots in my chest.

"Really?"

She sounds surprised. I can't tell if it's good surprised ("Wait—you actually want to sit with me?") or bad ("Wow—you're really going to make me answer that?"). Maybe neither; maybe Lauren's just shocked to hear I still *do* things weekends.

"What, um," she starts. She looks down and adjusts her handbag. I can't think of a goodbye that starts with "what," but I'm sure she's about to leave.

Until she hangs the bag on a chair and sits in it.

"What did you guys have in mind?"

And my chest fills up with such sudden, intense joy that for a moment my eyes water.

I cut a glance at Kody to make sure she's on board with this and incredibly, she is. Her smile is sympathetic, her raised brows encouraging.

Funny. When did she become the one helping me?

Lauren compliments Kody's lunchbox. Kody beams and asks her if she's read the books, and they get to talking, and all at once I see past swirl with present: a year of new traditions at a new lunch table, or maybe even off campus—we could induct Kody with a "toast" at Pippa's. Maybe Kody is into musicals and will join our obnoxious singing sleepovers. Maybe I'll end up liking the Killman books. It sounds like Lauren's gotten into them this summer—maybe we could all even see the first movie together?

I open my strawberry milk, and am about to make the suggestion when Kody suddenly stops smiling.

"Hello, Kisses," says a voice behind me.

I turn in my chair. Beside us, smiling evilly, stands Morgan with her latest cast of minions.

"Rachel noticed you left your present in the locker room," she observes, "so I thought I'd bring it back to you."

Something lands on the table in front of Kody: a full package of the silver-foiled candies.

"Do try to remember it this time. It hurts when you're so careless with my gifts."

The girls make kissy noises, then erupt in laughter and turn to leave. Kody flushes and tries to disappear into her hair. Lauren looks as if she'd gladly do the same.

"*Hey.*"

The posse stops and looks back. I realize I am standing and have challenged her without a plan.

Morgan sneers. "Do you have something to say to me, Juniper?"

She starts back to the table.

"Just . . . that . . . I think you're an awful person, and maybe you should keep your insecurities to yourself." I snap the bag of Kisses back at her. She catches it with a flinch, and then closes her eyes as if relishing the glove thrown.

When she opens them, she laughs.

"That's sweet, Juni. Shame you don't have quite the eloquence your sister did. Maybe you should leave the heroics to her. Oh wait, you can't—she's *dead*."

I feel my milk bottle crunch in my hand.

"That's low."

"No, Juniper. You know what's *low*?" Morgan slides closer but makes no effort to lower her voice. "Your sister two-timing Shawn. I heard that was why he broke up with her—caught her cheating with another guy. Slut needed *two* boys to—"

Splash.

Strawberry milk runs down Morgan's nose.

"Don't. Talk about my sister that way."

I feel unstable: head sick with adrenaline. Kody's slowly rising like she might need to restrain me; Lauren is receding, folding down, down, down into her conflict-free shell. Even now she has nothing to say?

"What way?" Morgan challenges. *"'Sluuuut'?"*

A strangled sound rips from somewhere—me, I realize—and in the next moment Morgan is on the floor and I am on top of her, not punching or clawing or pulling hair—just *shaking* her. I don't even hear the chants of "FIGHT, FIGHT, FIGHT!"—I just watch her head snap back and forth, back and forth.

Eventually strong arms pull me up and I see Morgan sprawled on the tile, small and winded and covered in strawberry milk.

"What's going on here?"

The demand is the first thing to register. More hands help Morgan up.

"Are you all right?" the voice asks her.

Morgan recovers and smoothes out her blazer. Then:

"Mr. Bodily!" she gasps. "Ju . . . Juniper *attacked* me!"

Mr. Bodily looks from her sopping face, to me, to the mostly empty bottle of strawberry milk on the floor. "Is this true?" he asks.

I know how it looks. I'm too furious to care.

"Come with me," he says.

I take my backpack and follow him out.

The adrenaline ebbs as we navigate the halls. I expect to be marched straight to the principal's office, but feel only hollowness as we move past it and toward Bodily's own classroom.

When we arrive he draws a chair for me before his desk. "Have a seat."

"Am I in trouble?" I ask, but more out of reflex than actual concern.

"Please, sit," he insists. I do. Mr. Bodily lowers himself on the other side and considers me gravely, chin atop folded hands. "I'm afraid detention is inevitable," he says at last. "That kind of attack on another student can't go unpunished, regardless of how provoked. Or merited."

"Merited?" I raise my eyes from the desk. "Are you saying Morgan deserved it?"

He frowns, but makes a gesture of allowance. "As a teacher, you understand, I have to be objective about these things. What matters is the attack and its consequences."

I nod and drop my head.

"But as a fellow human being, I think I should tell you that I heard what Morgan said. That it was terrible. And that I *know* Camilla would've been proud of her little sister for standing up for her like that." I look up.

Mr. Bodily is smiling.

At this, something in me shifts. It's like all my residual rage is suddenly pushed back, banished by this one little candle after so much darkness. To have someone remember Camilla with me—for a moment she's not just a memory, some dream I'm forgetting. She is real: confirmed by this stranger's validation, this piece of her he holds that fits with mine.

I look down so he won't see my twisted expression. "Thanks."

"Anytime. And Juniper"—Mr. Bodily lowers his chin as if looking over a pair of glasses—"I mean that. In the future, if you're ever upset about your sister at school or someone like Morgan is giving you a hard time, *please* come talk to me before wasting another perfectly good strawberry milk."

That wins a small smile. "Okay."

Exactly five minutes and seventeen seconds pass between the time detention starts and when Mrs. Davies, the pit bull–faced teacher who's supposed to be supervising us, nods forward at her desk and begins to snore like a chainsaw with a sinus infection. Three seconds later Brand is sitting at the desk next to mine.

"Like clockwork," he says. "Shall we?" He gets up without waiting for an answer.

"Shall we *what*?" I ask as he heads for the door.

"You wanna find that card of yours, or not?"

"Yeah, but—"

Brand's right. The clock is ticking: I only have until Tuesday morning before garbage is collected, and the weekend will be busy with watching Kody. This is one of my last real chances to search. Still . . . "I mean, we can't just—"

"*Relax*. She won't wake until quarter to four." He means Mrs. Davies.

"But if we get caught—"

"They'll what? Give us more detention?" Brand rolls his eyes. "Live a little, Lemon."

"I live plenty."

"Sure you do. How's Booster Club working out for you?"

My face sours. I'd remind him that I skipped the first meeting, but dumpster-diving's not exactly an improvement.

Brand smirks and walks out the door.

"You comin', or what?" he calls from the hall.

I glare after him. "At least I'm not a lifer in the fucking Breakfast Club."

With a last look at the hibernating Mrs. Davies, I slink past her and shut the door behind me.

"So why were you in detention?" asks Brand when we are again elbow-deep in papers and pizza crusts.

I blow a lock of hair from my face, annoyed it keeps trailing down even after I put it up. "I may or may not have attacked Morgan Malloy."

"Oh?" Brand stops trawling long enough to light a cigarette. "And what might have prompted this factual or fictitious display of rage?"

"She insulted Camilla."

"Mm."

"What about you? Why are you in detention?"

"Me? Still doin' time for your crime."

"Hey, you helped. And I thought you just got in-school for that—no after hours?"

Brand smiles, the cigarette clamped between his teeth while he digs with his hands. "What can I say? I'm a glutton for punishment."

I tie off a bag that is mostly cupcake wrappers, nacho sauce, and citrus-smelling flakes of orange peel and swap it for one full of French papers, notes whose authors whine about how bored (B-O-R-E-D and B-O-A-R-D) they are, and a box worth of Scooby-Doo fruit snack wrappers. Then, as I'm peeling through the verbs and misspellings and gummy Velmas, something slips to the ground. I dip to retrieve it.

A note.

I can tell right away this one isn't like the others; it's folded down into eighths, long-form, addressed lovingly in flourish to "Leo."

I open it and read:

Dear Leo,

Every day something new about you amazes me. One day it's that, in addition to being a painter, sculptor, architect, scientist, inventor, philosopher, cartographer, engineer, botanist, musician, mathematician, and general intellect you also wrote <u>fables</u>; another that you wore pink, which is so cool and ahead of your time but unfortunately makes me think that the rumors were probably true, and it would have never worked out between us; today that you were a vegetarian, and would purchase caged animals at market for the sole purpose of setting them free. YOU FREAKIN' ROCK.

If you have not been reincarnated into someone with one-hundredth your former intelligence, could you <u>please</u> manifest into some kind of sign—any sign—and point me to someone who has? At least ONE? I mean, my god. The only things the boys I know are interested in are Zombocalypse, boobs, and Instagram. Or other boys.

Help a girl out here?

Love,
A

A laugh-cough escapes at *Zombocalypse, boobs, and Instagram.* I clear my throat.

"You all right there, Lemon?" Brand exhales a stream of smoke.

"Read this." He takes the note and scans.

"What is this—one of those write-in advice things? Dear Abby?"

"*Leo's* no Abby. I'm pretty sure she means da Vinci."

"Da Vinci? The fuck is she asking a dead guy for dating advice?"

I rip the page back. "She's not. She's writing *to* him, not for advice—just admiration. Like fan mail."

"Uh-huh."

"She already knows what she's looking for . . ." I frown at the letter. "She just needs some help finding it."

A half smirk plays at Brand's lips.

"What?"

"Like you." Smoky exhale.

"Except I didn't *ask* for your help," I grumble.

"What was that?"

I smile and lift my shoulders.

Brand goes back to his bag, and I start to go back to mine, but the letter to Leo won't let go of me. Who is A? Doesn't *anybody* sign their name anymore? Whoever the author, it seems a shame to just throw something like this away . . .

I peek over my shoulder.

When Brand isn't watching, I fold the salvaged note down and slip it in a pocket of my jeans.

"Hey."

I jump and spin around too quickly. But Brand is preoccupied, crushing his cigarette butt with his shoe.

"So what's the deal with Kody?" he asks. I release my breath.

"Well," I say, considering a French printout I can read about six words of, "I sat with her at lunch today."

"And?"

I suck air through my teeth. "Started off okay . . ."

Brand looks up for the *but*.

". . . and then Bitchicane Morgan happened."

"'Bitchicane'?" He grins. "This Lemon's got zest."

I shrug. "I *did* invite her to see Lucy Killman tomorrow— Kody, not Morgan—but she was planning to see it tonight, and I don't know if she'll hold out for me."

"Sure she will." Brand hauls a closed bag back to the dumpster. "Be aggressive, Lemon Little. Call her house. Tell her what it would mean to you. Don't take no for an answer."

"My name is Juniper. And I think I can handle a little adversity, thank you."

"Says the girl who, *wearing gloves,* just flung a chewed piece of gum away like a hairy tarantula."

"It was not a *piece* of gum, it was—"

"Besides, 'Lemon' suits you. It matches the face you make every time you see me."

I feel my lips start to purse and chew them back, determined not to validate Brand's point. Unfortunately, this only adds to the impression I've just ingested something sour and am trying not to show it, and when Brand grins, my scowl gets the better of me. He leans against the dumpster with folded arms, awaiting—*inviting*—a retort.

When I don't make one, he says, "So? Kody?"

I assure him, face as even and pleasant as possible, that I will figure something out.

For the rest of the time we don't talk—just rummage. At 3:40 we put our scavengings away, still no 65. I offer Brand wet wipes. He offers me a head start before he sprays his Axe to mask the smell of cigarette smoke.

I don't have Kody's cell number, but once home I find her landline in the school directory. When I call it and no one answers, I leave this message:

"Hi Kody, it's Juniper. Uh, sorry we didn't get to finish making our plans today. But if you're still on for Lucy Killman tomorrow, I'd love to see it together! Call me so we can work out where and when." I leave my number, and emphasize that I'm looking forward to it. I figure at this stage a little guilting couldn't hurt any.

Then, because I think of Lauren and my murdered daydream that we'd all go together, I reach for my Index.

69

Happiness: 23
Breaking the ice with Lauren (+), only to
be forsaken two minutes later (---).
Mr. Bodily, re: strawberry milk (ha!) & Camie
proud of me (+++). Love letter to Leo (+).
Detention (-).
"Dead" and "slut" comments (-----).
Still no answer from Heather (-).
Brand Sayers (?).

As I'm reading the card over, I remember the love note from A to Leo in my pocket and take it out. Then I open my desk drawer to reveal Kody's card, the words "once and for all" in bold. I now have three notes that don't belong to me—two of which are undeliverable, and one which no one was meant to read.

What am I doing with them?

I file 69 away. As I pass the gap between 64 and 66, it occurs to me that I only found Kody's note because I'd been looking for 65. What if I'd never found Camie's letter? What if 65 had been like any other day, and I'd never brought the card to school with me and lost it and had to go digging for it?

Nobody would know about Kody.

A shiver runs down my arms. I know. I know and that means something. It has to.

I'll see to it.

I start to put the shoebox away, but just as I'm nestling on the lid my eye catches on A's letter again and I have an idea.

Inspired, I stop and I spider back to 69. Then, holding the open spot, I reach for the letter to Leo and add it in.

With 68 goes Kody's notecard.

At the hole where 65 should be, Camilla's letter. It doesn't fill the gap, exactly—in fact, it kind of sticks out like an ugly bookmark—but it holds the space, and feels marginally better than nothing.

I appraise my work. For some reason, the outliers remind me of the shards heaped in sacks in Ms. Gilbert's studio: I don't know what purpose they can possibly serve, orphan fragments that they are—but their existence, I am certain, means something.

At half past six, I hesitate outside Mom's door. Normally when Dad had some kind of dinner function, we—me, Mom, and Camie, that is—would raid the fridge for leftovers, combine whatever we could scrounge into mugs, then microwave and share our creations (chicken spaghetti, meatloaf parmesan, mac and chowder) at the coffee table over sitcoms or *Project Runway*. Tonight is the first late meeting Dad's had since . . . well.

I lift my fist to knock.

Stop again.

Mom's been shut in her room since she got home. Even if

she isn't sleeping, that makes me think that either she forgot about Mug Night, or she knows perfectly well what night it is, and just doesn't want to do it without Camie. I don't know which possibility hurts more.

But maybe I'm being unfair. I should at least try . . .

I raise my knuckles for the hundredth time tonight. The worst that can happen is that she'll say no, right?

I knock.

On the second strike, the phone rings.

Damn it.

I press an ear against the wood and rap more loudly. "Mom?"

Second ring.

Nothing . . .

On the third, I grunt and give up and hustle downstairs to grab the call in the kitchen.

"Hello?"

At first there's no answer; just the kind of silence that accompanies a wrong number. Then I hear a voice that is muffled as if turned away: "Yeah, it's ringing. It's . . ."

"Hello?" I repeat, hopeful.

A shuffle. "Hello? Juniper?"

Oh thank god. "Kody?"

"Hi, Juniper. Yeah, it's me."

"Kody, I'm so glad I caught you." She doesn't even know. "So, what do you think—are we on for Lucy tomorrow?"

Say yes, say yes, oh please if you don't I will show up at your house and things could get very uncomfortable.

"Um . . . yeah, actually. Would the three o'clock be okay? It's still a matinee, but late enough to sleep in, if you want."

"Three?" I'd watch it back to back all day if she asked to. "That's perfect. At the mall?"

"Yeah."

("Ask her if she needs a ride," says a loud whisper.)

("*Mom*," says Kody.)

("I can drive you," says the whisper.)

"Do you need a ride?" Kody asks. She sounds harried, but I envy her. I'd give anything for Mom to play helicopter right now.

"Nah," I say. "I'll meet you there. Thanks, though. Meet in front of the theater?"

"Okay. Sounds good."

"Okay." I put on a smile brighter than I am feeling before adding, "See you tomorrow!"

"See you tomorrow."

- 70 -

I arrive at the mall well before the 3:00 p.m. showing, but at a stroke of genius stall until twenty-five after: what I hope is just past the opening scene, too far in for a diehard fan like Kody to excuse, but not so far that she thinks I've bailed on her or I can't blame my tardiness on ludicrous traffic.

"Ludicrous traffic," I say when I find her on a bench in front of the theater. "Sorry I'm late!"

Sorry, not sorry. One showing missed = two hours more to work with.

When I greet her, though, and she lifts her head up in response, Kody doesn't look disappointed; she doesn't even seem angry that because of me she has now twice delayed seeing what she presumably feels is the only thing left worth living for. She finds my gaze indifferently, with eyes that look but do not see. I recognize them instantly: They're the same glazed-over, lost-in-the-fog pupils as Mom's. If Kody startled when I spoke to her, it was only because I'd caught her staring at the levels beneath us, at the people milling below, at nothing.

For all I know, at the drop.

"That's all right," she says, vaguely closing a copy of *Lucy Killman* she'd not been reading, and smiling in a way that is clearly more out of courtesy than excitement to see me. "We'll just catch the next one?"

"Great."

The next showing isn't until 4:55. Kody and I buy tickets, and then make awkward small talk while we ride the escalators back to central shopping. We talk about *Great Expectations*, its ungodly length, how lame it was that we had to spend the last of our summers on a book that could flatten three hamsters, even in paperback; about Mr. Bodily, who some of our classmates are already calling The Bod for his Abercrombian white shirt + washboard abs look; about, no eyes rolled, Rush Hollister and his own "caged oblivion" eyes (a direct quote from the book, if I'm not mistaken).

We do not talk about what happened at lunch yesterday.

By the time we reach the first floor, all that's left to discuss is *Lucy Killman* itself, which I am only pretending to have read and know next to nothing about, so when I see a directory in our path I nearly melt from relief.

"So." I loop my arm through Kody's in a show of enthusiasm. "Where do you like to shop?"

Kody eyes the listings like they're in Elvish. "I don't know. I guess I've never been much of a shopper."

"No?"

Suddenly, unexpectedly, something other than floating indifference crosses Kody's face. "Come on," she says, a cynical edge slicing through. "Where does a girl *this* big"—she holds her arms out in exaggeration—"go to find an attractive mini skirt?"

I grimace, but am actually glad for the punchy reply. Snark cares.

Now that I look more closely, Kody's clothes—a hippie skirt and a black tee under a jean jacket—seem strategically loose. It occurs to me she wears a lot of clothes that conceal her figure rather than show it, and might not even own anything more fitted.

I nod at a storefront ahead of us. "Wanna check out Forever 21?"

A spark enters her eyes.

We leave the store several bags heavier.

"Christ on a *stick*." Kody hefts hers back over her shoulders before we spot something else. "Is shopping always this much work?"

I nudge her with my own bags. "Come on, Kody. It's not like you've never been shopping before."

"Yeah, but not at a trendy store where everything's fitted. Where am I even going to *wear* these things? These are, like. NICE clothes."

Going to. Future tense. This is good.

"What's wrong with NICE clothes?" I ask.

"NICE clothes are for people who are . . . I don't know. Artistic. Preppy. Good-looking. People like you."

I stop in my tracks. Kody stops, too. I don't know where to correct her first. "So . . . what," I say, turning an eye at her, "you don't think you're *good enough* to wear the clothes you just bought?"

Kody looks at the floor. Suddenly the bags seem to weigh on her arms. "I don't know." Her voice is small. "I think someone like me needs an occasion to look nice, and doesn't have many."

I search her eyes, lips pursed.

"Come on," I say, and then escort her by the arm to the nearest restroom.

∞

I'm not one for motivational speeches, but given the sudden nature of Camilla's death, I believe it when I tell Kody that life *is* an occasion, damn it—and only what you make of it while it's yours. Therefore, it would be Perfectly Acceptable and Not at All Ridiculous for her to wear NICE clothes to a little old movie and maybe dinner afterward (still trying to buy whatever time I can here). Kody agrees, but only on the condition that I change into new clothes, too.

We leave the restroom in dresses and impractical shoes.

"Well," I prompt, arching a brow as we attract lingering looks from a passing group of teens, "how do you feel now?"

Kody rolls her eyes, but concedes a smile. "'I feel pretty. Oh so pretty. I feel pretty, and witty, and'—actually, pretty hungry at the moment. Shopping really takes it out of you."

As if on cue with her break from *West Side Story* lyrics, my stomach rumbles. "Wanna stop for something before we head up?"

We find our way to the food court and into line for smoothies.

"Why don't you grab a table?" I suggest. We're both shuffling our bags from arm to arm to remain comfortable. "These are on me."

"Really? You don't have to—"

"I want to. *And* I'd like to be able to feel my arms tomorrow."

Kody laughs. "Fair enough."

She tells me her favorite flavor—Strawberry Storm, same as mine—and relieves me of my purchases. Somehow, in the transfer of goods, I end up with Kody's purse, her copy of *Lucy Killman* sticking out of it.

"Can I look at this?" I call after her. Kody glances back and nods, smiling.

I *did* sort of let her think I'm as much of a Killmaniac as she is. I should probably have some idea of what I'm walking into in thirty minutes.

The jacket flap says:

> When a stranger buys her freedom from Bellingham Sanitarium, Lucy Killman swears one thing: revenge on those that murdered her family and had her committed. But the stranger has other plans. He wants Lucy to attend Scholomance, an elite school in Romania that admits only ten new pupils a year. What she'll learn there, he promises, will help Lucy wreak vengeance beyond her wildest dreams—a claim he proves with a gruesome magic trick.
>
> She agrees.
>
> But when Lucy arrives at the school, her escort—the Devil himself, its headmaster—reveals only *one* of the new pupils can be named his apprentice. If the ten want his mentorship in the Black Arts—and like Lucy, they all have very good reasons to want it—they will have to compete for it in the Consequences, an otherworldly contest of smarts, dark magic, and survival. To win, they must learn on their feet and fight until one is left standing.
>
> Let the selection begin . . .

Huh. That actually sounds . . . decent. If not for Rush What-Is-a-Shirt Hollister playing Vance Devore, fellow competitor/love interest, I might even say it sounded good.

"I can help who's next!"

With a start, I realize that's me and slip the book away.

"Hi," I say up at the counter. "Could I get a medium Strawberry Storm and Coconut Crush?"

"Medium on the coconut, too?"

"Ye—" I stop short.

Coconut?

I wasn't thinking.

I ordered *Lauren's* favorite flavor instead of Kody's.

"Yes," I finish hastily. Kody can have mine.

I pay as the order goes back, echoing my mistake. It blows through me like a wind, my best friend a ghost as I wait for our drinks by myself.

I stand to the side and hug my arms until they're ready.

"Well, if it isn't the little milkmaid," a voice surprises me when I grab them.

Morgan.

"Eating your way out?" She nods at my double order. The minions on either side of her snicker.

Still, I can't help noticing that she steps back a little. I permit myself a small smirk.

I'd love to upgrade that milk mask to real fruit.

But before I can say so, Morgan spots something else: the *two* purses looped on my arms. I try to divert her, but when she looks around, her eyes go straight to Kody.

"Oh! You're here with Kisses." She pouts her lips at Rachel, and Rachel and Minion #2 start the trademark kissy noises.

That gets Kody's attention.

"Leave us alone." I push past her, trying to signal to Kody that we should leave. Kody stands and begins gathering up our bags, but Morgan follows me over.

"I think it's sweet you two made friends. Must be nice knowing someone else who lost some *body* this summer, eh, Kisses?"

I smile at her, hard. "My friend's name is Kody. Though if your language setting wasn't stuck on Bitchalian, I'm sure you would have gotten it right by now."

I turn and guide Kody away, leaving Morgan behind us.

"You—" Morgan pips.

But she can only sputter.

When we round the corner, Kody bursts into laughter.

"'Bi—*Bitchalian*'?" She grins at me and wipes her eyes.

I smile back. "I have my moments."

In the darkness of the theater, we settle into our seats and watch the ads roll.

"Hey," Kody says after one. "Thanks, Juniper."

I replace my silenced phone in my bag. Still no word from Heather about who Camie might have been dating.

"For what?" I ask.

"For today."

I smile. "Day's not over yet."

"I mean," she says, "for standing up for me. Twice now."

I let the statement sit. I think about saying "It's nothing," or "You deserve it," or calling Morgan some other woefully uninspired bitch pun, but decide against it.

Instead, I say, "Don't flatter yourself. Yesterday I was standing up for my sister."

Kody laughs. Another good sign.

"You know, Juniper." She turns to me in her seat. "I'm really glad I came out with you today."

"Yeah?" A swell of warmth fills my chest. "Me too."

"I almost didn't."

I try to be casual: "Oh?"

"To be honest . . ." Kody smiles, guilty, "my mom heard your message on the answering machine and . . . and kind of *made me* pick up the phone and call you back."

"Good," I tell her. "I'm glad she did." And I mean it.

The lights go down and the theater quiets as the screen runs blank. In the darkness, Kody says, "If you ever want to talk to someone, Juniper . . . I mean, I know I didn't really know Camilla, but . . . if you want . . . I'm here."

My heart counts a few measures in the black. In the infinity of the lightless room, her offer is like a hand slipped into mine.

"Thank you," I whisper to her outline. "I'm going to hold you to that."

And then sound and special effects explode from the speakers, and the previews are too loud to keep talking.

The later showing leads to dinner, and dinner leads to Kody's house. Kody loans me the first *Lucy Killman*, her mom makes her model her new outfits (Kody makes me model mine with her), and before you can say "Netflix," the night is hurtling toward tomorrow.

I scribble the day's events on a borrowed index card while Kody is brushing her teeth:

Happiness: 5
Coconut Crush (−).
Morgan (−).
Still nothing from Heather (−).
But Kody & unplanned sleepover!! (+++).
Lucy Killman (OMG AMAZING I AM FULLY GOING
TO READ THE BOOKS NOW).
Rush Hollister (Um, +. He is actually kind of
hot in the movie).

In the morning Kody fixes crêpes Suzette, a delicious con-
coction fried in buttery orange syrup and lit in brandy
at the end. She's made it so many times she doesn't even
flinch when the flame belches out of the saucepan. I'm so
impressed (Kody juggled *fire* before noon; I grated orange
peel) that she even offers to teach me—maybe next weekend, if I'm free?

We shake on it.

But the more confident I am in Kody's safety, the more my
thoughts return to You. On the drive home that afternoon,
I take stock of my leads. Heather's beginning to look like a
dead end; after her, I have only Shawn and the letter itself,
which I go over and over in my head.

Dear You . . .

Here's what I think: Camilla was a smart girl. She wouldn't
have carried around incriminating evidence of a secret
relationship unnecessarily—and since the letter is neither
stamped nor addressed, I can only assume she intended to
hand it off to Secret Lover Boy in person. That would've
meant meeting someone at Shawn's, the only place we went
on July Fourth.

More reason to think she lied to get permission to go.

Could Shawn know something?

I'll ask him tonight.

∞

Dinner is as awkward a game as ever. I think, what with my returning to school, Dad imagined that there would be more to talk about.

There isn't.

"So," he starts. This is how pretty much all attempts at conversation begin around the Lemon house right now. "How was school this week, Juniper?"

I spear a carrot. "Okay."

"How're classes?"

"So far, pretty slow. Art's the only one we really did anything in."

"Art I? Isn't that the one your sis—"

STOP: Brick wall.

Go back three spaces.

"Er—" he amends.

I'm sure he meant to say art was the class Cam recommended to explore new mediums; to delve into my "doodle" brain, as she called it. And it was. But with Mom so withdrawn, the name of the game is Tiptoe—and we play every night.

"That's the one with the different mediums, right? Where you get to try a new one each unit?"

Great save! Collect Forkful of Pot Roast.

"Yeah."

"And what are you doing now?"

"Ceramics. But—"

"Oh! Like—" Dad inclines his head at our salt and pepper shakers: two of a pink-and-lemon-print set Camie made. There's a matching sugar jar and a bigger one for coffee on the counter.

"Well—yes, but, actually I opted out of ceramics. I'm doing independent study for the unit instead."

"Oh?" Dad looks at Mom. Mom looks at her plate. "What do you do for that?"

"Um." I glance down at my food. "I'm not totally sure yet. We're supposed to settle on a theme tomorrow."

Dad nods slowly. I can tell he's holding back, pausing to allow Mom a window.

She doesn't take it.

"Anything calling to you?"

I press my lips in to mask my disappointment. Mom used to weigh in on everything.

"Not really."

The table falls back into silence—or rather, to the sounds of forks and knives hitting plates. The absence on Camilla's side of the table is so strong, it's like a vacuum, slowly sucking even the memories from the room. Gone with her enchanting laugh and puppy energy is a former way of life: Mom's stories, Dad's lame jokes, familial teasing, the kitchen swelling louder and louder as she and Mom talked over each other with rolling, hysterical punch lines and the four of us honked and clucked and held our stomachs till it hurt. You wouldn't know it now, but before the accident Mom was as animated as Cam was.

Knife and fork. Knife and fork.

Roll again?

"The pot roast is really good, Dad." I feel bad for him. Dad hasn't just lost Camilla; he's lost Mom, too, and in some ways even me. My whole life, until ten weeks ago, has included a big sister. Topics from which she is cut out don't come easily.

"Thanks." Dad smiles thinly. "You like the rosemary?"

"Rosemary! That's what it is. I was going to ask."

He brightens a little. "Your palate's come a long way, Juni. You know, when you were little, the only way you girls would eat potatoes was fro—"

STOP: Mom inhaled sharply.

Lose a turn.

"Pot roast is great for fall," I cut in. Weather is Free Parking. Can't go wrong there. "This last week I've really felt the change from summer. It's cold enough for tea now, and for wearing boots and scarves and things, and it's so nice and crisp in the mornings. I think I saw the first leaves on the ground on my way to the bus—"

Sniff.

Uh-oh—I've mentioned a First. Firsts without Camilla are just as bad, if not worse, than dropping her actual name.

Now Dad hurries to cover me. "I think it's the wind, is what it is. The chill factor, even when it's sunny—"

But it's too late: Mom has stood and swiftly exited the kitchen. The door to the porch bangs shut behind her.

STOP: You upset Mom.

Game Over. Go directly to Room.

Once Mom has resigned herself to sleep, I don't have to wait too much longer for Dad. Twenty minutes after their light goes off, I ease my door open and pad soundlessly through the dark from my room to Camie's.

I hate that I have to sneak in like this. But with the way Mom is now, I don't dare set foot in Camilla's room even to reclaim an old sweater. It's a fluke I ended up with the handbag she took to Shawn's; I guess it was just lumped together with the rest of the things returned when they discharged me from the hospital.

Once, just two weeks after the accident, I walked in without thinking for a pair of earrings. Mom was just coming upstairs with laundry, and saw me going through her jewelry from the hall.

The laundry basket crashed to the carpet.

The worst part wasn't even her face, the black wave that slammed me as I remembered Cam was dead; the way the color molted from Mom's cheeks, or that she shouted "OUT!" before gripping her mouth.

The worst part is that while Mom was down the hall, crying in her room right after, I was crying in mine.

And she either couldn't see it—couldn't see I needed her—or didn't care.

I swallow back the knives in my throat. This is why I must tiptoe:

To remind Mom of Camilla is to lose her.

It's strange; outside her room, I almost feel I should knock.

But I know better.

I turn the knob and steal in, then pull the door closed behind me.

Inside, I hit the lights. Shawn Parker's cell number is exactly where I remember it, on the bulletin board tacked among a thousand images—photos with friends and family, clubs, volunteer teams; postcards from club trips and projects abroad: Venice, Athens, London, Dublin, Berlin, Tokyo. Camie's dream was to see the world, and with her various activities, she was well on her way.

I touch a photo from Splash Mountain two summers ago.

Mom, Dad, Cam, and I had had a log to ourselves and all posed with pirate props bought earlier that day. Mom's in front aiming a spyglass, Dad *yarr*ing in an eye patch behind her. I'm checking a treasure map. Cam's in back shouting orders, a captain's hat held fast to her head while Bristol, her signature Dala horse, clings to her shoulder like a parrot. Posing Bristol for snapshots had been a big tradition of Cam's, especially traveling.

I glance across the room for the real thing. On the shelf above Cam's desk are five Swedish Dala horses, a fraction of the many around the house since our grandmother began giving away her collection. Every Christmas, birthday, and visit somebody gets one, but Bristol is special. Bristol was the first and the favorite. Bristol is—

I look closer.

Four.

There are *four* Dala horses on the shelf.

The smallest in the lineup is missing.

I start toward the desk to investigate—maybe Bristol is just misplaced or behind a book somewhere—but down the hall I hear Mom cough and remember myself. I can't look for Bristol tonight for the same reason I can't look for YOU leads: because Mom and Dad are both light sleepers. There will be better chances another day.

For now I free Shawn's number from its tack and pocket it.

The line rings three times before it's answered.

"HELLO?"

I cradle my ear and hold the phone away from me. Not your usual answering volume. "Shawn?" I ask when I bring it back.

"WHO IS THIS?"

This time I make out the music and blare of voices I'm competing against.

"Shawn?" I repeat, uncertain. "It's Juniper. Juniper Lemon?"

A pause. Then:

"Juniper?"

"Yeah," I say. "It's me. You have a minute? I was just calling to see if—"

"WHAT?" I can't tell if he's addressing me, or someone in the senseless background. "Sorry Juniper, kinda loud in here. Just a minute."

There's a shuffle, more bass, several shrieks of laughter and shouted conversation—something about Delta Chis and Taco Bell—and then the music is distant, and all I hear is breath in the line like the speaker has stepped outside and is rubbing his arms with cold.

"Juniper?" Shawn is crisp now.

"Yeah."

"It *is* you. Shit—I'm sorry about the noise."

"No worries. It's the weekend, it's late, and I know I'm kind of calling out of the blue—"

"Is everything okay?"

I open my mouth and no sound comes out. That's a loaded question these days.

"Um. It's all right."

"And how are *you*, Juniper? I mean—how're you holding up?"

I always liked Shawn. Shawn's the kind of person who reads the daily comics and laughs aloud at them (I know because he used to read them at our house after school):

easygoing, personable, genuine. He was kind of the goofball yin to Camie's hardworking yang. With Shawn, what you see is what you get.

When someone like him asks how I'm doing, I know it's because he really cares about the answer.

"I'm . . ." I close my eyes. "I mean, it's hard. It's like . . ." It's like walking around with a piece of glass in your chest. "The pain is always there, but you just live with it. You know?"

"Yeah," Shawn says quietly.

Camilla and Shawn broke up at the end of their junior year, right before she left to build houses in Chiapas. Camie had had her eye on the future: In the next year she'd be president of the International Club, on debate, and running for student council (of which she became, what else, senior class president). She wouldn't have time for a relationship, she said, and it'd be easier to end things now than when they went their separate ways for college. Shawn said he understood, and they'd remained friends, but uninvolved.

Even so, he looked pretty cut up at the funeral.

"How are you?" I ask him. "How's college?"

A gust of wind—maybe breath—blows into the line. "It's good, Juniper. It's good. I just wish . . ." He can't finish the thought. Or he doesn't know how to.

"I know," I tell him.

A heavy silence settles in between us. I remember why I called in the first place.

"So hey, uh—I hope I'm not interrupting your night or anything—"

"Not at all."

"I called because I have a sort of . . . weird question to ask you."

"Anything," says Shawn. "Shoot."

"Well . . ." I haven't quite decided how much to share with him. I plant my feet and lick my lips. "About . . . your party that night, Shawn. The Fourth. Were there . . . any other lowerclassmen there? Besides me? Or—not necessarily lowerclassmen. Just . . . people that didn't graduate?"

"Didn't graduate?"

"Are still in high school."

Silence. For a long moment not even the thunder of music booms in the background.

"That *is* a weird question," he says at last. "But knowing you, there's a good reason you're asking. So, let me think. Other than you . . ."

I wait, anxious and oddly envious as he searches his memory.

Shawn clicks his tongue. "Sorry, Juni. I really don't think a lot of underclassmen were there."

My shoulders slump. I guess I wasn't expecting an easy answer.

"Oh, but you know, there was a big party over in Aloha that night. I think a lot of the uh, 'underclassmen' went there. Don't know if that helps."

I sigh, away from the receiver so he can't hear me. "Thanks, Shawn."

"Sorry. I know that wasn't really what you asked. Is there . . . is there anything else I can do?"

"Um . . ."

What I'd *really* like is to ask Shawn whether he has any

idea who YOU might be. That may be a sensitive topic—

But he's the only source I've got right now.

"There is one thing. Can I ask you . . ." I pull a breath in. "When you and Cam broke up, Shawn. It was for . . . purely academic reasons, wasn't it?"

"Yeah . . ." Shawn says, but he drags the end of the word like a question. "At least, that's what she told me."

I drop back against my bed, staring at the ceiling.

"Why?" Shawn's voice is the only living thing in the room, but it sounds far, a million miles away. "Was there someone else?"

"Actually . . ." I shut my eyes. "I was kind of hoping you could tell *me*."

There is another silence—then, unexpectedly, Shawn laughs. "Your sister sure knew how to keep a secret. Do you know, for my seventeenth birthday"—I can almost see him shaking his head and smiling—"she let me believe we were stranded in the middle of nowhere on some spur-of-the-moment road trip? A light had come on on the dash and the engine was smoking, so we pulled over. No cell reception. A few cars passed, but nobody stopped.

"Then, like twenty minutes later, this fucking *stretch limo* rolls up . . ." He laughs. "The window goes down and there's Young and Trey and Amy and a dozen other people . . . She'd brought the party to *me*! Young got out and popped the hood—it was just dry ice or something, there was nothing wrong with it—and we drove around in the limo for hours, talking, drinking, doing karaoke, taking stupid pictures . . . sometimes getting out and pretending to be somebody famous . . . God. She'd gotten everyone to chip in. She'd been planning the whole thing for *months*, Juniper, and I am telling you, she kept a straight face even when the dummy light came on."

I realize I am smiling when Shawn finishes. I knew all about the surprise party—like he said, Camie had been planning it forever, and when it was over she had had enough Birthday Princess pictures and videos of Shawn's Miley Cyrus falsetto to prevent him from ever seeking public office—but hearing him tell the story, hearing him remember her . . . it's like Camie is alive again: existing between us, in shared memory. In Shawn's memory, given to me.

And for the smallest moment, the holes shrink back a little.

On Monday morning, Kody is alive and well. I return her copy of *Lucy Killman: Underling* and exchange it for *Lucy Killman: Blackblood Heir*. Oh—and are you wondering who survived the "selection"? Spoiler alert: It's in the title. But don't worry: Frenemy/love interest Vance Devore has outsmarted the Devil, and returns in book two to show he isn't finished with Lucy just yet.

Unfortunately, instead of celebrating like I should be, I'm tapping my pencil and drumming my fingers and bouncing my foot all throughout classes to get to the dumpsters. Tomorrow trash is collected.

Today is my last real chance to recover *65*.

In French I, the class I switched to from choir, I'm cycling through worst-case scenarios—that my Index is lodged behind a heater somewhere, that someone has found it already, that the shame is being whispered around me even now—when my fret-a-thon is broken by a text. I check my phone below the desk:

1 NEW MESSAGE
SHAWN PARKER

My chest tightens. Did Shawn see something at the party after all? I open the message with trembling fingers.

"Excusez-moi, mademoiselle."

I look up. Before me stands Madame Remy, hands on her hips.

"Le portable, s'il vous plaît."

I don't know what *le portable* is, but from Madame's outstretched hand I am guessing it does not mean "the outhouse." I hand over my phone. Madame takes it with a dutiful grimace.

"Merci, mademoiselle. Bon, on y va au dialogue . . ."

She glides back to the front of the room and hands out papers with a script, then divides us into groups to practice it. In my group are Angela Waters, a girl with aqua nails and two yellow ones—the index fingers—gripping a book, and Sponge, whose pronunciation is so fluid, it could sweep you up and carry you away.

"Bonjour mesdames," he says, flawless.

"Bonjour." When I say it, it sounds flat and rubbery by comparison.

We both look at Angela, who reluctantly holds her place in her bodice ripper and adds, without removing her finger, "Bonjour."

Très original, this dialogue.

"Je m'appelle Lawrence," Sponge continues. His given name falls like poured wine. *"Comment vous appelez-vous?"*

We introduce ourselves, and with a round of enchanté(e)s move into a more variable section of script where we can choose words from a vocab bank.

"Avez-vous [un portable]?" Angela asks me, pointing

with her free hand at a picture of a cell phone. I frown.

"Non," I reply, and sadly shake my head whilst pointing at Madame Remy. Then, sounding out the words to Sponge: "Ah-vay vooz [un shee-ann]?"

Above "chien" is a picture of a dog.

"Non, je n'ai pas [un chien]. Mais j'ai un [gros] [chat]; il aime [le fromage]." He asks Angela about the next item: *"Avez vous une sœur?"*

I try out the phrase Madame Remy taught us for when we don't understand: "Kuh—cased kuh sest?" A thousand percent sure that's not how *qu'est-ce que c'est* is pronounced, but not all of us can glide through the French alphabet.

"'Sœur'?" Angela checks the picture in the word bank— a girl, but it can't mean girl, because "girl" is *fille*.

She and Sponge exchange glances.

"Non," Angela answers quickly—and then starts to ask me if I like her *boucles d'oreilles*.

But I'm already checking the textbook, finger trailing through the glossary under S. *Société. Soda.*

sœur sister (*f.*)

I set my book down.

"Oui," I whisper tightly. *"Elles sont très [jolies]."*

But I don't know how I'd have answered the other question.

I don't get to read Shawn's text until fourth period, when I'm alone upstairs in the art studio:

> hey juni, just remembered, there were at least a handful of guys that still go to Fairfield at the party that night.

WHAT? I thumb a text feverishly back:

> Who?

Shawn replies:

> idk their names, but the 4 seniors in the band. the band was
> Muffin Wars?

I straighten. Already knowing the answer in the pit of my stomach:

> Does the lead have kind of fox-colored hair and smell like an
> Axe factory?

Shawn:

> u would know better than me.

Me: "WHAT? What the Dickens does THAT mean?"

At which point Ms. Gilbert knocks on the door and I hurry to shove my phone away. I slap on a smile as she enters and pulls a chair opposite mine at the worktable.

"So. Have you cooked up some ideas for your independent work?"

I nod through my plastered smile. "Ideas."

"Great. Let's hear 'em."

"Okay. Well. I was thinking . . ."

But I am thinking of Mr. Mystery. Brand was at the party that night; could Camie's letter be to him? Is *that* why he's been so eager to help me?

And what does Shawn *mean,* I would know better than him?

Ms. Gilbert waits.

"Sorry. It's just . . ."

Brand breaking pots with me. Taking the blame. Insisting on helping me search. It couldn't be because he—? Camie's letter—?

"Could I do something with found objects?"

The idea slips out. It is unconscious, so unbidden, it almost feels foreign, like even though I'm hearing my own voice it was someone else who spoke just now.

"And—and arrangement," I add, reclaiming it.

"'Found' objects." Ms. Gilbert folds her arms. "What sort of objects are you envisioning?"

"Letters. Notes." Secrets. "Things like that."

"You think you can find such things so easily?"

"I've found them before. And if I can't, there're always antiques shops with old postcards and stuff."

"And how would 'arrangement' play into it?"

"I'm not sure yet. But I'm good at making connections; maybe that can be my theme? I can find patterns, or combine different pieces to make a statement, or make the parts talk to each other . . ."

Ms. Gilbert seems impressed—or at least she nods, and isn't frowning.

"I think that could make a very interesting collection," she says. "Let's say three to six finished pieces by the end of the unit, depending?"

I nod.

"Good." Ms. Gilbert smiles. "Then I look forward to seeing your first project."

∞

When I find Kody at her usual table by the milk machine at lunch, not only is she wearing one of her newly purchased shirts; she has put up her hair since this morning and now displays a pair of chunky green earrings in the shape of hollow teardrops. I smile at the sight.

"You look nice," I tell her, grabbing a chair.

"Thanks," she says. "I decided you were right. I bought all this new stuff, and now I'm gonna show it off!"

She turns her head from side to side as if posing for a camera. So I mime one.

"Fabulous, yes. Now look this way and give us a growl!"

Kody does. She hits about three more poses with a straight face before someone walks by and we both lose it.

"That was good," I tell her when I can breathe again. "You're a natural!"

"What can I say? Tyra taught me the smize."

The smize.

It hits me in a wave: the smize, or "smile eyes," was the same smoky look Cam and Heather and Lauren and I all used to practice in the mirror and for Lauren's Polaroids. We haven't dressed up and "modeled" together in years, but the four of us still used to join forces for makeover nights and sultry selfies.

"Juniper? You okay?"

"Yeah." I flash a smile and start to unwrap my sandwich, but can't help scanning the lunchroom for Lauren.

It's crushing to spot her upstairs—sitting at another table, with a group from choir.

So much for new traditions.

My glance does not escape Kody. She folds her arms, thoughtful.

"Can I ask you something?"

"Sure."

"What . . . happened between you two?" She nods up at Lauren.

Death happened.

"It's not . . . so much . . . what happened." A sigh I didn't realize I was holding escapes. "I mean, we didn't fight or anything. It's more like, after the accident, Lauren didn't know how to talk to me anymore. So she just stopped. Stopped inviting me out, stopped returning my calls and texts . . ." I shrug. "Death is hard to talk about. And Lauren's never been great at awkward."

"Still though. She's your best friend."

I stare at my food. Is she?

Or has that become a past tense, too?

Kody clears her throat. "But best friends are overrated. Who needs bracelets and lifelong confidants? LAME. Give me a mediocre friend any day of the week."

My lips twitch up a little. "Are we mediocre friends?"

"Hell, *sure* we are."

The twitch pulls higher.

"Juniper?"

I bite my dopey smile back and turn. Behind me stands a hair-gelled boy in all-American Converse, plaid, and jeans.

"Nate! Hey."

Kody pulls a face at me: *You know him?*

Nate sets his lunch sack and a bottle of pop on the table. "We missed you at Booster Thursday." He leaves the statement open, waiting for an explanation.

Crap.

"Yeah," I say, straightening. "Uh, something came up and—wait. *We?*"

"Me and Mr. Garcia. The supervisor. So are you coming this week? Like—still interested in the club?"

"Of course!" Still need to convince Dad I'm adjusting.

"Good." Nate nods to himself. "Because no one else came last week, and Mr. Garcia and I voted and made you secretary."

I choke on my sandwich. "What?"

Kody prods me. "Isn't a secretary, like. Supposed to take notes and stuff?"

"Yeah. Some start she's off to, eh?" Nate grins and extends his hand. "I'm Nate."

"Kody."

"You guys mind if I join you?"

Kody looks from him to me. I'm not sure which of us looks more surprised: me, at my new appointment, or Kody, at the fact that the boy about whom she is telepathically shouting WTF HE'S HOT has asked to sit at our table.

"Please," I say.

"Thanks." Nate scoots up a chair. Then, looking around and spying Kody's lunchbox on the table, "Oh," he says. "You like Lucy Killman?"

And Kody's eyes about fly from her head.

I am picking through a lunch sack in my gloves after school—ugh, scraped-off pizza cheese!—when there is an abrupt *kong kong!* behind me on one of the dumpsters.

I leap to my feet, swearing. I'd clamp a hand over my heart if it weren't covered in Fanta and cookie crumbs. "Can't you just say 'hi' like a normal person?"

Brand flashes his devil smile. "Hi."

I roll my eyes and crouch back down. The steady throb of *lastday, lastday, lastday* in my veins is too deep, too industrial to be disturbed by the likes of Brand Sayers—Mystery Man or not.

He rubs his hands together. "Any luck?"

I shake a lock of ramen from my hand as he helps himself to a bag. "None."

We work in silence. I want to ask Brand about the party, but I don't know how. From what Shawn said, it's almost like I ought to be acquainted with him. Did I take shots with Brand, or one of his band mates? Were we talking on the sofa? Doing something . . . other than talking?

Oh god.

"You okay, Lemon?"

"Fine." I cover my mouth with an arm. "Just got a whiff of Wednesday chili."

I change out bags and force my thoughts back to the search.

"Hey."

I look up. Brand is leaning against one of the dumpsters and regarding me intently. For a moment I wonder if he has somehow read my desperation to talk to him and my stomach flutters.

But what he says is, "Nice work with Kody."

"Oh." The comment is unexpected and feels strangely intimate, as though he has complimented me on my favorite books or the scent of my shampoo. "Thanks."

Brand lingers against the dumpster. The pause is a little too long, too heavy between us to be the end of the conversation. It feels like a transition: like he's opening up the stage for something to be said. Whether by him or me, I don't know.

I decide to take a chance.

"Brand?"

"Yeah?"

His blue eyes are intense, pale with sun.

"I realized the other day . . ." He waits. I take a breath. "The letter. Camie's letter. She had it in her bag the night of the accident. The night we were . . ." I lick my lips. "At this party."

"Shawn's party. So?"

I fight the urge to swallow. *Shawn's party.*

He knows.

"So," I press on, with difficulty, "she had only written it that day. I've thought about it, and I'm almost certain she meant to give it to somebody there. At Shawn's." I watch this sink in and try to analyze Brand's reaction. As usual, his hooded eyes reveal next to nothing. "And I remembered," I continue, treading carefully now as if testing my weight on a rickety bridge, "that the letter said she was leaving the guy in high school. That it was . . . someone younger than her."

I look him full in the eye now. The moments grow long and I wait, mentally clinging to the ropes on either side of me.

At last, Brand asks, "Why are you looking at me like that?"

My throat pinches, but I choke, "You were there."

"As were you. Why are you saying it like—" Brand closes his mouth, and after a moment cocks his head to the side. "You don't remember?"

A chill rolls over me.

"Remember what?" My faux support ropes fray.

"Remember *what*?" Brand moves his head back as if adjusting his vision. When I don't answer, he screws up his eyes and says, "Us?"

My stomach plunges.

"Relax," Brand says quickly. "It isn't like that." But I must look as unnerved as I feel, because he gets up from his slouch against the dumpster and walks over, leaning down to support me. "You really don't remember?"

I shake my head.

"Okay," he says. "Okay. Why don't we just sit down a minute."

I let him guide me to the curb.

"Here." Brand cracks his lighter and sticks a cigarette between his teeth, and when the end is lit he takes it out and passes it to me. I stare at it.

"I don't smoke."

"It'll help," he insists.

I look at his earnest face. At the stick in his hand.

Then I peel my yellow gloves off, wipe my hands along my pants, and take it from him.

"Just pull a little and hold it a minute."

I do. Only, after several moments, when I let the smoke out, my throat burns and I wheeze and cough on a hot, mangled cluster of brimstone.

"Did you even inhale?" Brand is trying not to laugh.

The tangle itches and I am coughing too deeply to answer. He can't keep from grinning.

"You're supposed to inhale it," he laughs. "Into your lungs."

I swat at him like a rakish-haired fly and thrust the cigarette back for him to take. Brand half frowns, half smiles at it, then sets it back between his own lips.

"So," he says when he blows out a drag, "July Fourth."

"July Fourth," I echo like a demented toast.

The night I can't remember.

"Did you—?" He breaks off as if checking himself. The smoke rises from the cigarette in his lowered hand. "Did you get a concussion that night, or something?"

"From the accident?" I take a deep breath. My chest raggedly deflates as I let it out again. "Maybe."

"Maybe?" He searches my eyes. "Are you being coy with me, or do you mean to say that you physically don't *know*?"

"I mean, there are hours that night I have no recollection of—and I don't know if it's because I drank too much and blacked out, or from the accident."

"Fuck." Brand eyes the concrete with distaste, as though it were an ugly throw rug. "That fucking sucks."

Brand doesn't even know. *He* doesn't see the holes eating away at the universe.

"Tell me what you do remember." He taps a bit of ash off. "Maybe I can fill in some of the blanks."

"I remember . . ." I close my eyes. "The party was already going when we got there. Music. Cups. People spilled across the sofas, drinking, dancing, making out . . ."

"That would've been us. The music," Brand adds when I open my eyes.

"Right. The band. I didn't see them—they were playing in the yard out back."

"You must've hung out in the house a while."

"Yeah. Camilla led me in—I remember meeting people,

shaking hands . . . getting drinks in the kitchen, talking to Shawn . . ."

"What'd you drink?"

"Jungle juice."

Brand winces.

"And that was just to start."

"What else?"

My shoulders fall in exhale. "We did shots—not Camie. She was gonna drive so I could try stuff and she didn't drink anything. But the rest of us—Shawn and some others, a bunch of their friends—we all threw back a few. Rum. Vodka. Tequila. Then Camie cut me off and said I needed to walk around and let it digest."

"Did you?"

"Sort of. We went around talking to people. I remember realizing I was buzzed, and thinking how fun and floaty it was—how I could joke with all these people I'd never met before, how fun dancing was, how I didn't care what anybody thought . . . the music was *so good*! I heard Queen and—"

Suddenly it dawns on me: "Don't Stop Me Now." "Another One Bites the Dust."

"Bohemian Rhapsody."

"That was you, wasn't it?"

Brand smiles. "Now we're getting somewhere."

"I remember wanting to go see the band, but we ran into Camie's friend Melissa. God, I don't even remember what we talked about . . .

"I think she had me try her drink, something fruity, and I liked it, and I ended up drinking the rest . . . Oh, and there was this big graduation toast. Camie wouldn't let me do another shot, so I just had Coke. After that . . ." I trail off, finishing with a shrug.

"You don't remember the request?"

"Request?" I tense.

"Yeah." Brand takes another drag, blows it out. "You came up to us not long after the toast. You'd heard us playing Queen. You wanted 'Bicycle Race.'" He leans forward, watching me to see if any of this is sounding familiar.

"'Bicycle Race,'" I repeat.

"You don't remember."

I shake my head.

"Well." Brand drops the cigarette on the ground and crushes it under his shoe. "You asked for the song, and you got it. We started playing, and . . . and then"—the corner of his mouth twitches up—"halfway through, you get up on the platform and tell us—or *me*, more specifically—*Nope, nope, WRONG, you're doing it all wrong*—"

My stomach cinches. "Please tell me you're joking." His smirk twists higher.

"It was the dialogue you were mad about. 'You know— wa-nah-NAH, wa-na-nuh—?"

I nod.

"You said my intonation was *terrible*, and you could do a *much* better Freddie Mercury, and—well, that was about the time your sister spotted you . . ."

I now am hanging on his every word. This footage of Camilla is new to me. Precious. It should be in my memory, but isn't.

I listen, fixing it in my head with everything I've got.

"I had thought she was going to apologize for you, but she didn't. She got right up on the deck and took the mike and said, looking at us, but talking to the crowd, *If Juniper says she can sing better than this guy, I believe her. Whaddya say? SING-OFF?*"

I feel myself redden and hold my face. "She did *not*." But even before Brand affirms it, I know it is just the sort of thing Camilla would've encouraged. "So what happened?"

"What else?" A wolfish grin breaks out across Brand's face. "We *sang*! It was this fucking badass, Bicycle *battle*. We did the whole rhyming back-and-forth: black/white, bark/bite—"

I bury my head.

"—and the crowd freaking LOVED it! You were fucking ridiculous."

I peer from a crack between my fingers. "Good fucking ridiculous?"

"Fucking *great* fucking ridiculous. After 'Bicycle' we did 'Good Old-Fashioned Lover Boy,' 'We Are the Champions'—"

"'Bohemian Rhapsody'?" My heartstrings pull taut.

"Yeah, of course we—wait. You remember?"

I bite my lip, suddenly ill again. When I can't open my mouth to answer, I reach an unsteady hand inside my raincoat. I take my phone from a pocket, but can't bring myself to pull up the file.

Brand looks from me to the phone's black screen. "You okay?"

Ropes are snapping. My cool dangles by a thread.

"In one week," I say, and I can't help it; a wry, bitter smile twists my lips, "I've gone from elite choir and lunches with my best friend to fucking *Booster* Club and daily dumpster dives with the *weird*est guy in school, who by the way INSISTS on a deodorant only marginally less suffocating than this elephant armpit of fermented chili, bullshat essays, and pizza crusts. I *think* I'm pretty far from okay."

Brand stares at me with an unreadable expression. I think he's relieved to see anger instead of tears.

He says, "You're a fan of the Axe, then."

I laugh.

Then I cry.

When my shoulders start to heave and my breathing is racked with sobs, Brand informs me I am making a scene and pulls me back into the building. I don't know where he's leading me; I am watching my feet and trying very hard to keep from letting anyone who might be around see me 1) upset and 2) hanging out with Brandon Box Cutter Sayers.

We turn one corner, then another, and eventually go through a door and up some stairs I don't recognize. At the top Brand fumbles something out of a pocket—keys, I discern from the jingle—and then there is the sound of teeth fitting and the turn and he pushes in, pulling me by the arm.

"Sit," he commands when we stop moving.

I find a beanbag chair at my feet and sink into it.

Wait.

Beanbag?

I look up from the floor. Brand has brought me to a long room with windows on adjacent sides, one looking out at the track and football field, the other into a tall room with rising rows of chairs and music stands. When I spot the filing cabinets and some instruments wedged in a corner, it's clear this must be the music loft: a dusty old storage space between the band and choir rooms.

Also known as Band Geeks' Paradise.

I sit up, suddenly wary of what might have been in this beanbag before me.

"Shit, Lemon." Brand is lifting stacks of papers as he moves from shelf to shelf, checking for something. "I'd offer you a hanky, but I left my gentleman's coat in the other decade."

My breathing is still somewhat haggard, but I manage to wipe my eyes with my wrists. Brand belatedly finds what he is looking for—a box of tissues—and offers it to me.

"Thanks," I tell him. Only, through the snot and grief, it comes out *tanks*. I take one and blow my nose.

"Feeling better?"

I stare at him, snot rag in hand. I know what I must look like right now, and "better" is a galaxy far far away.

"Here." Brand crosses to a shelf and pulls a slender case down by the handle: an electric guitar. I guess it must be his, 'cause he undoes the latches, lifts the instrument, and takes a plastic sack out from under it.

"Is that—?"

Brand takes a handful of its contents for himself, then lowers the open bag to me.

"Gummy bears?" I ask, identifying the colored globs.

"Yeah?" he says. "What'd you think I was offering you?"

"Gummy bears?" I repeat, still not over the fact.

Brand stares at me. I stare at him. Then, already broken and unable to censor myself, I laugh. My breath is still wobbly, so it comes out in dashes and stutters.

"What?" Brand demands.

"You ARE a suh. A suh-uh. Softie."

He frowns.

"I woul-uh . . . would've expected Warheads. *Sour Patch Kids,* at least."

"Fuck *off,*" Brand retorts. "I'm trying to be a gentleman here."

"I mean, Jesus. Flamin' Hah. Hot Cheetos . . ."

He folds his arms, sulky. But after a moment his face relaxes. "Since you've recovered your yap enough to criticize me," he says, evenly setting the gummy bears on the floor and dropping into the beanbag beside mine, "why don't you tell me why it is you've been crying?"

Now I can't meet his eye. "Do I need a re-reason?"

"Not necessarily." He drums his fingers along his jeans, and when I don't answer: "But you were doing pretty well until you brought out your phone."

When I look up, Brand is watching me.

I know I don't have to answer him. I know if I say nothing he will drop it, and probably never bring it up again. But we are alone in this foreign time and space—this dimension that is Band Geeks' Paradise after school—and something in his eyes tells me that this is a sacred place: If I leave a secret here, here is where it will stay.

I take my phone from my pocket.

"I haven't shown this to *anyone,*" I say, looking him hard in the face. He nods, silent as I hesitate with my thumb on the screen. After a moment I inhale, unlock it, and scroll through storage until a video is highlighted. A video received in a text July 5, 2:39 a.m.

I tap the file open.

The camera wobbles before settling on the girl in the passenger seat.

The person aiming it—the driver—tries not to laugh. "That's a pretty mean air guitar you've got there, Juni."

"*Electric* air guitar." The passenger blows a lock of straw-colored hair from her face, still jamming. "Or would it be air electric guitar?" Giggles. "Another thing I could probably do better than that haircut kid."

The driver cackles. "Oh my sister. You are going to en*joy* this tomorrow."

"Shhhh, shhh shhh! Here comes the air piano! *Dum, dum, dum, dum, dum, dum, dum, dum* I see a li-ttle sil-hou-ETTE-o—hey, green light—"

"Ohp! Yes it is."

The camera shifts as the hand holding it turns the wheel. An intersection curves away and then the view resettles, the night outside the windows slowing to a crawl. Streetlamps pass in occasional whitening glares, but not much else.

There are no other cars on the road.

"Juni, you are legend. Turn to me so I can see you in your full rock-out glory."

The blonde swats at the camera. "Shhhh! *DoDO DOdo DOdo DOdo*. Easy CO—Camilla!" She gapes at the camera, then up at the driver holding it. "Are you recording this?"

"What if I am?"

"*Camilla Alexis Lemon.*" The passenger folds her arms. "*This* is a vehicle in motion, which you are operating. Put that phone away."

A snort. "Yes, MOM. As soon as you finish your solo. We're coming to a red light anyway."

The star sticks her tongue out as the car rolls to a stop.

She shakes her finger in time with a blasting string of NO!s and the driver laughs.

"I love you, Juni."

But the passenger doesn't hear her; she is dragging out a high-pitched *eeeeeeee,* dancing, rifting on her air guitar to the tune of, "*DOO* doo doo doo doo doo, *DOO* doo doo doo doo doo . . ." while the camera shakes and shakes in silent laughter.

"So you THINK you—*Camie!*"

"What?"

"Drive!"

"Okay, okay, I'm sending it."

"Yeesh. If we get pulled over, let *me* do the talking."

A fresh spray of laughter. As the image blurs away from the passenger, a swell of light blooms from the other direction.

"God, that was classic. Tomorrow you're gonn—"

The screen goes black.

Brand raises his eyes from it to me in slow horror.

"That isn't," he says. "That's not when—?"

"That was the end of the video. She managed to hit send before the other car hit us. I know, because they recovered her phone in pieces."

"Jesus," says Brand. "Fuck."

"Camilla didn't even *drink* anything. But she was hit by some guy who did because she wasn't *watching* for the other guy; she was filming *me*."

I feel warm drops on my arms and realize I'm still crying. Not sobbing anymore—just tearing. I ball my fists and squeeze to oblivion. Brand looks away, either out of privacy or at a loss for what to say. I don't blame him. I wouldn't know what to say, either.

I wipe my face again and blink a few times. Brand shifts and reaches like he might put his hand on my back, but thinks better of it. Instead of saying "I'm sorry," or telling me it isn't my fault, he says, "And you've just carried that around on your phone this whole time?"

I nod. His expression tightens.

"Why?"

"It's the last I have of her."

That sits in the stale storage air a minute. Brand gazes ahead, seeing something that isn't there. "That's fucked up," he says quietly. "You should delete it."

"How can I? It's the last time she told me she loved me."

And I don't even remember it.

Brand's mouth shrinks into a line. He looks as though he's balancing something sharp on his tongue. He starts to say it. Stops again. Pulls his lips in and gets up instead, crosses the room. At his guitar case he stops, twisting on his heels like he can't quite decide something, and finally he pulls the lid of a compartment hidden beneath his instrument.

From it, he removes a small scrap of paper.

"What is that?"

Brand smoothes the crumpled scrap in his palm: a torn corner of something, white on one side, tinny silver and gumdrop colors on the other.

"In fifth grade," he says, hoisting himself to sit up on a filing cabinet, "I was rooting through my mom's desk drawer for some candy. She always had something—M&M's, Laffy Taffy, some ready snack to chew on over paperwork.

"When I looked there this one morning, I found an open

tube of Life Savers. I started to sneak a couple out, peeling back for the red ones, but as I was closing the drawer . . ." His nostrils flare. "I heard a sound. I turned, and she was standing in the doorway. She'd been watching the whole time.

"For a minute she just looked at me with this *face*. I'd thought she was mad at me. Trying to figure out a punishment.

"But when she came over, she just opened the drawer again, took the Life Savers out and closed the rest of 'em in my hand. She said, 'Keep 'em, honey,' and kissed my forehead." He stops, smiling thinly to himself. I can tell that this isn't where the story ends, though.

"What happened?"

Brand's smile lengthens a slice, but doesn't warm his eyes. "I thought it was my lucky goddamn day. I went off to school, Mom to work; I ate the whole package on the bus. After school, I came home and she didn't."

"She—?"

"Left us. Just walked out and never looked back."

I look at the wrapper in his palm. The plastic is worn with age, the colors faded, white along the creases. I think about what I might say to console him, to commiserate. But I know how hollow such words can be.

"And you've kept the wrapper all these years?" I ask instead.

The corner of his mouth tweaks. "It's the last I have of her."

I don't know what to say. "I'm so sorry, Brand."

Brand stares at the wrapper, his gaze turning inward. Then he crushes it into a ball and chucks it across the room.

"So am I."

Tuesday comes and goes, still no Index card. Grudgingly I resign myself to the idea that *65* is gone and *probably* not coming back to haunt me; if someone had found it and was going to say something, they would have by now.

But I continue diving, at least in the recycling out back, for "found" material for my art projects—and another reason.

One made of Axe and cigarettes and gummy bears.

I'm dying to ask Brand more about the party—about what happened, who he knew there, if any of those people might be YOU—but as soon as I'm actually looking for him, I can't seem to find Brand anywhere. Not even in Dumpsterland, where I'm sure he'll swing by for a smoke break. I wonder if he's avoiding me. If he thinks we got too personal before.

I hope not.

Fortunately I have other resources, and don't just twiddle my thumbs waiting on Band Boy.

"Hello, Juniper," says Sponge, clacking away at his laptop as I approach his table.

I nod. "Sponge."

He sticks out his hand, and when I deposit the Pieces there he graces me with his businesslike smile.

"Well?"

Sponge leans in as if to divulge something sensitive. "3 Hall," he says, and subtly nods like this is code for something.

"3 Hall?"

3 Hall is the westernmost of three central hallways at Fairfield. It's the wing where pretty much all of the arts (excepting art) are taught: theater, choir, band, literature, and, for whatever odd reason, weight lifting.

"3 Hall," Sponge affirms.

"Okay . . ." I frown and tighten my eyes. "What about 3 Hall?"

"Whoever your sister was seeing—she met him there after school. I'm sure of it."

"How do you know?"

"I'd always pass her on the way to Chess Club and AD."

"Can you be more specific? Like—what room? Which *end* of 3 Hall?"

Sponge clicks his tongue. "Sorry. I never turned to watch. I usually passed her on the A-Hall end, but she could've been going anywhere."

"*3 Hall?*" I repeat.

"3 Hall." Sponge nods.

"Is that seriously all you can tell me?"

"Juniper . . ." My informant reclines and turns up his palms. "My brain is not a search engine, okay. Got a lot in storage, but gotta sift through all the entries by hand."

"I know . . ." Boy, don't I.

Sponge opens his payment and throws back a candied shot. "If I come up with anything else, I'll let you know."

75

The next day I consider 3 Hall for myself. After school is the first Booster meeting for which I am actually present, so once Nate and I have drafted up fliers for our services ("Got cause? Get funds!"), our tour to put them up in the halls gives me ample time to look around and speculate.

Where, for one, had You been coming from when he met Camilla? Was his last class down the corridor? Did he drive here from another school? Camie could've gone to meet him out the visitor's entrance.

Or:

What if 3 Hall was more than a meeting point: a destination? Now that I'm looking, I see plenty of places for paramours: dressing rooms, storage spaces, a utility closet. Could You have had special access to one?

It does not escape my notice that the band loft is one such private place.

Or that Brand has a key to it.

"You okay?"

"Hm?" I snap to and realize I've been staring at the choir door, or rather elsewhere in thought. Nate stands ahead of me, looking back. "Yeah. Coming."

I shake myself and catch up with him. He hands me another flier, one of the last in the stack.

"Amazing that we almost missed *this*." Nate nods at a wall of cork between trophy cases, what's considered the most prominent news board at Fairfield. Directly opposite the visitor's entrance, it's the location of choice for announcements and spirit messages and sign-up sheets.

It was where they posted audition results for *Bye Bye Birdie* last year, and Lauren jumped up and down and uncharacteristically screamed with me when I got the role of Ursula, the main girl's best friend.

"Kind of crowded," Nate says, grounding me in the present. "Does no one ever take things down?"

Although the school year has just begun, he is right: The space is already plastered with try-out sheets, student campaign posters, fliers like ours.

"It's kind of change-as-you-go. Give me a sec, I'll find something old to take down."

I glance over the papers, inspecting dates, and am about to remove a flier for the Club Fair when I spy the word *Leonardo*. I peel up another sheet so I can read the rest: "THE ORIGINAL RENAISSANCE MAN: the art and inventions of Leonardo da Vinci." It's an ad for a museum exhibit in Portland.

"Find one?"

"No . . . " I trail off in thought. Has Leo's admirer A heard of this? "Still current. I was just—"

But then I spot something else: a portrait of a girl in a teal shirt with long lemon hair. A portrait I know every bit as well as the article it appears in.

Camilla's memorial announcement.

I drop the page above it as if burned.

"Juniper?"

Nate searches my face with concern. When I don't meet his eye he looks from me to the dropped page and peeks cautiously under it.

I sense, more than see, him stiffen.

"Oh," he says, quiet.

I smile through the moisture in my eyes. If I don't, I know he'll just ask me if I'm okay, and I am so, so tired and heartsick of answering Yes when that's so indescribably far from the truth.

"I guess you've heard," I say instead. My voice is steady, but its tightness betrays me.

Nate winces. "You might say that."

I mop my eye with a palm. "Might?"

For a moment, Nate hesitates. Then he says, "I thought you might appreciate the chance to be someone other than a surviving sibling for a while. Even if it was only with me."

I look down at the floor. He's right: It's hard—it *hurts* to be defined by your losses.

But it's also impossible not to be.

"If there's ever . . . anything I can do," Nate continues.

I smile at him weakly. "Thanks."

"And I'm not just saying that." The addition is quick, and he seeks out my eyes as if to prove himself. "I mean it. You think of anything, you let me know."

"I will," I agree, sniffling. "Thanks."

With a shaky exhale, I take up the Booster flier with both hands again. How do people recover from these public slips?

"Do you have siblings?" I busy myself with removing the Club Fair flier, then spread ours out over the space so I don't have to look at him.

"Had," he answers as I push in a tack. My ears perk up.

"A stepbrother. But we were never all that close. We only lived together about a year before our parents divorced each other."

"Oh." Not dead. Just estranged. "I'm sorry."

"Don't be. My mom was a lot happier once we moved back to Eugene, I think."

"Moved *back*?" We start down the corridor again, somewhere farther to put up our last copy. The relief is instant, like a fresh breath of air.

Somehow Camie papered over was even worse than a hole.

"From Aloha," Nate supplies. "Where my stepdad lived."

"Wow." And here I'd been hogging the hardship card. "I didn't realize you'd done so much moving. All that rooting and uprooting must be hard on you."

"It is." Nate frowns at the floor. "At least, until you make a good friend."

He peers up at me from the corner of his eye, surprisingly shy all of a sudden.

This time my smile holds its footing.

"So . . ." I indicate a spot near the auditorium. Nate nods and passes me the final flier. "Have you spent every year at a different school?"

"Sort of. More like split years." He snaps a piece of tape from a small dispenser. "Freshman year was half Eugene, half Aloha; sophomore half Aloha, half Eugene. Now Fairfield."

"Geez. What a whirlwind." I move my hand from one corner to the next so that Nate can tape them down. "Did it at least make the school year go faster?"

"Actually, I think it made it longer: The moves just sort

of all ran together, one forever blur of everything in boxes." He seals the last edge with his thumbs and shrugs. "I guess time's irrelevant when your terms of measurement change."

*Extra credit. Compare an element in *Great Expectations* to the same element in a book of your own choosing. Expand, and be sure to provide sufficient context.

Time

"Listen:
Billy Pilgrim has come unstuck in time."

So begins Chapter Two of Slaughterhouse-Five by Kurt Vonnegut. The passages that follow describe how Billy moves forward and back through the years, seeing his birth and his death and all events in between—though he has no control over which he'll visit next, and the scene can change as quickly as a stroll through the door.

This is the complete opposite of Miss Havisham, who stops all the clocks in her manor at twenty minutes to nine and shutters herself in to rot upon learning her betrothed has swindled her.

Billy is floating; Havisham is stranded.

I wonder: Which am I more like?

Unstuck: when the death of someone you love unmoors you from the present and you drift to either side of it—to the moments that were, that will be, that won't ever—and you can suddenly see, all of time spreading out before you like a stain, what a small, quick thing in the universe is the flame of a single, wild life.

Stranded: when the death of a loved one slams a

door between you and the world without her, shutting out reality. You can close your eyes to changes—to the falling leaves and new TV shows and rising gas prices—

But not to the cobwebs of time.

Not to the number on the top of your Index card, which only goes up.

New Units of Time

- days it's been
- holes discovered
- firsts
- secrets
- silences (Mom, Lauren, Heather)
- friends lost
- friends made
- traditions changed
- atonements
- topics talked around
- bad dreams
- careful dinners
- places Cam was papered over: the world forgetting

The first Friday in October, I'm diving for found materials when I uncover another strange letter from A—this one addressed to "Oscar."

> Dearest Oscar,
>
> Is there anything you've written that is not devastatingly perfect? <u>The Importance of Being Earnest</u> was hilarious. <u>The Picture of Dorian Gray</u> crackled with wit. Today I read "The Nightingale and the Rose" and wept.
>
> Where have all the poets gone?
>
> Love,
> A

I haven't read any of the works mentioned, but I've heard of *The Importance of Being Earnest* enough to know that "Oscar" is Oscar Wilde. First da Vinci; now this?

Who is this A person, and why can't she find a nice genius from her own century?

I turn the paper over. Although the back of the page is

blank, there's a faint impression of letters in the upper right-hand corner. I squint and bring the paper near my face, trying to make them out: "[something] *de l'eau*," it says. *"De l'eau"*? What is that—"of water"? "From water"?

A. Water.

Angela Waters??

Excited, I fold the page back down and pocket it. The other A note is in the art studio; I can easily compare them and determine if the authors are the same. My haul is getting pretty sizeable, anyway.

I tie off the sack I've been working on and redeposit it. But just as I stoop to collect the day's findings—

"What do you think you're doing?"

I whirl around.

"Seriously. What's with all the paperwork?" Brand indicates the armful of scrap papers I have all but dropped in surprise. "I thought you were looking for an index card."

I stare at him, fingers still tensed in start. "What is *wrong* with you?"

"Plenty. But let's not lose perspective—I'm not the one rooting through dumpsters and pocketing weird shit here."

"It isn't shit," I sniff, defensive. "It's . . . recycling."

"Says the one dressed for radiation." He tips his chin at my feet.

I'm still wearing rubber boots.

I fold my arms. "I had a bad experience."

Last week an Icee exploded right on my foot when I found it in with a recycling bag, felt something wet, and reflexively dropped it. I'm still not over my sticky blue Converse.

"Besides, if you'd talked to me in the last two weeks"—

even I am surprised at how bitter I sound that he hasn't—"you'd know I'm not looking for that card anymore. This is for a project."

"What project?"

I open my mouth to answer him—and then decide I don't have to.

"Hey," he says as I start away. "I'm talking to you."

"*You're* the one who's been gone," I fire back without turning. "If anybody gets to ask questions, it should be me." I had really thought we connected back in the band loft. But since then it's like Brand's dropped off the planet.

"Oh. I'm flattered you noticed, Lemon. D'you miss me?"

He follows, uninvited, toward the studio. I grumble under my breath. I still really want to ask him about who he might've seen at Shawn's party, or if he saw Camilla talking to anyone, but I also haven't totally ruled *him* out as Mr. Mystery, either. He's younger, he was there that night, and, as I realized putting up fliers with Nate the other week, somehow has access to a private room in 3 Hall.

"Brand." I bite back my irritation and face him. "I need to ask you about Shawn's that night."

"The party?"

"Yeah."

Brand makes a face. "I've already told you what I know. Besides, I spent the night playing—it isn't like I saw much."

"Yeah, but—" The words die in my throat as he catches up with me. "Brand, are you limping?"

The dip in his gait is even more pronounced as he swaggers to avoid a drain. "What of it?"

Now I hurry after him. When I fall into step beside him, I see the shadow around one of his eyes is a shade greener than normal. "Jesus, Brand. What happened?"

For a moment he looks confused; then something registers, and Brand's stern face slackens to neutral. He blows out a sigh. "I had to . . . settle up with this punk-ass sophomore last week. He pushed his stuff and tried to pocket the profit. Things got ugly."

I stop in place. "You—?"

Brand stops, too. "Fuck, no. I fell off my RipStik in the skate park. You believe that mafia shit?"

What, the rumors that he has uncles in it? With *his* cheekbones?

When I respond *"No"* a beat too late, Brand gives a crooked smile.

"So where's this 'project' of yours?"

"I guess it's more 'projects' than 'project,'" I confess when we enter the loft in the art studio.

The space is modest and crowded. A large worktable takes up most of the floor and drowns in my ongoing projects: a comic made up of sketches, doodles, and phrases cut from found notes and papers; a collection of java jackets stacked against a sprawl of red D and F grades (title: "Supply vs. Demand"); map templates labeled not with countries and capitals, but the cut-out names of people, events, and titles that belong to them. Stacks of used and unused materials lay everywhere, more in bulging folders in a drawer. Many pages I have cut things from hang on clotheslines, X-Acto holes revealing light like a city of windows.

Brand takes it all in. As he does, I step subtly toward the filing cabinet. Another project—the Secret Board—is stashed behind, but I don't want him finding it. On it, beside Camilla's letter, Kody's suicide note, and the love letter to Leo, is the Life Savers wrapper I picked up off the floor of Band Geeks' Paradise.

When he isn't looking, I quietly nudge the end that sticks out away.

"You're even weirder than I thought," Brand concludes after a minute. "But this is actually kind of cool."

"Thanks. I think."

He sets down a map of Europe—Hamlet in Denmark, Bastille Day in France, *The Prince* and Botticelli and da Vinci in Italy—and collapses into a chair as he eyes today's findings.

"So you . . . what?" he asks, putting his feet up. "Collect shit and cut it up and put it back together by theme?"

"Something like that."

Brand considers. The corner of his mouth turns up. "And you're getting a grade for that?"

I purse my lips, but can't help it—I smile back. And for a moment we're just looking at each other: no scowls, no smirking, no sass. Brand's china-blue eyes are a lot less frightening when he's smiling and not holding something sharp.

He says, "So . . ."

Something flutters in my chest.

"What was that one you stuck in your pocket?"

My skin prickles. I realize I am slightly disoriented. "What?"

"The sheet you folded and slipped away. Right when I found you."

The note from A to Oscar.

"Right." I shake myself, remembering that he might have dated my sister. I produce the page in question and Brand unfolds it and reads. "Remember that weird love letter to Leo?"

"Huh." His eyes linger at the bottom. "That was signed *A* too, wasn't it?"

"Yeah. And check out the top right corner." I tap the impressions carved by pen with my finger. "Angela de l'eau."

"Duh-low?"

"French. Means——"

"Water. Angela Waters?"

"That would be my guess." I'd grab the note to Leo now to compare it, but that one's still attached to the Secret Board and that's not coming out in front of Brand. Instead I say, "I had this idea."

"What?"

"Well——" I reposition in my seat. "I know Angela. She's in my French class. She's really sweet but super quiet, always has her nose in some steamy romance. I see her laughing at other people's jokes sometimes, but she never joins in on conversations herself."

"What's your point?"

"I was thinking, maybe she'd open up more if she got to know somebody outside of all these dead guys and bare-chested book hunks."

Brand considers me and frowns. "Is this a matchmaking session?"

"No no, nothing like that. But, you know——" I shrug. "I just think, like Kody, Angela could use a friend. We might—— *I* might reach out to her. I've been seeing this flier for a da Vinci exhibit——"

Brand scoffs. "Yeah. I'm sure you'll be bonding over dead guys in no time."

Whoa. Whiplash.

"Okay . . . what's with you all of a sudden?" He's the one who suggested helping Kody. I don't see how this is any different.

Brand takes his feet off the table. "Has it ever occurred to you," he says, leaning over it, "that some people are quiet because they don't *want* to talk? You can't just go around assuming you know what people need."

"But if I got to know her, it wouldn't be assuming."

"Like you got to know Kody?"

"I *have* gotten to know Kody. And I genuinely like her. She's fun."

"And how do you think she'd feel if she knew you only became her friend because you found her note?"

"That's not . . ." I start to say. But it is.

True.

"Good intentions have wiped out whole civilizations, Juniper," he says, standing. "Tread carefully."

And with that, Brand limps out the door.

Twelve days later, Ms. Gilbert assesses my finished projects for herself. It's the last day of ceramics and therefore my last of independent study, and I watch, anxious, as she circles around my worktable as Brand did, slowly, attentively following the interplay of details.

Unlike when Brand was here, the Secret Board is out.

Although it's been clear from the start that my materials were "found" on the premises, Ms. Gilbert doesn't question them. What she says when she finishes with the Secret Board is:

"Bravo."

She then critiques each piece with me—considering even, to my surprise, the gutted pages on clothespins to be a collection—and confesses that although the Secret Board is made more by its parts than because of how they're arranged, it is her favorite.

"It speaks to something deep," she says. "Something intimate . . . but universal."

I get a B for the board and an A for the unit.

"What's next?" I ask when she has noted my grades on her clipboard. "I mean, the next unit."

"Printmaking," replies Ms. Gilbert. "We carve linoleum blocks to make something like a stamp. Be thinking about your design—we'll start work on them Friday!"

If Brand was absent before, now he seems to be avoiding me. After school I look for him in the likely places—detention, the dumpsters, 3 Hall, on the stairs where he loiters with his band mates and occasionally tries to light and smoke his burrito like a meaty cigar—but find no sign of him. I wonder if he's mad about Angela; if my plan to reach out to her offended him somehow. But thinking back, I also remember how quick he was to insist he'd told me everything he knew about Shawn's.

Is Brand steering clear because he's angry—or because he doesn't want to talk about Cam and the party?

It occurs to me there are other places to look for answers.

I should have started in Camilla's room. It's the first place I thought to look for YOU, but it's also been the hardest to access. Between Dad working at home and Mom spending weekends in bed, I almost never have the house to myself anymore.

But tonight is their Grieving Parents Support Group; tonight, for the first time since I found Camie's letter, they're both out and won't be back for over an hour.

Tonight I can dig.

The air feels stale when I enter—staler even than when I snuck in for Shawn's number a month ago. The smell reminds me of old books, and everything from the windowsill to the rings and lipsticks on Cam's dresser are lavender with dust. I walk in and sink onto her bed.

The items around me are familiar: the yellow string lights that we put up together, which I reach to plug in; the hanging star lanterns she fell in love with at a crafts fair; the miniature Big Ben we both cracked up at regularly after discovering the real clock's unofficial Twitter page. I spy her guitar in the corner and can still see her laughing as she improvises lyrics to the tune of "Hey There Delilah"; the Paris snow globe on her nightstand and the way she'd pick it up, turn it, and whisper *un jour* through the falling glitter.

My eyes drift to the lineup missing Bristol.

Where the hell is she?

I get up to check the desk. Book by book I paw through the shelves, pulling one at a time to stick my hand in the space between them and grope for either horse or hidden paper, some secret item. Finding neither, I start in on the drawers. Inside: pens, markers, notepads, a stapler and USB cords; beaded bracelets, old school pictures, thumbtacks and a frozen wristwatch; envelopes, ear buds, stray batteries, a dozen *other* Dala horses and a dinosaur like a prize from a cereal box.

No YOU and no Bristol.

I shake my hands out and bounce up and down. If I were evidence of a secret relationship . . .

My eyes fall on her computer.

Of course.

I lift up the top and hit the power button. Nothing happens. I raid the desk again for the charger—but even if I find it, I realize, I'd still have to bypass Cam's lock screen. That could take hours.

"SHIT."

I slam a drawer in frustration.

With a hiss through my teeth, I fold the screen back down. Stupid. The charger could be anywhere: in one of her bags, cleared away like her toothbrush, maybe even with

Bristol. I guess I'll worry about the password once I find it. The files will keep.

But I'll be damned if I leave this room without something tonight.

I turn around to scan for other ideas. One prospect jumps at me—a row of photo albums in the nightstand—and I storm to it and begin blowing through. The relationship sounded serious enough; YOU and Camie must've had time to snap pictures. Whether they'd be in with all her other prints is questionable, but not impossible . . .

I move from one album to the next—but in the end, everything I find is old: shots of me and Cam in pajamas, carving pumpkins, sledding; on family road trips, Bristol posed by waterfalls and Ferris wheels and paintings; trick-or-treating, modeling outfits, trying lipsticks and liquid eyeliner with Heather and Lauren. The most recent one leaves off on her trip to Chiapas last summer.

It's like a whole year is missing.

That's when it hits me:

Yearbook.

I cross the room and rip down last year's volume from the desk shelf. If the guy goes to Fairfield, he'll be here.

No sooner do I start fanning pages than does a name in black marker leap out at me: *Brand Sayers*. My breath stops as I spot the three words above it—

Go to hell.

—and by the exhale I have already experienced at least four distinct reactions:

(Surprise) What? Did Brand have some kind of history wi—

(Relief) Oh yeeah. That's what he wrote in everyone's yearbook.

(Anger) RUDE!

(Rationale) It's not like he knew she was going to die in July.

When I finish scanning signature pages I check inside the covers, then the white space in front. No "love" sign-offs, no *I'll miss You*; no (romantic) sightings of the three little words.

Nothing.

Then, as I hold the book to the ceiling and fan it in a hopeless final pass, something drops and spirals to the floor—a torn piece of college-ruled. I set the book down to retrieve it.

Me

it says, in rich, blue ink at the bottom.

I sink to the carpet and read the rest.

Camilla,

It's always hard to say goodbye.
"It's No Use Raising a Shout"
W. H. Auden
v–vi

Love,
Me

I tear back to Brand's to compare handwriting. Polar opposites.

But why is YOU's on some throwaway shred of paper? An extra precaution? I glance at the book again and kick myself for being so careless; if I'd been paying attention, I might've found something telling about the pages it was stuck between. As it is, I've lost that lead.

Guess I'll have to seek my answers in the message itself.

I copy the lines onto a Post-It, put the scrap and the year-book away, and return to my room to look up Auden.

I hit the school library early the next morning. I now know "It's No Use Raising a Shout" is a poem, and W. H. Auden its author. I've read it several times, and even figured out that "v-vi" probably refers to the fifth and sixth lines:

Here am I, here are you:
But what does it mean? What are we going to do?

But they don't give me any clues.

So I decide to start checking hard copies.

I walk among the shelves in search of poetry. It's a long shot, but I'm thinking Camie could've followed the prompt just after it was written—while she was still at school. And if the yearbook was leading her to a physical book—one specific copy on location—there may be something more for me to find there.

Something that will point me to You.

Frost. Eliot. Dickinson. I follow the alphabet backward around a shelf.

I am almost on the other side when my eyes catch leather and Woke Up Like This hair by the computers.

Brand?

I double back and peer through the shelves. What's he doing here? Brand is not, as I might imagine, burning things or dozing or messing around with his band mates, but sitting quietly at one of the reading tables. No—talking with someone. A girl. The brunette is paging through printouts in her binder, tapping on some; Brand nods and makes notations in his own. They're . . . studying?

Since when does a truant study?

The girl laughs at something and touches Brand's arm. I feel myself flush, then wonder why I am flushing, and then flush even harder and curse at myself.

Focus, Juni.

I take a breath and remember what I'm doing here. The book I need should be in the next row.

Stepping around the shelf, I ignore Brand, think *Auden*, and very pointedly keep my eyes on the spines.

Which is why I fail to see the girl sitting crisscross on the floor and walk catastrophically head-on into her book stack.

Crash.

A gasp. I catch myself and apologize, quickly crouching to help pick it up. When a dark hand meets mine I recognize the aqua/yellow nail polish.

"Angela," I say, surprised.

A black curl trails from her up-do. Angela sweeps it back and smiles apologetically. "Hi, Juniper." In her other hand is an open book; on the cover are a man and a woman in an impassioned kiss. "Are you okay?"

"Just a little embarrassed." When I glance behind me, sure enough, Brand is watching us, shaking his head. Because I tripped?

Or because I'm talking to Angela?

Geez. It's not like I'm handing her a ticket to the da Vinci exhibit.

. . . That I may or may not have already bought her.

"Are you okay?" I ask.

Angela smiles. "I think the pile caught all the action."

"Are your books?"

"Think so."

She closes her current read to help me tidy. I look closer and the title surprises me.

"*Shakespeare in Love*?"

"Yeah." Her smile is a nervous flutter. "It's some of his love poems."

"Ah." The books in the pile, I realize, are also poetry—not the bodice rippers I'd taken them for. I feel my cheeks burn, guilty for judging her.

Then I have an idea.

"You read a lot of poetry, Angela?"

She hugs her knitted vest in, nods.

"Any Auden?"

"Auden?" Her back straightens. "He's one of my *favorites*."

"I don't mean to impose, but—is he around here?"

"Yeah!" She climbs to her feet and starts for the shelves. "You after something specific?"

I tell her the name of the poem. Angela finds the A's almost before I am standing. "Arnold . . . Ashbery . . . Atwood . . . Auden!"

There are several anthologies. Angela takes a slim one called *Tell Me the Truth About Love* and hands me a *Selected Poems*. We both start leafing.

"So is this for a scavenger hunt, or something?"

"Or something," I agree.

We browse the listings book by book until Angela says, "Found it!"

She taps the page of a paperback with a neon nail and holds it out so we can both lean over it. "It's the very first one. And look—someone even left us a bookmark!"

"What?"

I yank the book closer and pluck the slip from between the pages, hold it up like a diamond beneath the light: a check-out receipt, dated June 10 of this year.

June 10.

We would've had our yearbooks by then.

"You . . . okay?"

I snap to and flash her a smile. "Great. Just—excited to find it." Understatement. I will tear this book apart. "Thanks for your help, Angela—think I'm gonna go check this out before the bell rings. See you in French?"

"See you," she echoes, bemused.

I comb the Auden book all morning, sneaking glances at it in anatomy and French.

By lunch, when I pull it out at our table, I'm feeling defeated. I've scanned the entire text and found no obvious notes or markings; I must've read "It's No Use Raising a Shout" three dozen times by now. Still I have gleaned no hidden meaning from it—none, at least, beyond the lines the yearbook references.

Here am I, here are you:

But what does it mean? What are we going to do?

I think back to YOU's yearbook prompt and wonder if I missed something. Was there some kind of code in that message? A key that would've meant to read it differently?

What if "v-vi" wasn't lines?

I flip to page five. On it is a poem called "What's in Your

- 142 -

Mind, My Dove, My Coney"; on six, only half another called "Prothalamion." I read the first, and though it doesn't seem to carry any cryptic love notes, parts of it hit me with unexpected power—words of life, sudden loss.

I'm halfway through "Prothalamion," which seems to celebrate a wedding, when I hear the scrape of a chair pulled back.

"Whatcha readin'?"

I turn, surprised. Not because Nate's nodding at my book as he drops into a seat beside me; because the sound I heard came from the other side of the table. I look up.

No one is there.

But a chair is drawn.

And walking quickly away from it is Brand Sayers.

Did Brand see what I'm reading and bail?

Is that what YOU would do if he saw I was onto him?— spook and run?

"Auden," I mumble vaguely.

"What's that?" Nate cranes into my eye line like he didn't quite hear. I shake myself and meet his gaze.

"W. H. Auden." I clear my throat, sitting up a little. "It's, uh, poetry."

"I didn't know you were into poetry."

"My sister read it."

The words slip out. For an instant I regret them, but Nate doesn't look uncomfortable; he looks thoughtful.

"Juniper," he starts. "About your sister. I just . . . I wanted to tell you—"

"Hey, guys."

Kody heaves off her backpack and claims the seat beside me, Lucy lunchbox landing after her. "Ooh, book. Homework or fun?"

Nate pulls back. He seems eager to drop his awkward sympathy, so I let him, instead closing the book to show Kody the cover.

"*As I Walked Out One Evening*. Poetry?"

"I found the check-out slip for it. Camilla had it in June."

"Whoa." Kody's eyes widen. She glances at Nate, but he just raises his brows. "Find anything interesting?"

"Some good poems so far. Not so much on which spoke to her."

I close the book and set it down to start my bento. No sign of YOU yet, either.

But if he's there, I'll find him.

By English I am trawling the pages of *As I Walked Out One Evening* one by one, checking for creased corners, pencil ghosts, underlined words, and margin notes when Mr. Bodily's back is turned—anything that could be part of a trail left for Camie. At this point I don't really expect much, but it isn't like I've got something better to go on.

I work gradually from front to back, one stolen minute, one page at a time, until suddenly binders are closing and class is over.

"Juniper."

I look up through the bustle. Mr. Bodily motions for me to meet him at the front of the classroom.

Hmm. Perhaps my ninja reading was slightly less ninja than I imagined.

"Uh," I tell Nate, who lingers to see if he should wait for me, "I'll see you at Booster."

"Cool. Don't forget, meet at Pippa's today!"

I flash a thumbs-up. When Nate waves and joins Kody,

I close *As I Walked Out One Evening* inside my notebook, stack both beneath the book I should have been reading, and walk to the front of the classroom.

"You wanted to see me?"

"Yes." Mr. Bodily is erasing the chalkboard. He dusts his hands, then drags up a stool and sits on it. "How are you doing, Juniper?"

"Uh . . . doing?"

The question catches me off guard. It's been weeks since the strawberry milk thing; does he mean that, or just how I'm doing in general?

He'd be the first teacher to ask.

"I'm all right."

"I couldn't help but notice *The Scarlet Letter* didn't appear to be holding your attention."

Guilty.

I shrug.

"And did my eyes deceive me, or were you sneaking glances at another book as we discussed the riv-et-ing story of Hester Prynne?"

His subtle smile is contagious: I feel my lips contradict themselves while my eyes give me away.

"May I ask which one?"

He's already caught me. Might as well.

With a wobbly smile I remove the poorly concealed anthology from my notebook.

"Auden?" Mr. Bodily's brows go up. It's probably not every day he catches someone *reading poetry* under the table. "Well," he laughs, "at least it's literature. You like him?"

I squash my lips together. I wish I'd spent more time

reading the lines than searching between them. "What I've read so far."

"He's a good one. Any favorites yet?"

"'Prothalamion,'" I vamp, recalling the wedding one I read at lunch. "What about you?"

"Me?" Mr. Bodily folds his arms, pensive. "'Funeral Blues,'" he says after a moment. "It wasn't always my favorite, but it's gotten me through some hard times. Perhaps you would also find it meaningful."

Without intending to, I stare. I didn't realize Mr. Bodily had lost somebody. He's what—twenty-two? Twenty-three? It's hard to imagine someone so young having suffered a significant loss.

Then again, look at me.

Maybe *that's* why he's been more sensitive than other teachers.

"Thanks," I say.

I hesitate a moment, wishing I could ask him who, what shape hole the person he's lost has left in his life—there are so few in my circle I can relate to—but suddenly this feels personal. Too personal.

I say, "My next class is in G Hall. I better get going."

Mr. Bodily says, "Okay. Have a nice weekend."

After school I head to Pippa's, the first on a list of places Nate and I will be soliciting for contributions to Booster causes. I arrive before Nate does, so I order a drink and sit down to look up "Funeral Blues"—on page 43, according to the table of contents.

I take a quick sip of coffee and flip to it.

Then I shiver so hard, I nearly lose the book.

The first four words are *Stop all the clocks.*

How—I didn't even *turn in* that Pilgrim/Havisham response. I stashed it between the cards of my Index. There's no way Mr. Bodily could have seen it. Coincidence?

Or is grief just like that for everyone?

I grab the blank card holding my page and scribble down:

TIME

The first words of "Funeral Blues" by W. H. Auden are "Stop all the clocks."
Havisham 1.
Pilgrim nothing.

I write so fast I smear the ink with my hand. The blurs remind me of another rush job on an index card.

I wonder . . .

My eyes trail up toward the bulletin board by the register. It, like the one in 3 Hall, is as crowded as a city telephone pole.

Could my card still be there?

I get up to check. I don't recall exactly where we stuck it, but I'm encouraged when I start peeling up layers to find fliers from as far back as April.

Lost dog. Spring concert. Zombocalypse tournament . . .

Then—

My handwriting.

I unbury the rectangle, removing just enough tacks and staples to work it free, and smooth the corners to read over the first side.

In moments I am grinning from ear to ear.

"Did I miss something funny?"

I look up to find Nate at the counter, a paper coffee cup in hand.

"Oh." I laugh. "Uh, hey Nate. No, I was just remembering something."

"Remembering what?"

I shake my head and show the card. "About my sister."

"Oh?" Nate arches a brow. He sits at a table and folds his hands like I should go on.

I press my lips together. I don't want him to feel uncomfortable, but he *did* offer his support before . . .

I decide to take him up on it.

"Well, we were here last Valentine's Day, and"—a laugh escapes me as I steal the seat across from him—"and I wasn't in a very loving mood . . ."

I slide him the card. Nate looks over the side facing up:

Things I just LOVE about Valentine's Day ♥ ♥ ♥

1. the classy, original verse each year. Roses are red. Violets are blue. This poem's a lie. Violet's PURPLE, FOOL.
2. couples kissing in line.
3. couples frenching in line.
4. couples exchanging Juicy Fruit, oxygen, and other worldly goods in line.
5. like is that boy a dementor 'cause I think he's sucking out her soul (like a horse sucking bubble tea through a straw)
6. when they share a milkshake <u>Lady & the Tramp</u> style and/or SIT ON THE SAME FREAKING SIDE OF

THE TABLE WHAT IS WRONG WITH YOU

7. the special few who feel moved to serenade their valentine with song, despite being five-screeching-cats tone deaf

8. WHEN THE GIRL CALLS BRAIN-MELTINGLY OFF-KEY SONG "CUTE" UGH GAG.

"Oh my god." Nate wheezes and holds his sides. "*A horse sucking bubble tea through a straw*?"

I grin again. "I was *trying* to write a speech for health. I'd had this massive headache and there were these gross couples everywhere and they were im*poss*ible to ignore when—" I jab a finger at #7. "So I started this list instead. Camie—she was here studying with me—caught on, and she swiped it and said—"

"Valentine's Day's about love, *Juni! Write down some positives and maybe you'll have a better time."*

I laughed darkly. "'Positives'? I have a headache, a speech to write, a test to study for, they're out of my coffee and I can't. Focus. On anything. But Marty Mc-freaking-Slurpface over there. What do I have to be happy about?"

Camie considered me as if accepting a challenge. I knew that look.

That look was dangerous.

"Okay." She stole one of my Index cards. "I'll make you a deal. No one can match your mind for patterns or peppy pessimism—"

I harrumphed.

"—but let's make things interesting. I challenge you to a race: a positives race. We each take a card, and on the count

of three, fill them up as fast as we can with good things about today."

"Not fair. You have bigger handwriting."

Camie rolled her eyes (which actually made me smile). "Three things, *then*. C'mon. It'll be a snap."

"For you, maybe."

"If you win, you can grouch all you want. I'll even buy you a shake."

"And if you win?"

"If I *win* . . ." Camie smiled, a mix of mystery and charisma you could never say no to. "You have to use your powers of observation for Good for the next three months."

"*Three* months? Why three months?"

Her lips curled slyly. "That's how long it takes to form a new habit."

I gaped at her. "You evil genius."

"So? You game?" She took her pen and twirled it between her fingers. "Or are you afraid you might actually enjoy yourself?"

"Tsh. I'll do it just to prove that I won't." I turned the LOVE list over.

"Ready?"

"No!"

"On the count of three. One . . . two . . . THREE!"

"Camie won, naturally." I flip the card over so Nate can see the reverse. "I only got one."

1. Noise-isolating ear buds

Nate grins. "To block out Tone Deaf, right? And, uh—

what did you call him?" He flips the card back. "The bubble tea kid."

"McSlurpface."

"Yeah."

We both laugh. It feels good to share the memory with someone.

This might be the most I've talked about Camie with another person since she died.

"So did you manage?" Nate asks me.

"What?"

"Your three-month penalty."

I smile. "Yeah. I mean, I made some adjustments—I did both positives and negatives, that just felt more honest to me—but I got out an old shoebox and filled it with cards like this and did one every day. I didn't always get three good things, but I made the effort."

"I bet your sister was pleased."

Snort. "Thrilled. Camie called it my 'Happy Box.' After a couple weeks, I started rating days one to ten just to spite her: a number that fluctuated like the Dow Jones based on events. I called it my 'Happiness Index.'"

Nate grins. "I like it."

For a moment, I feel a swell of pride. But as I keep remembering, my own smile fades a little.

"I meant the name as a joke—part sarcasm, part attempt to make the thing feel more dignified. But in the end, the joke was on me. I still do it."

"Do?"

"The cards. One a day. The habit *did* stick, the sneaky genius."

I take a breath, and on the exhale shake my head. "Anyway. Thanks, Nate. I think I needed that."

"Anytime."

He regards me thoughtfully. For a moment he looks as if he might add something, but then he closes his mouth and shakes his to-go cup—empty.

"Well, I don't know about you, but I could use a refill. Should we go talk to Pippa now?"

"Let's."

Nate pays for a second cup. As he does, we chat with the owner, and she agrees to donate pastries to several school events: award ceremonies, staff meetings, Chess Club tournaments.

Throughout the exchange, my eye strays to the bulletin board. My old V-day list is safe in my pocket, but even so, the place it used to be and now isn't eats at me, a burning hole beneath the papers. It doesn't feel right to leave it that way—to have taken something of my sister out of the world and left a new hole behind—so on a whim, I check myself for something to replace it.

The first thing I find is a keychain: the miniature Dala horse on my backpack. It isn't Bristol, but the classic red reminds me of her and of Camilla.

While Nate is getting his coffee, I unclip the horse from its zipper.

Then I hang it on the tack where the card used to be.

Two days later, my da Vinci ploy comes together.

I tell Kody that my mom won some tickets at work, and Saturday morning we hand them over to a lipsticked official who stamps our hands and tells us to "Enjoy."

In the first room of the exhibit, an illustrated timeline of da Vinci's life and work, I start looking for Angela. Beside me, Kody leans in to read something. "'Da Vinci filled over six thousand pages with notes, sketches, and ideas. But he only ever realized a small percentage of them, and started many more projects than he ever finished. In the seventeen years he worked for the Duke of Milan, for example, he completed only six paintings.' Whoa," she says. "I thought *I* had commitment issues."

We move through hallways of lesser-known paintings (that is, expensive canvas copies of them) to the next room, an open space with blown-up journal pages and structures realized from their contents.

No sign of Angela.

In efforts to stall, I enthusiastically note every contraption with an interactive lever, rope, or crank and insist that we go pull it.

"Is that a DEATH RAY?" I ask, eagerly pointing at an illustration of a mirror redirecting a sunbeam onto a ship. A moveable counterpart sits beneath it.

Kody makes a face. "Okay, seriously—what was in that latte you had?"

We continue through rooms of invented tools, weapons (not interactive), vehicles, and flying machines. I stop at every display, secretly sneaking glances between them.

When we get to the bigger paintings—a life-size copy of *The Last Supper* and a whole wing in homage to *Mona Lisa*—I know we are nearing the end.

Then we reach the video room.

The change is immediate, the darkness plunging us into another world. Our eyes adjust, and the soft light of images stirs a feeling:

I have been here before.

I've been so busy keeping Kody occupied—looking for Angela—that I haven't thought at all about the last time I was at the Portland Art Museum. It didn't even occur to me that the gallery used for the Tuileries Garden exhibit last spring could be the same I have been walking through all morning. Nothing looks the same.

We take two chairs in back. I close my eyes to da Vinci's paintings and inventions, and when I open them I see long avenues and fountains and summer-yellowed trees instead.

I see not Kody, but Camilla beside me.

"Macaron?" she'd asked, proffering a fancy box as if popcorn.

"What!" I'd stared at the confections in surprise. "I thought the gift shop didn't sell food!"

"They don't," Camie'd said.

"So where'd you get those?"

A cunning smile. *"C'est un secret."*

We'd done cookie cheers and eaten. I hadn't thought of it again until just now.

I wonder if that "secret" was that they were from YOU.

"I can't believe all I knew about da Vinci this morning was *The Last Supper* and the *Mona Lisa*."

The memory vanishes as Kody points to images of a diving suit, a piano with strange insides, a pyramid parachute brought to life from da Vinci's sketches.

"Full of surprises," I agree.

As the montage runs, a troubling thought occurs. Room after room of the exact hall I explored with Camie six months ago, and it took me *this* long to remember something. I mean, sure, I thought of Tuileries this morning—but not of the macaron Cam'd offered. That required cues: the heavy curtain doors, the rows of chairs, the video walls. What about the rest of the gallery? Did I lose other memories just because the cues weren't there?

The furniture changed and Camie's footprint here was almost erased.

Where else will I lose my means to remember her?

When the images loop, Kody and I rise and exit through the thick black curtain. Outside is a carnival-style poster with the face cut out—this one of *Lisa*.

"Want a picture?" Kody asks me.

It takes a moment to put my enthusiasm back on.

"Uh, *yeah*!"

Kody takes one of me, I take one of her ("Imagine if Lisa had been ginger"), and then, just as I am putting my camera away—

"Excuse me."

I turn, placing the curls and neon nails in a heartbeat.

"Could I ask—oh hey!" Angela smiles at me, surprised.

"Hey, Angela."

YES. Finally, some luck.

I nod at the camera in her hands. "Did you want a picture?"

She grins and lifts the strap from around her neck. "Would you mind?"

"Not at all."

I take it from her and Angela prances behind the poster (yes, "prances"—her actual giddiness is ten times the strength of mine feigned) to mimic the world-renowned smile.

"And . . . got it."

Angela prances back and checks the screen. "Thanks, Juniper."

"Sure." Glancing around: "You here by yourself?"

"Yeah. I mean—" She smiles sheepishly. "I don't *usually* do stuff like this alone, but I found this ticket in my locker Friday, and of course there were only two days left in the exhibit . . ."

Kody, who wears an amused expression (I assume because she did not think it possible to find anyone here more enthused than I've been pretending to be), says, "What a coincidence. Juniper's mom just won tickets from a drawing. Good thing we were all free this weekend."

"You guys know each other?" I ask, inwardly dancing as my plan comes together. "Kody, this is Angela. Angela, Kody."

The two exchange nice-to-meet-yous and our parties converge. Unfortunately, my prediction soon proves accurate; we round a corner and the end of the exhibit is in sight. All that remains are a few plaques and a crowded station.

"Oh!" ejects Angela. She nearly gallops into the lead. "I *wondered* when they'd get to this."

The table ahead is furnished with hardcover journals, pens, and hand mirrors. When one of the visitors aims a mirror at what she's written, I realize that what I've mistaken for guest books are actually part of the exhibit. I spot the sign as we circle around: "Mirror Writing."

"Da Vinci was a freakin' genius," Angela gushes. "He wrote left-handed, from right to left, and *backward*."

"What?"

Kody and I regard the table again: the sample pages, the hand mirrors, a couple trying and grotesquely failing to write I LOVE YOU more legibly than five-year-olds. In other books: "Aki rules," "I HAVE TO PEE," and "Jessica was here."

The last sparks an idea.

"Some say he was dyslexic, but others think he was trying to protect his ideas in case someone got their hands on his journals."

I flash to 65, my deepest secret laid bare in plain English. I have a sudden new respect for Mr. Renaissance.

Angela takes a marker. "Ever try it?"

She flips one of the books to a clean page, smoothly writing HI, I'M ANGELA in backward capitals, then holds a mirror up to it. Sure enough, they are the flawless work of someone who's done this before. Kody and I exchange glances.

"This gives 'the da Vinci Code' a whole new meaning."

We uncap Sharpies, trying to emulate Angela's smooth penmanship. We fail. Miserably.

"You know," I say, struggling to picture which way an *s* should go, "you would *think* I'd be better at this. In elementary school my sister and I had a new secret alphabet every other week."

"My brother and I have a code." Kody nods, squiggling several confused *e*'s. "We knock. One knock means 'Dinner.' Two knocks means 'NOW.' Three means 'GET OUT OF MY BATHROOM AND STOP STEALING MY BRAS, BUTT-MUNCH.'"

"Siblings," sighs Angela. "Can't live with 'em, can't live withUHHHH, I mean—"

"It's all right," I tell her quickly. "It's a good saying."

Angela holds her breath, perhaps waiting to make sure I won't explode into tears in the next several seconds. When I don't, she closes her mouth and studies me.

"You must get tired of hearing that," she says after a moment. "I mean—of people censoring themselves around you."

Waiter? An extra-large YES, please.

I shrug. "It's not the worst offense."

"No?" Angela chews her lip, like maybe she wants to ask what is.

I tell her, "Someone at a support group once told me 'You should be grateful. Your sister is with God now.'"

It was the first and only time I ever attended a support group.

Angela's jaw drops. *"No."*

"Oh yeah."

She shakes her head, at a loss for words.

"AND ON THAT NOTE," says Kody, loudly patching over the heaviness, "I vote we all pick up one of those fluffy sunshine, rainbow-lens lattes and eat pastries and play Find the Hot Boy now. Who's with me?"

Angela raises her hand.

"Juniper?"

I smile.

Couldn't have planned it better myself.

We cap our pens and take up our bags again, and, to the tune of Angela's eager da Vinci facts ("Did you know Bill Gates bought one of his journals for over thirty million dollars? The Codex Leicester. 'Leicester' came from an earl . . ."), leave the exhibit behind us.

At the writing table, in an open book, the page I have left says half forward, half backward, and very illegibly:

Camilla was here

In art class on Wednesday, I finish carving the same words on my linoleum sheet for printmaking. Well, not the words, but the areas around and between them: the negative space. Ms. Gilbert warned us that with linocuts, you have to think in terms of positive and negative because anything you cut will show up white, while whatever you leave will grab ink and print on the page.

That's exactly what happens when I roll a brayer of red over my work and press a sheet of paper down on top of it: I lift the page back, and what peels up is a red-and-white Dala horse, the words CAMILLA WAS HERE inked below.

It seems paradoxical, doesn't it?—that the positive image—this challenge to Cam's absence—was only possible through the act of carving empty spaces?

When Nate and I meet after school the next day to continue our soliciting work for Booster, there are four Camilla Was Here prints in the front of my binder. Nate sees them sticking out and asks:

"Are those fliers?"

I start to say no—that the prints were something I made for myself and have no intention of putting up like ads or campaign posters—but then I hear what I am thinking and stop short because *that is effing brilliant*. Why *not* put them up? How better to reassert my sister in the world?

"You're a genius," I say instead, and promptly start from the flagpole toward Pippa's.

"Hey!" Nate jogs to catch up with me. "I thought we were hitting the library today?"

At Pippa's, I find my Dala horse keychain exactly where I left it last Thursday—mercifully. I don't know what I'd do if even that was gone, too.

Nate watches, bemused, as I set my binder on the counter and pull out one of the prints I made. I lift the keychain just long enough to pin the inked horse under the wooden one.

"Camilla was here," Nate reads.

"Because she was," I explain.

Nate considers me with a head tilt. I can't tell if he's unsure what to say, waiting for elaboration, or trying to decide if I've lost it.

But before I blurt something even weirder about holes or the museum or what I realized in the video room last weekend, he saves me with a nod. "So she was."

Across the way, several voices whoop with laughter. I glance toward them and see four boys—Brand and the rest of Muffin Wars—at a booth heaped with backpacks and instruments. Two of them are aiming French fries at a third's—Keegan's?—open mouth and cheering.

Brand is watching me.

When Nate turns to see what I'm staring at, he looks away.

"We should go," I hear myself say. "I told the librarian I spoke with that we'd be coming in straight after school."

"Sounds good. Let's boogie."

The Fairfield Public Library is crowded when we get there. Nate and I take our place in line behind some other students, a woman with children, a man whose basket is full of hardcovers, and—

"Lauren."

She's just leaving the counter. I spin away to a display of free bookmarks: Rush Hollister again. This time, I take one and eagerly examine it.

When I judge she is gone, I glance up front again. Safe.

But when I face back, I see her by the entrance: stopped to hold the door for someone. Lauren looks inside to be sure they've cleared it—

And sees me.

And then pretends she doesn't.

I look away just as quickly.

"So," says Nate. He can't have missed that painful exchange.

But he doesn't comment on it.

When he says, "Tell me something you remember about her here," I'm pretty sure he means—

"Camilla?"

"Yeah. If you want." He gestures at the queue in front of us. "We've got the time."

I consider the offer. It *did* feel pretty good to share the Valentine's story at Pippa's last Thursday.

I look down the checkout line.

"In third grade," I remember, seeing the wait, "Camilla saved my butt. I had checked out *Coraline* and dropped it in this Jurassic *crater* puddle at the bus stop—completely ruined it."

"Eeek."

"Yeah. So, the next day, my mom made me bring it back here. I was mortified—had the book in a plastic bag like dog poop or something the cat killed. So there I am, sweating bullets and nervous and gripping the sad, soiled sack for dear life—but then *just* as I'm walking up to the counter, Camilla swoops in and plucks the bad news from my hands and says *she's* the one who dropped it. She even paid to replace it—with what was probably a few weeks' allowance back then."

"Awww."

"I know! I think my mom lectured her about depriving me of my chance to be responsible, but you could tell she was proud, too. She took us out for ice cream after."

Nate smiles as the line migrates forward. "That's sweet."

"It was. Is." I draw an unsteady breath. "Thanks, Nate. For listening again."

"Sure. And you know, you don't have to thank me— especially if we make a habit of this Thursdays."

"You . . . actually want to? I mean—you don't mind hearing all my sad girl sister stories?"

Nate shifts a little—almost like a flinch.

"If . . . if it helps," he says at the floor.

I feel my brows come together. What's with him all of a sudden? Nate's looking away like he's upset, or—

Or hiding something.

What if there's another reason Nate wants to hear my Camie stories?—like because *he secretly dated her*?

Now I have trouble meeting his eye. "Of course it helps."

The line moves forward. We walk with it in silence. Am I projecting here? I didn't just imagine that dishonest vibe. But I don't see how Nate could be YOU; he just moved here from Eugene, and Cam's letter made it clear that her relationship was local, or at least not long-distance. The Lemons would've noticed if she'd been making any two-hour road trips.

He's probably just being kind to me.

Or maybe Camie's not the sister he's interested in.

"I can help you over here!"

We're summoned to a check-out desk.

"Hi," I greet the librarian behind it. "We're from the Fairfield High Booster Club. I spoke to Inga about going through donations?"

"Oh yes!" The woman who called us over checks a sticky note. "Juniper and Nate? She said you're welcome to come back and look. She's gone through them already, so if you find a book you want, it's yours."

"Awesome. Thank you!"

Nate and I start for where she indicates, but then I glimpse the countertop and stop again.

"Question?" asks the woman.

"Y . . . eah." I glance around at the other desks. Every one of them displays photos, book lists, and events news beneath a clear sheet of glass. "Would it be possible to borrow some real estate?"

The librarian raises a brow. "What did you have in mind?"

I unshoulder my backpack for a Camilla print. But on a quick search inside—

"Shoot," I realize. "I think I left my binder at Pippa's."

Nate nods at the exit. "Let's go get it, then."

With apologies and thank-yous, we tell her we'll be back.

Back at the bakery, getting my binder is as simple as asking the first employee I see—Pippa herself—for it.

What I don't expect is the scoop that comes with it.

"One of the boys over there saw you leave that," she explains as she passes it back to me. "He handed it in right away."

I don't have to turn to know that she means Brand, but I do, anyway.

His eyes cut up at me.

Pippa nods at the prints in my hands. "Did you make those yourself?"

I pull my gaze from Brand. "Yeah. They're from a block I carved in art class."

"They're very good. I think your classmate thinks so, too. He was admiring the one up there for some time." Pippa tips up her chin at the bulletin board. I glance at the print there, then back at the boys' table. Funny.

Now Brand won't look at me.

First he avoids me 'cause I'm reading the Auden book; now he's interested in my Camilla prints, but doesn't want me to know about it?

Am I collecting coincidences here—

Or am I starting to glimpse YOU?

Happiness: 5

Lauren at library (−).

Brand as You?? (+/−) (If I find 10 coincidences,
do I get a piece of evidence free?).

Remembering with Nate (+).

Prints left at lib. and Pippa's (+).

IDEA: can use Camilla Was Here prints to strengthen
Camie's presence in the places she was?? (+++)

MAKE MORE PRINTS

Instructions for Remembering Your Sister

1. Visit somewhere she's been. Recall a memory of her there.
2. Leave a token of her (Camilla Was Here print) on scene.
3. Take something found on site. Ex: "Things I Just LOVE About Valentine's Day" list, da Vinci ticket, library bookmark.
4. Use souvenir to keep that memory closer.

By the end of our third Thursday soliciting for Booster—this time to secure Grimaudi's pizza for a tailgate party—it is no longer a question of if, but where Nate and I will remember Camie next. I show him a list of Places She Was I've drawn up, and Nate offers to work through it with me: one stop, one Dala horse print, one Camilla story at a time. At least, when the places are local and can be looped in with Booster work. I'm too grateful to refuse, even if I *do* still question his motives.

I can't think of anyone who'd want to hear my Camie stories more than YOU.

Brand may have been skeptical, but only two weeks after my da Vinci scheme, Angela and Kody and I are all playing Truth or Dare in Angela's attic and eating junk food in a ring of beanbags and candles. The occasion?

Halloween.

"*Angela*. Truth or dare?"

Angela and I are still howling, tears squeezing from our eyes. Angela dared Kody to call Nate with the cheesiest pick-up line we could find ("Hi, this is [prank alias]. We met last night?" "Huh?" ". . . In my dreams?") and not only was Nate home; he called back. Three times. I guess "Alicia Pepper" really made an impression.

Kody is unamused.

"*Angela*." She whacks her with a pillow. I squawk and have to hold my stomach as Angela goes face-first into a bowl of Cheetos.

"*Okay*. Yeesh." Angela rights herself and picks puffs from her sweater. It takes a few tries, but eventually she says, through her laughter, "Truth."

Kody: (eyes narrowing in vengeance) "Who do you *like* at Fairfield?"

Angela stops laughing.

"Nobody," she says too quickly.

Kody and I exchange glances.

"Is it Nate?"

"What? No!"

"The Bod?"

"N—" Angela reconsiders. "Handsome, but not my type."

"What *is* your type?"

"Mm—" Angela sighs at the ceiling. "Well, I *thought* it was dinosaur, but—"

"Dinosaur?" Kody wrinkles her nose. "Prehistoric?" I know what she means, but Kody hasn't read her notes to Leo and Oscar.

Angela beans her with a doughnut hole. "Not old. I mean *extinct*! How many juniors do you know with the passions of da Vinci, the wit of Wilde, the sensitivity of an Auden or Frost?"

"None?" Kody ventures.

"Exactly."

"But you do," I realize.

Angela folds her lips in. I study her intently. What modern genius has managed to catch her eye?

At last she winces. "Please don't make me say who. Every time I admit to liking a guy he turns out to be gay. It's like a curse or something."

Kody cracks a grin. "Are you sure they just don't like you?"

This time Angela throws a whole doughnut at her. Kody yelps as it glances off her cheek, smearing chocolate and rainbow sprinkles in its wake.

She checks the candied smudge and gasps as if it's blood.

"Oh, it is ON!"

She grabs the rest of the box. Angela shrieks and shields

herself with a blanket as Kody aims doughnut holes at her, the powdered sugars leaving dust prints on the fabric— although after a few Angela thinks better of it and gropes along the floor for the pizza, which she finds and pulls in with her and arms herself with.

"You guys do realize that if you throw the food, we can't eat it, right?"

Splat.

A pepperoni unsticks from my chin.

"Well, then."

In moments the attic is a war zone: Kody dives behind some boxes, popping up to pelt us from over the top; Angela hugs an armchair and retaliates with a rain of pizza chunks; I hunker behind a desk, aiming Cheetos. Unfortunately, those only float in useless arcs to the floor, and Angela and Kody see this and gang up on me.

"Mercy!" I cry through flecks of frosting and pizza sauce.

"NEVER!" they rejoin together.

In a desperate move, I empty both of my bowls at them, candy corn clattering across the floor while Cheetos crunch underfoot. Angela and Kody take up their boxes, preparing to do the same when—

"Angela?"

The trapdoor falls open. Angela's mom calls up to ask what we're doing.

"Experimental spa treatment!" Angela calls back.

Kody and I catch each other's eye.

"Could you please 'experiment' a little more quietly?"

"Sorry, Mrs. Waters!"

When she's gone, Angela turns to us. "I . . ." Her laughter flatlines as she surveys the attic. "Am so-o-o dead."

Luckily, there are rags and cleaning supplies inside one of the (now bespattered) boxes, so we get to work cleaning up before any stains can set in.

Angela sticks one of the unthrown slices of Grimaudi's in her mouth. "Truth or dare, Juniper?"

"Truth."

Angela chews, thoughtful. The sound of rain filters in through the rafters.

"If you had the chance," she says at last, swallowing, "if you could see Camilla again—what would you say to her?"

I feel my body lock, a burglar caught in a spotlight. A pepper falls from the piece of pizza I've just rescued from the top of a wardrobe.

"Oh god," says Angela quickly. "I didn't—god, *sorry,* Juniper. I can be so clueless sometimes—my mom says I have the social sensitivity of a seagull—"

"It's okay."

Angela closes her mouth, lips pressing together so fiercely, it looks as though they have barricaded themselves in for winter.

"Really. All's fair in Truth or Dare. And it's not a rude question, you don't have to apologize—it just, surprised me, is all."

Angela's mouth remains boarded shut. She and Kody watch me, riveted.

"I would say . . ." The rain beats around us like a thousand hands; children laugh as they splash along trick-or-treat routes below. "*I love you.*"

I close my eyes again.

"I would tell her I'm sorry."

So, so sorry.

"I would ask her . . . why she didn't tell me."

Thunder consumes the attic. After a pause so long and enveloping, I start to wonder if this isn't a dream, Kody leans in and asks, gently touching my forearm, "Tell you what?"

I look from one friend to the other in the candlelight. Both grip so tightly to whatever I'm about to say next that I might be at the height of a ghost story.

Well.

I guess I kind of am.

I tell them about Camie's letter to You.

When I finish, Angela swears. "And you think this guy went to Fairfield?"

"Goes," I correct. "The letter said You was still in high school. But yeah—I'm almost positive. Sponge says Camie spent an unusual amount of time in 3 Hall after school."

"3 Hall?"

Angela and Kody raise their brows at each other.

Kody asks, "Any theories who it is?"

I bite my lip. Their eyes widen.

"Who?"

I toss my hair from my face. "Okay. Don't freak out on me, but—" I drop a hunk of maple bar in the trash and reposition. "I think it could be Brand Sayers."

"BRAND SAYERS?"

I walk them through the mounting stack of evidence:

1) He's younger, and more importantly was at Shawn's party the night the letter should've been delivered;
2) He's known as both unstable and concerned about his image, which might explain why neither he

nor Camie would have wanted their relationship
public;

3) He's been uncharacteristically nice to me on mul-
tiple occasions;

4) He has a key to Band Geeks' Paradise, which is,
as Kody and Angela well know, a secluded and
notorious sex haven *in 3 Hall*.

And that's before you account for Brand's walking away
when he saw me reading Auden, or his apparent interest in
my Camilla print at Pippa's.

But Kody only shakes her head. "I just don't see it. I feel
like Camilla was too clean, too . . . *ambitious* for someone
like Brand. Or, not ambitious—academic. Good grades, tons
of clubs and activities, senior class president . . ."

"But then," Angela counters, "wouldn't that just be
another reason to keep it quiet? Because it would rock the
social scene?"

Kody frowns. "Maybe . . ."

"You know what I think?" They turn to me. "I think
there's one only way to find out for sure." And it's long over-
due.

Angela asks me, "What?"

I answer, "Ask him."

When I look for Brand after school that Monday in detention—he did say he's a glutton for punishment—he isn't there. I try out back, thinking maybe he snuck off for a smoke break.

Nothing. Not even an Axe cloud.

I fold my arms. I may not know my suspect perfectly, but I *can* think of one other place to look for him.

A quiet little place in 3 Hall.

When I climb the steps to Band Geeks' Paradise, I hear music. It's electric guitar, a song I don't recognize. There's a lot of quick notes, bending, vibrato. It's smoky. Melancholy.

Blues.

I knock on the door of the storage space.

"Lemon?" Brand looks up as I enter, but he doesn't stop playing. "This is a surprise."

I cross the room, drag up a stool to sit on. "Is that a Muffin Wars song?"

"Nah," he says. "Just improvising."

"That's *improvising*?"

I think of Camie and the way, on slow afternoons when we were lazing around the house or raiding the fridge for a snack, she would suddenly start rapping out a rhythm on the countertop. After a few measures she'd add a half beat, a clap, a beatboxing vocal or a line of notes. Then she'd look at me, a cue. I would jump in with variations.

If we were in the car, she'd ad-lib harmonies with the radio. It always blew me away. I was convinced there was some trick to it, but when I asked her how she did it, Cam just said, "You hear a song enough, you can just kind of feel it."

It was the skill that prompted me to join choir.

Nowadays, thanks to that experience, I can find a harmony myself. Still, I doubt I'll ever really *feel* a song like Camie could.

Like Brand can.

Maybe they would've been good together.

"So." Brand's fingers scale the neck of his guitar, ending on a high bend. "I'm guessing you didn't drop by to hear me play." He stands, unplugs and lifts off his instrument, and takes it over to lay back in the case.

"No," I affirm. "I came because . . ."

Brand is fiddling with keys at a low cupboard. On the floor beside him are an unrolled mattress pad, a pillow, and blankets.

"Is that—?" I crane closer.

"What?" Brand unlocks it and hurriedly stuffs the amp, then the bedding away. "Sometimes I come up here to nap."

"How is it that you haven't flunked out of the district?"

"I keep a 3.7 average, thank you."

"What the crap? How?"

Brand shuts the cupboard and twists the keys. Grinning, he confides, "The smarter you are, the more you can get away with."

My mouth bends down. Smart, too? You can bullshit a paper, but you can't fake a GPA. He's sounding more like Camilla's type by the minute!

I decide to hit him with it straight in the hopes of startling out the truth.

"Brand, were you dating my sister?"

He stiffens visibly. "What?"

"If I said 'Auden,' you'd say . . . ?"

"Is . . . that someone I should know?"

"Or if I asked about Pippa's. She said you were lurking around my Camilla print."

Brand scoffs. "Since when is it a crime to appreciate good art?"

"And I'm sure it only *seems* like you've been avoiding me since I brought up Shawn's again."

"That—" Brand closes his mouth and looks down, a sudden smile playing up his face. "Is not what you think."

"No? And just what do you think I think? What aren't you telling me? *Why are you smiling?*"

Brand crosses the room without answering, still clearly savoring my agitation. He takes his time straddling the stool he'd been sitting on to face me.

"Actually," he says, "until just now, I'd been under the distinct impression that *you* were avoiding *me.*"

"What?"

If he means that as a curveball, it's working.

Brand says, "Well yeah. You haven't been coming by the dumpsters anymore. I thought that maybe you'd found what you were looking for. I was gonna ask, but then I saw you hanging out with that flannel champ and thought—I thought—" He stops short, looks away. "Never mind."

Is Brand . . . *blushing*?

"Is that why you jumped ship at lunch that day?" Not because he'd seen me reading Auden—but because I was with *Nate*?

I guess I'm not the only one who's wondered about him.

When Brand doesn't answer, I clear my throat. "I got a grade for those projects I showed you. That's why I haven't been around the dumpsters—not trawling for materials any-more. And Nate—Nate and I started hanging out mostly because of Booster."

I'm not sure why I feel compelled to add this last part. But as much as I've questioned why he's been such a good friend to me myself, that is all Nate's been: a friend.

Brand says, "Oh."

He looks considerably less surly.

"Anyway," I cover, heat rushing to my face, "don't change the subject on me. I want answers."

"What answers?"

I opt not to tell Brand about the Auden lines or 3 Hall. Instead I remind him I know Camilla's boyfriend is still at Fairfield, I have a pretty good idea she was meeting him at the party, and that the only younger person I know was there besides myself is—

"Me," he finishes.

"And your band."

Brand shakes his head. "Look—I'm not the guy. I don't know how to convince you of that except to say that if I *was*, I would've told you already. I'd want to read the letter, and I wouldn't want to mislead you or deprive you of your closure. Douche thing to do."

My shoulders slump.

Yeah. I guess it would be.

"As for the rest of Muffin Wars"—he tilts his head, frowns—"Tyler only joined this summer, and Derrick and Keegan were both dating other people. So that's that."

"Did you see Camilla talking to anyone that night?"

"We were playing. It's not like I was watching her."

"You must have noticed her once she picked up the mike and said I could sing better than you."

A scowl.

"Please, Brand. Anything could help."

Brand crosses his arms. I wait.

"I guess . . ." At last he exhales. "I *did* see her talking to some guys when you were up on the deck with us."

My eyes spring open. "What guys? Who?"

"Dunno, but they looked older. One of 'em had a Fullbrook sweater."

"Fullbrook?" What would Cam be doing talking to guys from the local university? "Anyone else? Someone younger?"

"Jesus, Lemon, I told you. I was *playing a gig,* not taking a fucking census."

"Please."

Brand frowns. After a moment he sighs and drags his hand back through his hair. "Other than us and Sponge . . ."

"Sponge?" I sit up straighter.

"Yeah. He's our sound and lights guy. But it isn't him, okay. Sponge is—"

But I don't hear him. I am galloping down the stairs, pieces falling into place.

Sponge is the sound and lights guy. And not just for Muffin Wars—for most of our school productions.

Which take place almost exclusively in the auditorium *in 3 Hall*.

"Where are you going?"

I don't answer him. There is swearing, keys, and a hustle of steps behind me as I stalk for Ms. Gilbert's, but I hardly notice; my head is buzzing with Sponge, the theater, possibilities. The sound booth is only one place those in drama might have access to: under stage. Dressing rooms. Costume loft. Not to mention it was Sponge him*self* who clued me in to 3 Hall.

How better to mislead me than with truth?

"I found something weeks ago," I explain when Brand catches up with me, panting, outside the studio.

"What?"

I jerk my head. Together we enter and clomp up the stairs to the room I used to use for independent study.

"Here."

I hit the lights. When the bars flicker on, I pull the drawer with all my scavenged materials, riffle through, and find what I am looking for—a single page with Sponge's name on it—in a folder marked "poetry."

I take it out and pass the sheet to Brand. "What if it's about Camilla?"

Brand takes the page I offer him and scans it.

We touched by chance one afternoon
And neither of us was immune:
The spark inflamed to fevered flu 'cause
Boy, I had a crush on you.

Your shining eyes, your golden hair
You caught me watching from the stairs
And waltzed right up and said you knew that
Boy, I had a crush on you.

We kissed, we danced, the seasons changed
Our hopes and dreams and fears exchanged
You were my butter, bread, and moon
Oh boy, I had a crush on you.

Our secret love did not deter
A secret lover's French whisper:
Je vous aime, chéri, et si beaucoup
Boy, I had a crush on you.

But on one fateful summer night
You vanished from my world in flight
And didn't even say goodbye—though knew that
Boy, I had a crush on you.

It even does the repeating lines like "It's No Use Raising a Shout"!

Sponge Torres

"I think you're seeing what you want to see." Brand hands the paper back to me.

"Maybe," I admit. "But *look* at this stuff. 'Secret love'? 'Golden hair'? 'One fateful summer night'? You can't tell me that this doesn't all line up." And that's not even counting the French bit.

Brand looks at me. His chest swells and empties with a heavy breath.

"Just don't try to 'fix' things for Sponge like you did with Angela."

I blink at him. "What's that supposed to mean?"

"What it sounds like," he says.

I stay till five to hit the auditorium in 3 Hall. If Sponge is You and Camie used to meet him in the theater, she'd have surely been sighted by those in school productions. Maybe even *with* Sponge. I never saw her around when I did *Bye Bye Birdie* last fall, but maybe she and You weren't dating then. Maybe they only started dating after.

Maybe someone who was in the spring play can tell me something.

Unfortunately, when I try to question any likely informants—the cast and crew now in rehearsals for *Fiddler on the Roof*—a new director kicks me out faster than you can say "cast list."

The only other way I can think of to catch them all is to wait until full rehearsals—the last two weeks before the show. Those practices are more grueling, and the cast almost always goes out for Pippa shakes after.

The only caveat?

Full rehearsals won't start until about a month from now.

Damn it.

It sucks I can't just ask Sponge.

By mid-November, Nate and his wintergreen charms have suckered both Angela and Kody into helping us prepare for Booster's first real event, the annual bake sale. As the four of us mix, knead, drop, and decorate various pastries at my house the night before, he doesn't seem to notice the way they keep getting lost in his eyes.

Everything's going well until, midway through biscotti, scones, and the redundant but exquisite-looking cookies 'n' cream cookies, Angela asks about more baking soda.

"Is there some in one of these?" She indicates Camie's pink-and-lemon-print canisters.

"That one's sugar, and that one's coffee."

"Up here?" Angela spot-checks a few cupboards. "Uhh . . ." she says when she gets to the one above the stove, where most people keep spices.

Ours is full of our more unusual-looking Dala horses.

"One sec. I'll check the pantry."

I flip the light and step into the closet. All the baking stuff is up top and I have to stand on tiptoe to see, but I catch a glimpse of Arm & Hammer orange in the very back. I push aside cinnamon and vanilla and bring it down.

"Wha—?"

The box is feather light. I shake it, and am about to ask who put it back empty when I realize it isn't.

Empty.

Something rustled inside.

I pull the flap at the top and peer in. Wedging my hand through, I tip the box toward me and work out the two spare papers that cling to the edges.

The sheets are thin. Newspaper. I unfold the first, and as I brush off the baking soda, my eyes go to the date in a corner.

July 6.

And even before I turn the slip over and see her picture, the commemorative words I helped write, I know I am holding Cam's obituary.

My heart accelerates and I feel green. What's it doing here? Did Mom or Dad put it here?

I fumble the second piece over. Another senior portrait, a boy, stares back at me. I don't recognize him, and can't fathom why Mom or Dad would have some other kid's obit in our pantry—until I catch the date for the memorial service at the bottom: July 10.

The breath goes out of me.

Same age. Same burial date.

Same accident.

He's the other driver.

"Find any, Juniper?"

I jump at Angela's call from outside, but somehow find my voice to answer her. "Still looking!"

My eyes dart up the clipping.

AARON CHAMBERLAIN

Aaron was born in Aloha to Sam and Jocelyn
Chamberlain. He loved swimming, stand-up, music,

pizza sandwiches, and many an adventure in the great outdoors. A talented comedian and athlete, Aaron took pride in his videos and making people laugh, learning to snowboard without instruction, and playing water polo for the AHS varsity team.

He is survived by—

I hear feet on the stairs.

"Smells good down here!"

Mom.

I nearly drop the empty box. Shoving the clippings back inside, I just barely replace it, grab a cylinder of baking powder, and step out before she enters the kitchen.

"So," Mom quips when she does. She eyes our spreads along the counter. "Which of these delightful-looking treats is the culprit?"

My pulse pounds in my ears as my brain shorts. Not only have I uncovered someone's secret stash of grief; this is the first time I've had friends over since Camie's death. For Mom to be down here, socializing—chatting not just with me, but with strangers—

It isn't just a big deal.

It's monumental.

"That would be the cinnamon roll shortbread," Nate informs her. "Kody's recipe." Kody beams.

"They look delicious." Mom inhales their aroma above the tray. "And they smell even better. May I?"

Kody gestures *help yourself,* so she does. The four of us look on, unconsciously quieting. Kody and Angela know how withdrawn Mom has been and their looks go out to me, and though I meet their gazes gratefully, there's no way they can guess the real storm spinning behind my eyes.

The obits are Mom's. They have to be. Dad would rather talk about his grief—not stash it in some hidey-hole. But why would Mom keep them (and why in the baking soda)? Why keep Aaron's?

Maybe to remember that he was a person, too?

In the quiet of the kitchen, Mom chews. Nate lifts his brows at us, joining the circle of discreetly exchanged looks, but he is smiling. Probably he's just waiting to ask how many stars we get.

And the verdict is . . .

"Divine!"

Kody passes me a smile.

"You think those are good. Wait till you try my teacakes!"

Nate leads Mom along the counter. Angela accompanies, offering suggestions for what to try next, and Kody gets out an old cookie tin for Mom to collect what she jokingly refers to as her "kitchen owner's tax" in.

I lean against the fridge, processing. Mom hasn't been this outgoing in months. But more staggering is what's just occurred to me: All this time she's had the obituaries, this dark remembrance squirreled away—just like I've had the secret that I wrote on 65. It kills me that we both have things about Camilla we keep from each other.

Will we ever be able to talk about them?

"So." Mom fits the lid on the tin when the tour is finished. "Aren't you going to introduce me to your friends, Juniper?"

"Uh, yeah." I clear my throat and regroup. "Mom, this is Kody, Angela, and Nate. Guys—my mom."

Nice-to-meet-yous and Thank-you-for-the-kitchens are

exchanged. Then, a sharp rise as if suddenly perceiving something, Mom stands taller and furrows her brow.

"You seem familiar," she tells Nate, studying him. "Did you know Camilla?"

Whoa. That grief group must really be helping.

Mom *never* brings up Camilla.

"No, ma'am," Nate replies, easily, blissfully unaware of the cosmic forces it must've taken to form the question. "My family only moved here this summer."

"Oh? Where from?"

"Eugene."

"Eugene?"

"You're probably confusing him with someone from a Gap commercial," I say lightly, half hoping for a smile or a laugh. When was the last time I made Mom laugh? "It's the hair flip."

"And the jeans," Angela adds.

"And the *name*," agrees Kody. "'Nate Savage' could sell scarves and sport coats on sound alone."

Nate grins. "What—but not with my dashing face?"

"Savage . . ." Mom frowns at the floor.

Abruptly her expression changes.

"*Nathan* Savage?"

"Just Nate," Nate says quickly.

Crash.

The cookie tin clanks against the counter, rattling to a stop. The kitchen goes still, and when I look up Mom is gripping her temples.

"Mom?" What just happened? "Are you—?"

"Air." The word is dry, a whisper. Mom clears her throat and lowers her hands. "I just need some air." And it looks true; as she reaches down the counter for her purse I can see her face has gone off-color. "I'm just gonna—" She scrabbles for her keys. "I think I'll run to the store."

"Are you sure, Mom? I can get you som—"

"I'm fine." She glances once around the kitchen. "You kids need anything?"

Angela looks askance at me, and before I can warn her not to, says, "Baking soda?"

I wince and lower the powder tin. So much for discretion.

"Baking soda." The motion is not missed by Mom. Her eyes dart my way and off again, and then she mumbles, "Call me if you think of anything else," and slips out the door.

"Is it just me," says Angela when the sound of her car has faded, "or did that get a little weird just—*ow!*" Kody's knocked her on the foot.

"Sorry, Nate." I feel awkward and embarrassed and don't really know what else to say. How do you apologize for grief? "My mom's still really sensitive about my sister—the randomest things set her off sometimes. You probably just reminded her of one of Camilla's friends."

"Right," he says. You can tell he feels guilty, though.

"It's nothing personal."

Nate nods, stoic.

"Speaking of Camilla . . ." Angela foots awkwardly into the uncomfortable silence that follows, "Have you found any more leads on that guy, Juniper?"

Nate's frown changes shape. "What guy?"

"The one she was secretly seeing and wrote a letter to before—*OW!*" Kody has kicked her again, too late.

I heave a sigh as my gaze meets the pantry. Where there's Camilla trouble, You can only follow.

I tell Nate about the letter.

"A secret boyfriend," he repeats when I finish. "So—*do* you have any leads on this guy?"

Right now my prime suspect is Sponge—but if I share that with the class, I'll have to explain why.

And where I found the evidence.

"Bits and pieces. Nothing solid yet."

"Have you, like," says Angela, preemptively shifting her shins away from Kody, "looked in her room for pictures? Notes?"

"ANGELA."

"*What*? If it was my sister, that's what I'd do."

"I have," I say, halting the two in their grapple, "but never for long. My mom is really weird about that stuff."

"Weird?" Kody releases Angela's shoulders. "Weird how?"

I tell them about the jewelry incident. How one day the door was just shut after that, an unspoken barrier like a string of police tape.

"That doesn't seem right," says Angela. "At least, not to me."

Kody asks, "Did you guys share clothes and stuff?" I nod. "Don't you ever—I don't know—want to wear one of her shirts or something?"

"All the time." In fact, I think Camilla would feel a lot less like a shadow if I had more of her things to physically adhere to. Things I could touch and carry like the bag she took to Shawn's. "But there's no way my mom wouldn't notice. And she'd flip."

"What if we all went in?"

Each of us turns, surprised, to Nate.

"I'm not saying we *should*," he adds quickly, "I just think

Angela has a point. It seems like a logical place to look for evidence of a secret relationship."

"*Thank* you," says Angela, looking pointedly at Kody.

Then all gazes move to me.

Nate cautiously continues: "If the four of us looked now—you, me, Kody, and Angela—we could all search faster and cover way more ground. Be out before your mom gets home."

The others hold their breath. I chew my lip, looking from them, to Nate, to the tin Mom abandoned on the counter.

I may not get another opportunity like this.

At last I concede, "Okay."

I go in first. Our steps are measured, muted as if out of respect, and the mixture of humility and reverence on everyone's faces makes it seem more like holy ground than a teen girl's bedroom. Angela and Kody regard the ceiling, a collage of Paris—its splendid palaces and curbside cafés, bright flowers and fruit stands, the old shops and long windows and elegant women in skirts and peacoats—like *The Creation of Adam*. This does sort of *feel* like a pilgrimage.

Or trespassing.

The sheep look to their shepherd. I draw a half-hitched breath.

"Let's get started."

I move for the dresser. Tentative, Kody goes for the bed. Nate and Angela take the bookshelves and desk respectively.

"Look for pictures, a message, anything coded," I instruct despite the knot in my chest. "Especially addressed to 'You,' or signed 'Me.' Oh—and if you see a mini Dala horse with a star on its belly, would you let me know? It was Camie's favorite and I haven't been able to find it."

We work in silence. I don't find much in the dresser, apart from some scarves I'd like to borrow and the occasional horse that isn't Bristol. I even check inside the socks, beneath underwear, in all the nooks and crannies of her jewelry boxes.

Nothing.

The others find as little as I do.

"Did you say you found the letter in a purse?" Nate asks, replacing the last book on the shelf.

"Yeah, I—"

I follow his gaze and stop short.

The bags.

I cross the room to where they hang off of hooks in rows, opening the closet to reveal more. "Jackpot."

I deal them out like a hand of cards, and for the next several minutes we are all combing through clutches, cross-bodies, drawstrings, and shoulder bags, periodically announcing our finds:

"Sunglasses."

"ChapStick."

"A book."

"Change purse."

"A flask and a bottle of soap bubbles. Bet that was a fun afternoon."

"Three pens, tissues, and seventy-two cents."

"H&M receipt."

"Uhhhh," says Nate, holding up a pink-wrapped feminine product.

When I get to a camel-colored backpack, I feel something in a pouch before I see it: stiff paper, too rigid to be a receipt. I unzip the pocket and pull it out.

A ticket stub.

"Guys."

"What is it?" Kody and the others gather round.

"Concert ticket. To . . ." I break off.

"What?"

"Arctic Monkeys." I check the date to be sure and bring it down. "I *invited* Cam to this. She told me—she said she had other plans."

"Yeah, with somebody else. Ow!" Angela rubs her shoulder where Kody hit her.

"What plans?"

"I don't . . . I can't remember. She said it was something she couldn't get out of. Club stuff."

"Hey." Angela paws through a clutch. "I found one, too. To . . ." She holds a yellow scrap out in front of her. "*Zombocalypse 3*?"

"What?" I seize the stub. Like the one for the band, it's also dated in the last year. "Well, she definitely didn't see *that* one with Melissa and Heather. I think we're getting warmer."

Another couple minutes and the tickets are cropping up like weeds: movies. Concerts. A play. The zoo. The fair. The art museum. Always just one: half of the equation.

Always with a hole where its twin should be.

"Yo," Nate calls after a while. "I think I found something else."

We turn to see him holding a paperback in one hand, a crumpled slip of paper in the other. His finger's on the open title page, a handwritten line at the top:

Camilla,
Saw this and thought of you.

Yours,
Me X

The four of us exchange glances.

"And get this." Nate closes the book—*Les Misérables*—and holds up the paper that was in it. "The receipt is from Fullbrook."

"*What?*"

The four of us crowd around the tiny font.

Fullbrook University Bookstore.

"But that doesn't make sense." I scrunch my brow. "The guy Camie was dating is still in high school. Why would he be buying books there?"

"Maybe he was touring campus," Angela suggests.

"Or taking a class," offers Kody.

"Maybe—"

But Angela stops talking. There's a thick, leathery crinkling noise, and Nate and Kody and I all freeze, pivoting to face whatever silenced her.

Standing in the doorway, hand tightening around a paper grocery sack, is Mom.

We are holding half a dozen of Camilla's bags between us.

"Juniper," Mom says, jaw tight and voice small but frighteningly even, "it's time for your friends to go home now."

Happiness: 0.2

Friends who support me (+++).

Being caught in Cam's room (−).

Mom upset (−).

Dad taking her side (−−).

Fighting (−).

Confrontation (−).

Struggle over baking soda box; losing my grip; crashing into & breaking Camie's handmade pink & lemon sugar jar (−−−).

The look on Mom's face when it happened (−−−).

The look on Dad's before he went after her (−−−).

When I arrive at West Rose Mall the next morning, site of the Sunday farmer's market and the GSBC bake sale, Kody reads in my expression that things went badly.

"How bad?" she asks.

I set down the first box of cookies. "Bad."

I really don't want to dredge up the details since we're prepping for eight hours of pushing pastries with a smile, but I give Kody, and then Angela and Nate when they arrive, the short of it:

1) Grounded. By Dad, though, not Mom, because
2) Mom prefers to shut out reality, including me, and
3) I blew up when Dad accused *me* of not respecting *her* needs, and
4) I am now formally forbidden from entering Camilla's room.

I don't even touch on my big accusation—that Mom and Dad pretend Camie never existed—or what happened in our struggle for the baking soda. Too much explaining.

And too painful.

"Shit, Juniper." Nate looks bleak, as worn-through as I feel when I finish. "I'm sorry. If I hadn't suggested—"

"If you hadn't suggested it, I would have done the exact same thing later, but without the support of friends."

A pause. Then—

"Aww." Angela touches my arm, the other hand going tenderly over her heart.

"Aww," Nate echoes, girlishly imitating Angela.

Kody rolls her eyes. "Are we all going to hug now?"

"Aww," chorus Angela and Nate, both reaching for Kody.

The whole thing's about as cheesy as a cracker platter—but it's the best I've felt since July.

Fairfield is a small suburban town, but by ten o'clock, the bake sale is bustling. Word of Kody's cinnamon roll shortbread is wafting out from here, like—well—like the scent of hot cinnamon roll shortbread. A few times, I think I even catch Lauren looking over from across the street, where she and other choir members are washing cars to raise money for San Fran.

"You okay?" Kody asks when she catches me staring. Her eyes move across the street, where Lauren looks quickly away.

I turn and smile automatically. "Great."

But there's a disconnect. I feel like that's my old life over there, and all I can do is watch it from outside. For the last two years, that was me washing cars and waving signs and belting musicals with the group. Laughing beside my best friend. Spraying—

—the hose in at one of the customers?

A shriek.

"WHAT THE HELL!"

The window of a red coupe rolls the rest of the way down and a sopping Morgan Malloy glares out.

"Whoops," says Lauren loudly. "Didn't see your window was open. Sorry!"

Her eyes cut to mine.

I feel a bit better after that.

In the meantime, our group has its own antics: Nate, for example, noticed early this morning that customers with brightly colored shoes tend to buy complementary confections. Somehow this evolved into a game of guessing everyone's perfect pastry based on footwear.

We're now calling matches for nearly every shoe we see:

"Gingersnap!"

"Peanut butter!"

"THAT PB PRETZEL ONE WE AGREED NOT TO CALL CAMEL POOP!"

—debates the club about a single woman's tan-colored sandals.

We're still watching the ground when a pair of classic Timberlands approaches.

"Deej?" a voice asks.

Nate looks up. His face splits into a wily grin. "Garrett Bowman!"

He stands, and Nate and the dark-skinned boy in hiking boots clasp hands and bro-hug. The rest of us exchange glances.

"Deej?" I ask.

"DJ," Garrett offers, also grinning. "'Cause this kid can *mix*."

"What? You mix music?" Angela is as surprised as I am.

"Not music," Garrett laughs. "*Drinks!* Ask him to make you a mojito sometime. So what's the deal, Nate? You living in Fairfield now?"

Nate darts a glance back at us, reddening. The three of us smile and promptly look away like we're not listening, or if we are, aren't judging.

"As of July," he returns, still embarrassed.

Apologetically, he asks if we mind if he steps aside a minute to catch up with Garrett. He hasn't seen him since his year in Aloha.

"Sure."

Nate smiles and claps Garrett on the shoulder, guiding him away. Garrett asks, "July, huh? Anything to do with the Shark?" and for some reason I swear the tips of Nate's ears go even redder.

I realize I'm leaning after him to overhear when a voice up close startles me.

"I hear you have gummy bear cupcakes."

I jump in my seat. I've been so intent on eavesdropping that I failed to notice Brand Sayers stroll up, smiling, an unlit cigarette between his teeth.

"Wow," I say.

"What?"

"I think that's the first time I've seen you before I smelled you."

The kid paying beside Brand, some freshman in a Stallions hoodie, guffaws. Brand silences him with a Remember,-I-have-mob-relations squint and he hastily scrambles off with his cronut.

I fold my arms. "Why are you here? Come to make fun of me?"

"Of your Betty Crocker Bakes gig with Booster? Never."

"Go away."

"You're very egocentric."

"Excuse me?"

"You heard me. You see me and automatically assume I have no better way to pass a Sunday than to prod at you? *Some* of us came to do the shopping"—he holds up a plastic Lauer's sack as evidence—"and, if all went uninsultingly well, to buy a pastry."

I scoff. "You're here to buy something."

"I *do* have a life outside of you, Lemon. One that, if you'll trouble yourself to remember, includes the occasional indulgence in gummy bears. So do you have gummy bear cupcakes, or not?"

I sigh and retrieve one from a carton in back. "Two fifty."

Brand begins to pull out the bills, looks at the cupcake; sees another guy carry off six in a plastic to-go box; looks back at his single serving and frowns.

"How much for that?" he asks, pointing.

"Fourteen."

"Fourteen . . ." Brand assesses his wallet. "A bit steep," he says, removing his only twenty, "but I hear the cause is a good one." He nods at the *Help fund the St. Valentine's Shaker!* sign across our table.

I exchange the single for a half dozen, take his twenty, and give him change. He pockets it, takes the box, and starts to go.

"Brand."

He turns, the cupcakes halfway lowered into his bag.

". . . Thanks."

For the briefest moment I see a hint of a smile. Then Brand salutes, lights the cigarette still in his mouth, and saunters off, trailing smoke.

"Did you just sell cupcakes to Brand Sayers?"

Kody and Angela are both watching me with rapt expressions.

"Heeey," adds Kody, a thought occurring, "wasn't it *you* who wanted to bake with gummy bears?"

"Y—yeah, but—" I falter under their gazes. "So?"

Angela and Kody chorus "Ohhhhh!" like someone's just scored a goal.

"She blushes and does not deny it, Angela, repeat—"

"Does *not* deny it."

"Whatever. It—coincidence," I fumble.

"What would you call that color she's turning, Kody?"

"I don't know, Angela—'Crushing Crimson'? 'Denial Red'?"

My cheeks burn deeper. "You know what, I'm feeling kinda thirsty all of a sudden. I'm gonna go grab an iced chai at Pippa's. You guys want chai?"

I get up without waiting for an answer. But I get one, anyway:

"But wait, she's—yes—*changing tack*! An evasive maneuver toward Pippa's—"

"Selflessly promising mochas for her friends—"

I'd promise them a finger if we weren't out here for a school event.

I'm so flustered, I nearly miss Nate and Garrett over by the tamale booth. But then I hear Nate say "Thanks, man," and see the two clasp hands and bump shoulders again. For a moment I think they're saying goodbye; it's the same way they greeted. But then the hug goes longer, fuller than their last—almost like they're trying to squeeze something across it.

Almost like there's something they're missing.

∞

A few minutes later Pippa takes my order, and once I pay, I stand off to the side to check the bulletin board. If my Camilla Was Here print's been buried, now would be the time to fix it.

The first thing I notice is that my keychain is still there. That makes me smile.

The second is that almost all of the print is still showing. Only a flier for Oktoberfest has nosed up on it, and that much I can quickly remedy.

The third is what I see when I lift the flier: that somebody has written on the print.

That beneath the Dala horse and words CAMILLA WAS HERE in red are three words I am not responsible for, hand-written in black:

I miss You.

The message from YOU lights a fire under me. If knowing he still cares about Camilla is powerful, knowing he is local's a powder keg. Here I've been, raiding my sister's room and chasing old notes and interrogating Camie's friends for clues to his identity, and all along I have overlooked something far more useful: the fact that if YOU is here in Fairfield, he could be talked to.

Why spin my wheels trying to learn who he is?

Why not reach out to him directly?

Maybe I have finally found a use for all the extra Dala horses lying around the Lemon house.

First I write an answer under YOU's on the Camilla print at Pippa's. Lightning's already struck there once; maybe he'll actually see it.

Then I start writing the same words on horses.

On Thursday, four days after I've discovered YOU's message, Nate and I remember Camie at the local swim center. I tell him about how, when I was six, she taught me to keep my eyes open underwater with a game, dropping coins in the shallow end. Then I leave another actual Dala horse— this one larger than the keychain at Pippa's—along with a print at the front desk. The girl on duty puts the image on the wall and says they'll keep the horse out on the counter.

A note is written on its belly, right where the star on Bristol would be:

I have a Message for You. -J.L.

I watch Nate's reaction carefully as I show him the words on the underside. If he is You, his easy nod and countenance do a hell of a job convincing me otherwise.

When we leave and Nate heads home, I spend the next couple hours leaving Message horses at all the places we've already been—

And then a dozen more where we haven't.

By the following Thursday I have left a horse and Camilla Was Here print at every place on my list within a thirty minutes' drive, and even added some more mundane ones: the grocery store, gas stations, the post office. Putting them out and checking for replies makes me feel proactive, like I am finally making progress and closing the gap between me and You (even if he hasn't returned the contact yet). Perhaps more importantly, that progress gives me strength today, on what may be the most embittering First without my sister yet:

Thanksgiving.

Touring the Places She Was and now isn't, especially without Nate, it's hard to see anything but the holes, let alone something to be grateful for. And Camie's absence is extra sharp at home after Booster; if Mom didn't want to talk about her before, now she won't even look at me.

The words on my linoleum block become more mantra than ever: *Camilla was here*. Every time I put up a print I repeat them, reminding myself that their image—positive shapes on white paper—was only possible via contrast: by carving out the blank space around them.

Would I see more of Camilla, I wonder, if I focused instead on her absences?

Portrait of Thanksgiving Using Negative Space

- Absence of aunts, uncles, screaming cousins, friends, and neighbors dropping in with tofurkey and pies and half a dozen stuffings all day

- Absence of gaudy apple pie candle Camie won from school carnival one year and INSISTED on lighting every holiday since

- Absence of sweet potatoes (Cam's favorite with the candied walnuts)

- The empty side of the table

- Empty chair moved from kitchen to study

- Absence of Mom's stories about Thanksgiving growing up: the year Chevy got the turkey on the floor and carried off a leg; the Eggnog Potatoes Disaster; the time her brothers switched the salt and the sugar as a joke and everything but the cranberries was ruined, and Grandpa made them eat it all as punishment while the rest had dinner out

- 0 ads scoured, lists made, coupons cut for Black Friday

- 0 plans/strategizing for same

- Absence of conversation

- Absence of eye contact

- Absence of "This year, I am grateful for_____"

The one hope I hold on to through Thanksgiving is that five days later—today—I'll finally be able to follow up on my Sponge/Camilla investigation. Mandatory *Fiddler* rehearsals start tonight, so if I'm lucky I might catch the cast and crew for questioning at Pippa's after.

By 7:00 p.m.—when practice ends—I'm in place at a table.

By 7:30 I've seen a few people in Fairfield sweaters, but none I recognize from the theater department.

By 8:00 I am dispirited: even a hell director wouldn't keep everyone this late on the first of eight full rehearsal nights.

Right?

My coffee goes cold. I get another cup.

When 8:30 rolls around, I decide to pack it up. Maybe I'll have better luck tomorrow.

Gathering up the homework I have brought (but not made much progress on), I toss the rest of my coffee and head out.

It's only when I start for my car that somebody says:

"Lemon?"

I turn around.

Brand.

"Hey." Looks like he's just heading into Pippa's himself.

"Hey," he says. His arm is on the door, but he doesn't push in.

After a pause, Brand lets go. "Those gummy bear cupcakes were killer. From the bake sale," he adds, like I might not remember.

"Good," I return. "I'm glad you liked them."

We're both facing each other now.

"You, uh . . . here by yourself?" Brand looks around as though expecting to see someone else.

"Yeah. I was just . . ." But I can't tell Brand why I was really here. He was weird when I connected Sponge's poem to YOU before. "Studying."

"You do that often? Come here to study?"

"Sometimes." Or at least, I used to with Lauren or Camie. "What about you?"

"Just picking up dinner. It's an easy stop. I mean—on my way home from practice at Keegan's."

I nod. "Kind of late for dinner, isn't it?"

"Not when everything in the case is half price before closing."

"Good point."

Brand looks off to the side, considering something.

"But maybe . . ." He frowns, wads his hands in his pockets. "Maybe I'll come a little earlier next time. Catch you for a coffee break or something."

"Y—yeah," I fumble. Glad it's dark out. Hopefully he can't see the heat I feel flooding my cheeks. "Coffee."

Maybe I *should* start studying here again.

"Cool," says Brand. "See you round, Lemon."

"Yeah. See you."

With a hand goodbye, we turn back to our respective business. As I start toward my car, it's with a tiny smile.

I didn't get what I came for tonight.

But I no longer feel I'm leaving empty-handed.

Eighteen days later, my You leads are looking dismal. When I finally did catch the *Fiddler* gang at Pippa's, nearly half were underclassmen and never knew Camie, those who did just shook their heads when I asked if they'd ever seen her behind the scenes.

I've gone back there a couple nights since to study, but I haven't seen Brand.

Perhaps most discouraging of all is that it's now been a month since I started leaving Message horses everywhere and I *still* haven't heard from You. I'm losing faith that I will. In fact, I'm close to pulling my hair out. All the horses I've smuggled out of the house or ordered online; all the places I have visited and left them; all the time and energy and hope I've poured into this, and for what? To see it fall through like Heather and Sponge and Shawn and Brand and *As I Walked Out One Evening*?

What *kills* me is knowing that You was at Pippa's—that I was *this* close to him and missed him. Maybe I've been that close to him since, I don't know. I hate not knowing. I hate that all I can do is broadcast. I hate just sitting around and hoping and waiting for You to bat the ball back!

The Saturday before Christmas, when Mom and Dad leave the house for a special Grieving Parents' Support Group,

I am frantic for new blood: something—*anything*—that might be linked to You or could help me reach him.

And as soon as the garage door touches down, I shoulder into Camie's room to look for it.

I start with the computer, now desperate enough to guess passwords. I remember Camie posting *some* pics from the last year online; fun with Heather and Melissa downtown, sightseeing with Bristol, trips including New York, our cousin's wedding, and even Chiapas, where Camie's real albums stop. There have to be others—ones she didn't share publicly—in her files.

Now if I could just find that bloody charger already—

I ransack the desk again with no luck. Failing that, I try other likely places: backpack. Large handbags. A duffel for sleepovers.

No dice.

In a rage, I throw open the closet. Hangers, jackets, purses fall before me as I shove aside coats, rip down sweaters, pull out shoes and folded pants and hats and toss it all on the floor after turning out pockets. Screw the charger; I'll take whatever I can find.

I root through her laundry.

I empty her drawers.

I check beneath her mattress, in the pillowcases.

I unlatch her guitar case so fast, the instrument *thring*s, muting only when I grab it by the neck to see what's under it (nothing).

I return to the shelves I have already raked, now removing their contents altogether.

No secret photos. No cryptic messages.

No evidence of dates or anniversaries or even Bristol.

It's only when I take apart the nightstand that something falls from a photo album: a Polaroid. It isn't of some Mystery Man—I recognize myself, Lauren, Camie, and Heather all showing off cat eyes—but just enough of it slips under the bed to make me lift back the edge of the blanket.

Revealing, in a coil like a dusty snake, Camilla's laptop charger.

Bingo.

Hurdling the mess I've made, I finally plug it in and power up. On comes the password prompt. With a squint, I venture:

Bristol

Wrong.

callalilies

Denied.

But of course:

Paris

Now a tiny line of text appears below the login box:

Hint: You know . . .

asdfhgklh;rweogb

I shove myself away from the desk. This is starting to feel like one of those infinity paintings where all the stairs chase each other and you can't tell which way's up and which is down: no beginning, no middle, no end. Just a labyrinth of unanswerable questions.

Unless . . .

Maybe this is a chance to test a few theories.

Hopeful, I scoot back to the computer. Fingers poised, I try:

natesavage

Nothing.

NateSavage, NATESAVAGE, NATHANSAVAGE

Nope.

brand, Brand, BRANDON, BrandSayers

sponge, LawrenceTorres, lawryT

Auden, WHAuden, itsnouseraisingashout

And nothing.

Finally an unbidden thought occurs, catching me like a sock to the stomach: I really didn't know my sister.

I close the laptop.

When I finish picking up the disaster I have made, I return to my own room and collapse onto the bed. In moments, laptop propped against my knees, I'm clicking through the most recent of Cam's public photo albums: "NYC," from her trip there with International Club last spring break.

It takes several minutes, and it isn't obvious at first, but then it happens:

I start to see him.

It isn't obvious at first; I never actually see YOU's face. Not even the back of his head, a silhouette. But he's *there*. In the pictures taken after the rest of the club left and Camilla stayed on, I see him. I find him at Times Square. The Empire State Building. On the ferry to the Statue of Liberty. There he is at Grand Central Station; again stopping off for a hot dog, roasted chestnuts, a butter-glazed pretzel from a street vendor.

He's in Camilla's eyes, her rosy smile: that glowing, intimate expression only one person summons.

He's the one holding the camera.

And once I see it, I can't stop seeing it: YOU is everywhere. He's there, with Camilla and Bristol, dozens of other places throughout the previous year: on hikes. At the grill. Shopping Saturday Market, sharing Dutch Bros, on volunteer projects—almost as far back as Chiapas.

Who is that smile for, Camie?

The next several days are more of the tense, loaded silence that was Thanksgiving. Winter break would've been a difficult time anyway, but things have been extra strained since Mom caught all of Booster Club in Camie's room and we had it out about her.

No effort has been made to continue that conversation—probably because Mom doesn't want to, and Dad doesn't know how. Things have been tenser even between them since that night; I overheard Dad coax Mom into showing him the obits, and when he'd asked her why she'd kept them, she'd spat back, "What else should I have done? *Recycled* them?" She'd cut them out because she couldn't get rid of them; she'd hidden them because she didn't want to talk about them.

"We have to talk about it sometime." Dad had gently reminded her that Dr. Prasad, the therapist we'd tried once, would see her anytime—alone, or as a family.

Mom had said only: "I can't."

And so we haven't. And we don't.

And instead of hanging around the house and its perpetually crushing silences, I spend as much time out of it as humanly possible: at the library, Kody's, Angela's. But of course the winter break means holidays: family time. Kody's and Angela's families have always been welcoming, but I don't want to impose, and being around them—especially Kody's now bratty, now adorable little brother—makes me hurt for what I'm missing.

So on Christmas Eve—when my friends are celebrating, and my usual haunts are closed, and I just can't bear to be in the house any longer—I take my keys from their hook in the kitchen and announce I am going out.

"Late shopping?" Dad asks.

"No. Just out."

He stares at me long and hard. I can tell he's conflicted, weighing my needs against Mom's, eager to avoid a repeat of the Blowout. "It's Christmas Eve, Juniper," he says at last, quiet. "Family time. You should be home."

I cast a glance at Mom on the living room sofa. She sits stooped, staring across the room at the fireplace where only three stockings hang this year. A glass of untouched wine before her winks with constellations of colored tree lights.

"I don't think I'll be missed," I say.

And I shoulder my bag and go.

I get on the freeway going north and just drive. I travel in a daze, knowing that no matter how far or how fast I go I can't leave my problems behind me. After about an hour I start seeing signs for Hatton, and decide on a whim to run an errand I've been meaning to get to, anyway.

I take the exit and begin following signs to Fullbrook.

I'm relieved to find the bookstore open when I park along College Way. Despite the winter lights and holiday displays in the windows, the shop doesn't appear to be doing any business. When I pull the door and enter I actually have to look around for a salesperson.

"Hi there!"

A door closes somewhere in back. A tall, scruffy man with thick black frames and a smile appears and crosses the store to greet me.

"Is there something I can help you find?"

"Yeah, I—"

But I'm at a loss for what to say. All I know is that Camilla's secret boyfriend bought *Les Misérables* here. How am I supposed to ask this bearded hipster ("WILL," according to his nametag) if he's seen the guy I know next to nothing about?

Before I can even try, WILL says, "Hey, have we met before?"

That throws me. "I . . . doubt it."

WILL: (trying to place me) "No, I'm sure I know you from somewhere. Were you in Intro to Psych last year?"

I shake my head.

"Brontë sisters?"

I shrug. WILL looks thoughtful, then snaps his fingers. "Jan term: the Hitchcock class."

At last I smile. "I don't go here."

"What!" He grins. "Where do you go? Are you in school, or—"

"Fairfield."

"Fairfield *High*?"

"That's the one."

"Ah-ha." WILL nods, a look of understanding coming over him. "So, are you here to see the campus?"

"No, I . . ." I hesitate, debating what tack to take, and then decide the truth is the most straightforward. "I found a book someone bought here. It has this thoughtful, really beautiful inscription in the cover, but it doesn't say who it's to or from"—okay, the strategically modified truth—"and I guess I'd like to figure out who bought it so I can get it back to them."

"What book? Out of curiosity."

"*Les Misérables.* Oh, and I don't actually have it with me," I realize belatedly. "But would that be possible? I mean, if I brought in the receipt, could we look up who bought it?"

"Mm . . ." WILL looks off to the side, doubtful. "There *are* certain records, but even if the buyer used a credit card, we wouldn't be able to disclose their name. Legal reasons."

My shoulders drop. "Right."

I bow my chin a moment, spinning the gears, trying to come up with another angle. Before I have anything—

"Got it!"

WILL claps his hands together. Thinking he has found a loophole, I straighten attentively.

"You're the Bicycle girl! From Shawn's thing? With the band?"

"Oh god." I hold my face, half in laughter, half in mortification.

"I knew it," says WILL. "I knew I'd seen you before! I'm pretty good with faces."

"You *are*," I realize.

And if WILL was at Shawn's that night, maybe he saw something . . .

"Do you remember seeing her?" I show him one of Camie's senior portraits, a photo I still keep in my wallet.

The same one in the obit.

WILL looks at the picture, frowning.

"Uh . . . yeah," he says after a moment. "You know her?"

"Do *you*?" It comes out more accusatory than I'd intended.

"No. I only met her at that party."

"You talked to her?"

"Uh, briefly, I think. Why?"

"What'd you talk about? Did she say anything about meeting somebody?"

"Meeting somebody?" WILL's frown deepens. He looks as though he's beginning to feel uncomfortable.

"Please. If you can remember anything—*any*thing she said—it would be a huge help to me."

WILL considers me, eyes screwed tight. "She's your sister?" He nods at the photograph.

"Yes." I don't trouble myself correcting his choice of tense.

Rather than comment on my answer or ask why it is I'm asking *him* these questions instead of her, WILL seems to decide something. He exhales at the floor.

"Honestly, I don't remember much of what I talked about with anyone that night. I mean, Fourth of July, that was what—six months ago?"

My disappointment must physically weigh me down, because WILL shrugs and adds, "Sorry."

The bell at the front of the store clangs, announcing the arrival of a girl with an armload of books. WILL calls to her, "Hi! Be right with you," and asks if there is anything else he can help me with. I tell him no. He wishes me an automatic *Happy holidays,* and heads to the till.

It's just getting dark as I drive back into Fairfield. I sit a moment at a light that's turned green, debating, and instead of taking the turn for home I go straight, toward school. A couple minutes later I pull into a space outside 3 Hall, turn off the engine and just sit there, the only person in the only car in the lot.

I can't go home yet.

I drum my fingers along the steering wheel. When that makes me feel too trapped I unbuckle my seat belt and lean back, pinch my forehead, loll my head around from side to side. All I can think is that there's nowhere to go, there's nowhere to go, there's no—

—reason the lights should be on in the band loft.

Why are there lights on in the band loft?

When I try them, the doors leading into 3 Hall are locked. Inside is dark, and when I cup my hands and peer through the glass I can't see anybody.

But the light in the band loft burns steady.

I walk back a ways and try the exterior door of the choir room, which is really more of an emergency exit and never used except on concert nights and muggy afternoons.

It opens.

I tense, waiting for an alarm. When there isn't one, I stare.

"Hello?" I call in, and instantly regret it.

But several moments pass; nothing happens.

So with a final glance around, I slip inside.

A dim light spills from the staircase between the band and the choir rooms. I approach and find the door to the band loft wide open, a bright yellow square at the top of the stairs.

"Hello?"

Reflex. Can't help it.

I start up the stairway. When I reach the top, I knock and ask more quietly, "Is anybody here?"

No one answers, so I step through the doorframe. Instead of a person, I find a mess: empty bottles, soda cans. Wadded fast-food bags, wing-stained paper plates, Cup Noodles with plastic forks sticking out, and a tower of sushi trays stacked so high, it leans. The room reeks of pizza and taco sauce, and looks like the backseat of someone who plays Xbox more regularly than he washes.

I walk through it, gawking.

Then I see the bedding.

The blankets, pillow, and mattress Brand said he uses for naps sometimes—all of it's out on the floor.

Slept-in.

The bottom cupboard he'd put the bedding away in is open, too, keys left dangling in the lock.

Thinking of Brand, my eyes lift to the shelf where his guitar was. Sure enough, the case is open, and I recognize the black-and-white Fender inside it as his. Beside it is a plastic sack with oranges, several boxes of instant rice and mac and cheese, and—

A large, open package of gummy bears.

Suddenly I don't want to be here; don't want to have to explain myself to him, or Brand to explain himself to me. I backtrack through wrappers that crunch like fallen leaves and hurry out.

Back in my car, I close my eyes and grip the steering wheel. The night's grown dark, the air's turned chill, and though I find it oddly tranquil, I know I can't stay much longer. It's getting close to dinner. As much as I don't want to, I had probably better—

A knock at the window.

"JESUS CHRIST."

I release the wheel, eyes wide at the shaded face outside. Brand smirks at me, his devilish smile faintly blue in the December night. He motions with a gloved hand for me to roll down the window.

"What?" I demand, still on edge.

"Car trouble?"

I realize what he must be seeing and that he's trying to help me.

"No," I sigh, relenting a little. "I just . . . needed to get out of the house for a while."

Brand grimaces. "I hear that."

A lamp flickers on in the parking lot. Brand and I match gazes in its orange ray, each as if waiting for the other to say something. I ask, "What are you doing here?"

"Me?"

Brand holds up a white paper Lauer's sack, something from the deli. Fried chicken, by the smell of it. I think of all the fast-food bags, the instant meals and takeout strewn across the band loft and wonder how long he has been staying there.

If the grocery store fried chicken he's holding is his Christmas feast.

If he is eating alone tonight.

Tomorrow.

"Just picking up dinner," he says. "The old man isn't big on cooking."

I nod. I'd like to ask him some of what I am thinking, even invite him to join us for dinner tomorrow, but I can't think of a way to do that without revealing I have seen his hideout or making him feel like a charity case.

Not that Christmas dinner with the Lemons would be a real improvement.

"Hey," Brand says suddenly, rubbing his hands together. "What are you doing for New Year's?"

"What?"

"New Year's. Got plans?"

"Uh . . ." Beyond staring at the ceiling and talking to no one because I can't even talk to my parents anymore? "Not really."

"Good. There's something I wanna show you. Pick you up at ten?"

"Oh. I'm, uh, kind of grounded right now. I don't know if . . ."

"So sneak out." Brand's eyes search mine, their faint china blue illumed strangely in the harsh orange light. A cold wind drafts through the open window and I get a waft of leather and forest and cigarettes.

"And dress warm, Lemon," he finishes, leaning back and knocking on the roof of my sedan. "The forecast says snow."

"Brand," I call after his back.

He turns.

"I'd say merry Christmas, but . . ." Nope. There's just no getting around it. "It would feel kind of shitty and hollow."

A small smile.

Brand holds out his arms in regal gesture, the fried chicken still clutched in a hand, the other lifting an invisible hat as he sinks into a bow. "Then merry fucking Christmas," he says. "From the heart."

I smile back. "Merry fucking Christmas."

Merry fucking Christmas:

174

Happiness: 0
Camilla $(+-+-+-) \times \infty$

Portrait of Christmas in Past Positives

• 4:00 a.m.: recon with Camie—sneak into living room with flashlights to snoop out stuffed stockings and Santa presents. Sneak cookies. Back to bed.

• 6:00: Cam'd bounce on my bed singing JU-NI-PER, JU-NI-PER, JU-NI-PER, PRE-SENTS to the tune of "Jingle Bells" until I rolled out and/or hit her with pillows. If slow to rise, "Jingle Bells" followed by annoying Top 40.

• Family presents in pajamas.

  ° Relatives' presents first. Aunt Jane: HATS. Always hats. Queen of England, Sunday best, Luncheon with the Ladies of Tea and Dainty Pastries hats. Gramma Lemon: Dala horses.

  ° On opening a horse: annual rewatching of When Camie Got Bristol video. [Script. Six-year-old Camie: "A HORSE, A HORSE!" *gets up and runs around, gallops it through the air* Mom: "Careful, honey! That's a special horse—she's older and more fragile than your other ponies. She's <u>collectible</u>. You have to take good care of her so you don't scratch the paint." Camie: "Okay!" *runs back to couch, plunks down, begins picking at discarded gift tag* Dad: "What are you doing, Cam?" Camie: (peeling off sticker) "My horse is special and I'm . . . I'm gonna give her a star." <u>Zoom in: Camie plants star sticker on horse's</u>

<u>painted underbelly.</u> Cam: (grinning toothily) "See?" Mom: (under her breath) "Damn it, David, I <u>told</u> Sandy she was too young for this!" Dad: *laughs*]

• Warm cinnamon rolls from Lauer's. Coffee for Mom and Dad. Hot chocolate for me and Camie.

• Santa presents last. Camie = screamer.

• Try on clothes. Model. Trade.

• HAT WALK. Cam <u>insisted</u> we parade our Aunt Jane creations each year, not only around the house, but out in the neighborhood. It could be surprisingly fun: We'd get honking cars and huge thumbs-up, shouts like "Which way to the Hatter's?" and "GLORY HATTELUJAH!" and once, cookies from an amused Santa.

• Make dinner. Everyone helped: Dad did the roast and vegetables; Mom the cranberry bread and bread pudding; Camie the sweet potatoes; I made pie.

• 4:00 or 5:00 p.m.: eat. Dinner followed by pie and more coffee/ hot chocolate, respective food comas.

• Card games. Cam = reigning Rummy champ.

• Cam and I ended the evening with a last hot chocolate and a Christmas movie. Took turns picking. Last year I chose <u>The Nutcracker</u>. Camie's favorites: <u>The Holiday, Elf, The Muppet Christmas Carol.</u>

• Never made it to the end; always fell asleep in blankets on the living room sofa.

On New Year's Eve a rock clangs against my window at promptly 10:00 p.m., successfully startling the bejesus out of me. I lift it open and lean out.

"Could you *be* any more cliché?" I hiss down at Brand in the grass below. "If you're trying to be discreet, next time use a pinecone—or maybe some of those gummy bears you like so much."

"I'm on time, aren't I? What more do you want, roses?"

I roll my eyes and shut the window.

"I thought you were sneaking out?" he says when I walk out the front a minute later. "If I'da known you were gonna use the door, I would've knocked."

"My parents and I aren't on great terms right now."

Life at home has hit an all-time low since Christmas Eve. My walking out on "family time" (even though Mom was in the exact daze I left her in when I got home, with the exception of less wine in her glass) appears to have fouled whatever rapport Dad and I had left.

"You don't care if you get in trouble?"

I shrug. "What are they going to take from me?"

Brand unlocks an ancient Pontiac and stares at me before opening his door. "I think you've been hanging out with me too much."

∞

We drive to a neighborhood where the yards are narrow and strewn with children's toys or beer bottles, occasionally in fragments that catch the headlights, and mean-looking chain-link fences keep out visitors.

Brand pulls into the driveway of an unlit property—one of the larger homes at two stories—and even in the darkness I can see the peeling strips of paint, the moss that grows in clusters on the roof, the weeds in the cracks of the pavement.

A dog barks down the street as we get out.

"Your house?"

Brand nods. "Just gotta grab a couple things."

We carefully climb the steps of a sunken, frost-covered porch, and as Brand turns the key, I wonder what it is he's been avoiding at home.

If we'll encounter it.

"After you," he says, holding a door that creaks on its hinges. I enter and he shuts it behind us.

"Are you . . . *baking*?" I ask as an aroma registers.

"Special occasion."

I follow him into the kitchen. The clutter hits me like a smell: dirtied plates, bowls, beer bottles. Mugs heaped over with used silverware. Every surface is stacked, and by the opaque, sudsless water in the sink, I would guess that the pans and glasses sticking out of it have been there for several days. Something shrill begins to buzz—the oven timer—and Brand quickly shoves aside an armful of bottles to make room for two hot trays of cookies on the counter.

"Pumpkin chocolate chip?" I'd smelled the chocolate, but am surprised to see they're orange.

Brand throws down the oven mitt. "You're not gonna say anything about the mess?"

His eyes press at mine. I meet them, neatly *not* gawking at hardened mustard stains on the counter, the dried noodles, crumbs, wedges of crunchy bread on the floor. I'm glad to be wearing boots, and wonder vaguely if cookies are a cover for the stench of mildew and booze. "Should I?" I ask, uncertain.

"Won't apologize for it"—Brand reaches past me, pulls a spatula from a drawer—"because it isn't mine. Well—most of it. My dad drinks enough for ten. Don't worry," he adds, "Father Boozy is out right now. Every New Year's he throws 'em back at the Firehouse till closing."

I nod, even less certain how to answer this. "What do you usually do?"

"For New Year's?"

"Yeah."

"Me, I make something hot and go up where my mom used to take me."

"Where's that?"

Brand's smile reveals his canine. "You'll see. Get the coffee while I box these? There's a thermos in that cupboard." I follow his gesture and, half bracing myself for rats, claw the cupboard open and find the canister. Brand directs me to the opposite counter, where a pot of fresh, hot coffee sits beneath a glowing light. I transfer it to the thermos.

"All right then." He shovels the last of the cookies into a Tupperware container and snaps on the lid. "Let's just grab a few sugar packs and—"

Headlights flash through the window. Brand stops cold.

"Who's—?"

"Shhh."

Tires crunch to a stop outside. Then the engine shuts off and a door slams.

"Fuck."

Before I can ask, we are moving, Brand steering me swiftly toward the stairs.

"Brand, wha—?"

"Go go go," he urges.

We make it to the top and into a room, the door of which he slams behind us and secures with two latches, a bolt, and a chain as someone—I assume his dad—unlocks the entrance below. I'd ask again but a sort of numb foreboding's taken me, and instead Brand and I just look at each other, breathless, waiting for whatever's to come.

The front door bangs shut again with a force that rattles the house.

"BRANDON." A few heavy steps, then a jumbling like collision with furniture. "BRANDON, I KNOW YOU'RE UP THERE."

Brand doesn't answer. He looks soundlessly at me as the footsteps resume and approach the stairs.

"Get down here, you little shit, know what's good for you." The threat is mumbled, slurs together.

It's also closer.

"BRANDON." The wall quivers with each step. "Brandon, if you don't get your sorry ass down here NOW—"

Even given all I know or have heard about Brand Sayers, his next move surprises me:

He cups his hands around his mouth and hollers, "MAKE ME."

"Piece of—!"

The slow thing on the stairs suddenly animates, clambering wildly as if on newly sprouted limbs. Brand runs for the dresser and yanks it toward the door and I hurry to help, and together we slide it into place just as the knob judders and a palm strikes the wood from the other side.

The voice that comes is unsettlingly even. "Open the door, Brandon."

"No."

"I'm not gonna ask you again."

"Good."

A snarl. The knob rattles in its socket and the wood bucks with punches. Then it stops, and you can tell the speaker is lowering his fists and sidling up to the door to whisper threats through his teeth.

"You've got some reeeeal nerve, you little shithead," the voice hisses. "Think you can run away from home and then drop in whenever you feel like it, help yourself to my kitchen? My wallet? You been STEALING MONEY from me, wiseass?"

A slam. I swear the door jumps in its frame.

"I support myself. I ain't stolen shit."

"Bull*shit*." Something drops with a thud. Maybe a picture frame. "Missing a fifty just today, Brandon. You gonna tell me it just got up and walked out on its own?"

"You probably spent it on booze already, you drunk."

"OPEN THE FUCKING DOOR!"

The wood shudders and heaves in beats, straining against the locks. The knob saws back and forth so violently I worry it'll fly off. But Brand looks more annoyed than concerned; he takes a remote from the navy bedspread, aims it at a stereo, and hits PLAY. A wave of angry electric blasts from huge speakers at the end of the room.

"I'M GONN—" The sound becomes unintelligible as Brand cranks up the volume.

"Sorry," he yells to me. "Easier to ignore this way." He casually braces the thumping dresser with his back. There's still shouting, but it is indeed muffled now, drowned by the wails of guitars.

"He'll tire himself right out," Brand mouths.

Sure enough, in less than a minute the charging and shaking desist. Brands scales the music back almost imperceptibly—just enough to be less than an assault on the ears—and crosses the room to the window. Headlights soon snap on below, flurries of falling snow lighting up in their glare, and the dark truck to which they belong peels back and off into the street.

Brand clicks the loud music off. The quiet that follows is worse.

He says, without turning to face me, "And the night was ruined in record time."

"Hey." I circle around him till he looks at me. "Who says it's ruined?"

Brand holds my gaze.

He leans closer . . .

Then he shakes his head and moves for the dresser. "Every time," he says to himself, grabbing an end. I go to push the other. "Every time, I tell myself, 'This is the last time I let Emory Sayers fuck something up for me.'" We wedge the dresser back into place and he moves to the door, undoing its latches. "And yet—aw, shit, not again."

"What's wrong?"

Brand is turning the doorknob. And turning and turning it. It spins like a plaything, around and around. He grimaces. "Second one this year. Something's busted inside so the knob isn't gripping the bolt. Man, I gotta start keeping a screwdriver in here."

"How do we get out?"

"Well . . ." Brand crosses the room, peers out through the glass. "Normally I'd say the window . . ." He slides up the bottom panel. A blast of cold air and snowflakes whips in under it. "But given the ice, I'm a little iffy on dropping down from the ledge just now."

"How far is the drop?"

"C'mere."

I join him at the window and look down. The snowy ledge looks low enough to drop from, but not so low that you couldn't break something if you landed badly.

"Here." Brand shoves the window up the rest of the way, ducks through it so he straddles the sill.

"What are you doing?" I demand.

"Testing. Give me your hand."

I offer it and he takes my forearm more than hand, sets down a tentative, feeling foot along the roof. Seems okay. He swings the other leg out and slowly rises, checking his balance on both feet. Takes a few tiny steps.

"Mm," he says. "Maybe it's o—"

His foot slips.

He slides like a deer on a roller rink.

"Shit! Shit! Shit!"

"Gotcha."

I ground my feet against the wall and pull. Brand eagerly grips both my arms now, legs tripping helplessly beneath him. I reel in, straining, and drag him back to the sill, level with it, and with a final oomph, over.

We both land, winded, on the floor.

"Oh god." Brand pushes himself up. For a moment he hangs over me, checking his limbs. Then he seems to remember me and meets my eyes.

The smell of his Axe, I happen to notice then, is a lot less unpleasant than I remember.

We stare at each other.

"Sorry," he says after a beat, and backs upright into sitting position. Helps me achieve the same. "You okay?"

"Fine. Just got the . . ." I gesture because even my thoughts feel suddenly dizzy. "Breath knocked out of me." I push my hair back and straighten my off-the-shoulder sweater. "Guess the roof is out."

Lacking a screwdriver, we try a variety of pens, keys, paperclips, and even his box cutter on the screws in the doorknob—all without luck.

At last Brand swears and pulls out his phone.

"What are you doing?"

"Texting Keegan. He's filling in for a guitarist in Portland tonight and won't be done until after midnight, but . . ." Brand sucks his teeth and hits SEND. "Better late than being stuck here till the snow melts."

"He's . . . gonna come here?"

"Yeah. I'll toss him my keys out the window so he can come in and let us out."

I loll my head at him. How many times has Brand done this before?

"In the meantime," he says brightly, eager to change the subject, "the goods are in here with us. So c'mon. Stop staring at me like that and enjoy a cookie. Pumpkin choco chip is your favorite, right?"

He retrieves the Tupperware and sits back against the bed, proffering the box to me.

"How'd you know that?"

An offside glance. "I may or may not have consulted Sponge."

"And why would you do that?"

He regards me without speaking. A sly expression twists his lips. "Because it's cold outside," he answers, "and hot cookies would defuse, if not entirely remove, the temptation to put the moves on me to get warm."

"'Put the moves on you'?" I scoff. "Someone sure thinks highly of his haircut."

"Have a fucking cookie, Lemon. It will make me feel like less of a jerk."

Rolling my eyes, I join him on the floor and comply. I am not disappointed: The cookies are still warm and melt like a pumpkiny, chocolate butter in my mouth. I wash it down with coffee Brand pours for me in the thermos lid.

"You know it isn't your fault," I say when I lower it. "Getting stuck here."

"I know." He stares ahead, not meeting my eye.

"Brand . . ." I don't know if there's a delicate way to say what needs to be said now. Brand knows the same. "How long has this been going on?"

No answer.

"That day you were limping—when I showed you my independent study stuff. Was that because . . . did he hurt you?"

Brand says nothing.

"Brand—"

"He doesn't scare me."

I open my mouth to respond, but then my jaw sets and I feel myself harden.

"So you think you're being brave?"

Brand blinks at me, surprised. "I didn't say—"

"It isn't *brave,* Brand. It's stupid."

His face contorts. Suppressing a reply, he sighs and gets up to stalk away from me. It's a short sigh—frustrated—so when he spins back, I assume it's to lash out at me.

It isn't.

"You asked how long," he says instead. He turns to the window and looks out through the flakes floating down. "He used to hit my mom. She left. He started hitting me."

"Brand, I'm—"

"Sorry?" He glances back at me over his shoulder. "*Sorry* is just a word. It doesn't undo the things that that bastard has done. It doesn't bring her back. It doesn't change anything, or make things right again."

To that I can say nothing.

I know these things better than anyone.

"Besides." He shoves his hands in his coat and walks back, "I'm almost eighteen. I've been saving money from gigs, odd jobs. As soon as I graduate, I'm outta here for good."

"Where will you go?"

"Don't know." He drops back to the floor and leans his head against the bed. "Anywhere's better than here."

We sit in silence awhile. It occurs to me I should tell someone about Brand, about his situation at home, his living out of Band Geeks' Paradise—but before I can even consider who, I remember what Brand once said about Kody:

that if we went to somebody, she would have to deal with the consequences. And what was it he said when I found Angela's Oscar letter?—"You can't go around assuming you know what people need"? He even warned against helping Sponge when I showed him the thrown-out crush poem.

Was Brand talking about Kody, Angela, and Sponge—or himself?

He asks, as if reading my thoughts, "You're not gonna tell anybody, are you?"

I study him. "You don't want me to."

"Believe it or not, a couple people know already. Certain school keys didn't just fall into my lap, you know."

My eyes widen. "Who knows? You mean they *gave* you the keys?" Hearsay depicts Brand Sayers as both a pyro and a klepto.

He grins. "A mobster's nephew never reveals his secrets." He refills the thermos cup and takes a steaming swig, watching me. "So? You won't tell anyone?"

I hesitate.

"Brand . . ." I begin, with difficulty, "if you're threatened at home . . ."

"I'm rarely *at* home," he counters. "I stay at friends' places. If not there, the band loft. You heard what he said about 'running away.'"

I frown. I'm glad the secret about staying at school is out in the open, but I'm far from reassured.

He waits, anxious. I bite my lip.

"I guess . . . if you're not in danger . . ."

"I'm not."

"And you have people and places you can go to . . ."

"I do."

- 239 -

"And you really don't want anyone to know . . ."

"I think I've made that clear enough."

I draw my knees up in front of me and watch him, wishing I could see into his thoughts. "It makes me uneasy, Brand. But if that's what you want . . ." I lift my shoulders. "Okay."

"Good."

"And, like, I'd say you're welcome at my house anytime, but I'm technically grounded, and even if I weren't I'm not sure the oppressive silence would be much better."

"I guess things aren't quite Brady Bunch round the Lemon house, either?"

"Do you know why I'm grounded?"

I tell him about Camilla's room.

"That sucks."

We lose ourselves in coffee and cookies awhile, neither of us knowing what to say to make things better for the other, and watch the snow stick in feathers to the window.

Brand says, "Wanna see what I was gonna show you tonight?"

He reaches past me and pulls something from between CDs on a shelf: a glossy photograph. In it are a small boy and woman who must be his mother picnicking in the shade of a giant oak tree.

"Is that . . . Oak Hills Cemetery?"

"That's right." Brand sits back beside me. "It was one of Mom's favorite places. We'd go up there for picnics, sometimes just for the view: the fall colors, holiday lights, fireworks—"

"At New Year's?"

Brand smiles. "Ever been?"

I shake my head. "Not up the hill."

"Well, let me tell you—you can see all of Fairfield, from Lauer's and our ugly-ass high school to the fancy-pants high streets and shops up on Main. Big blue-green hills on the horizon, a few city lights winking through after dark . . .

"When we got up there, my mom—she was kind of spiritual in her way—she used to look out at everything and say it was a special place: on one side, the town and life; on the other, the cemetery and death. The hill had a foot in both and neither."

"Sounds poetic," I say. "This place and your mom."

Brand shakes his head. "When my old man was with us, he'd cut her off and say to stop filling my head with her New Age mumbo-jumbo. But it rubbed off on me, anyway."

"Is that why you go every year? 'Cause she used to take you?"

"Yeah. Plus, the fireworks are good. You can see them in every direction. Unlike—" Brand smirks to himself a moment, wry.

"What?"

He nods across the room. "Unlike from here." I follow his gaze to the window. The glass is frosted and milky with fog.

"Psh. Fireworks are overrated."

We finish the coffee. Brand opens his closet and comes back with two plastic water bottles, hands one to me.

"Do you miss her?" I ask.

"Huh?"

"Your mom."

Something about the question seems to bother him.

"The difference between my mom and your sister," he says after a moment, "is that your sister didn't *choose* to leave. Yeah, I miss her. Sometimes. Other times I'm angry. Mostly, though . . ." He shrugs. "I've said goodbye." He looks meaningfully at me, and for a long moment we hold each other's eyes. Then—

"Oh, hey."

He jumps back up, nods at the alarm clock on his shelf. 11:53. "Almost time. You want a beer or something?"

"Or *some*thing? What all do you have in there?" Brand is rummaging back through his closet.

"I like to keep it stocked. For . . ." He casts about, jerks his head toward the door with its bolts. "Unforeseeable conditions. So? Drink?" He pulls a few bottles, listing names.

"Hmm. Closet beer. Tempting, but no."

"No?" He wrestles deeper, disappearing up to his shoulders in T-shirts, and in a moment reemerges with two brown bottles. "Cream soda?"

I blink at him. "Did Sponge tell you that, too?"

"Tell me what?"

"Vanilla cream was Camilla's favorite. She used to drink it with . . ." I smile to myself, remembering.

"With what?"

"Lemon."

Comprehension dawns in the form of a half smile, half frown, like I have made a regrettable pun.

"I'm afraid the only Lemon here is you," says Brand, "but if you want one of these bad boys, it's yours."

I laugh. "I'm pretty sure that is the only time in the history of the universe anyone has called vanilla soda a bad boy."

He passes me one and we twist off the lids with our shirts. We sip them a minute and then, voting to brave the snow for a chance at glimpsing fireworks, lift the window again and lean out along the sill. It's a close space for two, so our arms, and sometimes hips, brush.

The heat from Brand's leg somehow tickles up my spine. 11:58.

"Has the accident, like," Brand starts, "ruined drinking for you forever?"

He shifts to face me, making my skin buzz. I look at him; at the open soda in my hands.

Even as I do, I can still see the blood on them.

I set the bottle on the floor. "I'm sure I *will* drink again. Maybe even before I turn twenty-one. That's what scares me: that I might one day drink without remembering her, without feeling her loss. Right now I can't even imagine that. But one day . . . one day, what if time erodes that pain? What if it's like the sea sanding the edges from a piece of glass?"

"What if you're happy?"

"What if my pain is all I have left of her . . . and I lose it?"

"Hey." Brand straightens and puts his soda on the sill.

Then he reaches for my hands and pulls me upright.

"Pain," he says, squaring me to look him in the eye, and my bloodstream sparks and spins at his warm touch, "is like the good times: something that comes and goes. There's nothing you can do about that. The important thing"—he draws a breath, and it's almost like he took it from me—"is to live each moment for what it is."

Outside, a rocket screams. Brand's thumb grazes my cheek.

Then the rocket explodes and we are connected, mouth to mouth and hip to hip and hand to hair, and his breath is hot and his lips are soft and his taste is stars, stars, stars, the vanilla tingle left from the soda fizzling and crackling like the colors in the distant sky.

When we part I am spiraling, dizzy, one of the whirling white pieces in the wind.

"Happy New—"

I kiss him again.

180

Happiness: 9.8

Kiss kiss kiss kiss (+) and I kind of got yelled at (−), but kiss kiss kiss <u>KISS</u> KISS

KISS

The next night I am washing the dishes as punishment—one of many in a line that await me for breaking my grounding again—when the doorbell rings. Dad goes to answer it, and when I hear the voice that greets him, my dishrag falls into the sink with a splash.

"Hi, I'm Brand. I thought I should introduce myself before I picked up Juniper for our date tonight."

Date?

"Date?" I hear Mom echo in the living room. I strip my gloves off and hustle out into the entryway.

"It's very nice to meet you," Dad is saying to a figure sharply dressed in darks, "and I'm sorry that you've gone to the trouble, Brand. But Juniper is groun—"

"Can't stay out too late."

Dad and I both turn, surprised, to Mom. She's standing in the hallway, hugging her arms, and pulls her shrug more tightly to her.

"Home by midnight, Juniper?"

I gape from her, to Brand, to Dad. Mom and Dad exchange a series of looks.

What is *happening*?

"Definitely," Brand agrees.

His grin is like a wire, a rush of yesterday and soda fizz stars. In spite of myself and our audience I grin back.

I should take advantage of Mom's generosity before she changes her mind.

"I'll just . . ." I attempt to contain my smile. "Go grab my bag."

I head upstairs as neutrally as possible. When I'm around the corner I jump up and down and silently squee, and then hurry to my room to pull on boots and a sweater.

On my way back, bag in hand, I pause by Camilla's door. I wish I could share the events of the New Year with her.

"Ready?" Brand asks when I come back down. I nod, a little more subdued.

"Juniper?"

I stop by the door. Mom is watching us with a strange expression.

"Yeah, Mom?"

"Just . . ." Something wells behind her eyes—pride? Pain? It's hard to tell, but she looks kind of like she's seeing me off to school for the first time. "Take a coat, honey."

I do.

Brand shows me to our ride—not his car, but Keegan's, as Brand has stayed with him since yesterday—and Keegan says hello and starts the engine. We buckle in and pull away.

And when I see Mom at the window, I cry a little.

Neither Brand nor Keegan enlightens me as to where we're going until we're practically there—but once we park in a by-the-hour lot in Portland and they open the trunk to remove their instruments, it's pretty clear that it involves music.

"You're playing a show," I guess.

"Not quite."

"Auditioning for *The Voice*."

"Colder."

"Can I at least trust there will be no public serenade?"

"We're here!" Keegan announces.

I look up at the building we have stopped in front of: black bricks with the neon purple sign *8-Ball Pizza*.

My brows go up. "*8-Ball*? I thought you said you weren't playing!" I've been here a few times; most recently with Camie to see a coworker's band. I know it mostly as a stop for rising underground groups.

Brand smirks. "You said 'a show.' I said 'not quite.'"

He guides me to the door. A reader board with flashing bulbs declares *Open Mike Night* in bold letters overhead.

A flicker of doubt passes over me. "This isn't an attempt to get me back into singing, is it?"

"Lemon, Lemon, Lemon. Always thinkin' about Number One. I'll have you know that *this*"—Brand gestures at himself, at Keegan and their instruments, the venue—"is about making you fall for me, and it is en*tire*ly selfish."

I bite my lip as he holds the door for me.

It's working.

He grins and adds, "Just don't tell my fan girls."

Inside, we're greeted by Derrick and Tyler, the bassist and drummer of Muffin Wars, respectively. When I see them plugging in, the secret is at last revealed: The band is *opening* for tonight's event. Brand and Keegan join the sound check in progress, and then—after some good-natured ribbing about whether or not to expect any guest vocals tonight ("Thanks, but I'll leave this one to the professionals")—the four begin warming up.

"This is 'Bitter/sweet,'" Brand says into the mike.

He wasn't kidding about the "fall" part. The song they play is slow but sly, full of hips and dark allure, and from the moment Brand starts singing I'm pulled under, strung by his smoky voice from word to savored word: *kick, relish, kiss.*

I don't miss the references to rain boots and gummy bears—especially when Brand looks right at me as he sings them.

By the time the song is over, a crowd has gathered in front and it cheers and bursts into applause. Brand grins, prompting several shrieks and wolf whistles. Not kidding about the fan girls, either, apparently.

When they strike up a dialogue with the audience, I slip quietly toward the back of the space for a better look. I want to remember this night.

I snap some pictures with my phone, then edge back even farther for a wide shot. When I glance behind me to be sure I won't hit something, I see not the wall, but its contents, and lower my phone. Even the last time I was here I was taken by the sprawling collection: a collage of photos, fliers, and album art, a gallery of the bands who have played here. Some who've made it big.

I explore the wall instead, taking it in. When I find a duplicate flier for tonight's event—*Open Mike Night, ft. Muffin Wars!*—I take it down and replace it with a Camilla print from my bag. Tonight it's more out of habit than in hopes of reaching YOU; I didn't even bring a Message horse, and besides, I've started to accept that YOU may be *choosing* not to answer them. Still, the campaign means something to me.

The band is about to start again when I hear:

"Lauren? What's wrong?"

I turn to see a girl with long black hair at a table facing quickly away from me.

But I recognize the slightly older girl across from her.

Heather recognizes me at the same moment. I can feel Lauren sweating from here but don't care, and will not be deterred from questioning one sister by a little awkwardness with the other. Why didn't it occur to me that Heather would be home for the holidays?

"Juniper," says Heather, startled as I stalk up to them. I'm so focused that I *almost* don't notice the shopping, Voodoo Doughnuts box, and Powell's bag at their feet—exactly what I'd be doing with Cam if she were home this break. "This is a—I mean, wow, it's good to see you."

"Is it?"

I can't keep the resentment from my voice—or avoid a pointed look at Lauren.

Lauren starts, "Juniper, I—"

"It's okay, Lauren. I get it. You don't have to apologize. But if you don't mind, it's actually Heather I'd like to talk to." I tilt my head at the entrance, indicating Heather and I should take a walk. With Muffin Wars' new song starting up, it's difficult to hear.

Heather and Lauren exchange glances.

"I'll be right back," Heather shouts.

I signal the same up at Brand on stage—*one minute*—and then Heather and I are pushing out into the night to stroll the block.

When the music is distant, "Why didn't you answer my e-mails?" I ask. I'd sent the same to both her old and new school addresses to be sure she got it. "Do you know something about the person Cam was seeing?"

Heather doesn't deny it. Instead, she seems to study the pavement with interest.

"I . . . *suspected* Camie was dating someone," she sighs at last. "But I didn't know who, and you didn't, either; I figured—well, if neither of us knew, I think it's pretty clear she would've wanted it kept secret. What good would come from uncovering that secret now? And would it really mean more to her than their privacy?"

I consider. "But what if I didn't *need* to know the guy's identity? What if I knew just enough to know where to find him, or someone who knows him, and then they could deliver the letter instead?"

"'Letter'?"

Heather stops walking.

"You didn't say what you'd found was a letter."

I stop, too. "Well, what else do you 'deliver'?"

"I don't know! I thought you meant, you know, a song or a poem she'd written about them or something. For all I know you could've meant pizza."

"Yeah. She really wanted him to have her last slice of supreme." I roll my eyes, but know it isn't helping, so I add, "It was a breakup letter."

"A *breakup* letter?" I wonder at her indignation: if it's because I didn't say so before, or because her best friend kept that serious of a relationship a secret from her. "Okay." Heather resumes walking, so I follow. "I think I'm starting to see where you're coming from. I can tell you what I know, but I warn you, it isn't much."

"Anything."

"All right, well—I was downtown one weekend for a class last winter. Maybe February?"

"Travel Spanish," I remember.

"Yeah. Anyway, I was early, so I stopped in at this little café on my way. Camilla was there; she was waiting down at the counter where they call your order."

"And?" My impatience is a grabbing child.

"I went over and said hi, asked her what she was doing there. She said she was meeting a conversation partner for French. But she seemed fidgety, too; more than from lack of caffeine. When the barista brought her order, she practically jumped on it—cut the guy off mid-sentence. You know: 'Lattes for Camilla and—!'" Heather cuts the air like that's all there is.

"For who?!"

"I don't know! She grabbed the coffees—*both* of them—with a 'Thanks!' before I could see what was written there."

I could kick something. Another dead end.

"*But,*" Heather adds, "in her hurry to get them, she dropped her keys. Her hands were full, so I went to help her, and—guess what?"

I urge impatiently.

"*They weren't her keys.*"

"What? How do you know?"

"They were on an FHS lanyard like hers, but the keychains were different. One was U of O: *Oregon Ducks.*"

"What?"

Camilla hated football. But more importantly:

U of O and the Ducks are from Eugene.

Just like Nate.

"And I'm thinking," Heather continues, "why would she have somebody else's keys—particularly somebody from Fairfield's—unless they had driven there together? Or maybe he had a postbox nearby? I don't know. Whatever the case, those were *not* some random language partner's."

"And she didn't want you to hear the name," I realize, "because she must've thought you'd know them."

Or could find out who it was.

Heather slows to a stop and folds her arms. We are back in front of 8-Ball already.

"I'm sorry I can't tell you something more helpful."

"No, I'm glad you did. Any information is good information."

And it may have been more help than you know.

Heather smiles at me—a saddened, downturned smile.

Then, without warning, she reaches forward and hugs me.

"It's really good to see you, Juniper."

I don't realize until that very moment, with her arms around my back, how much the feeling is mutual; how Heather, Camilla's best friend and my familiar senior all these years, is like a sister by proxy.

I feel suddenly choked up.

"You too," I say tightly. "Tell Lauren—" But I don't know what she should tell Lauren, so I just shake my head.

We go inside and go our separate ways.

At the end of the month and finals four weeks later, Heather's tip has led me exactly nowhere. Or, if you want to be really specific, it has led me in a big fat circle and back a step. The Ducks fob she mentioned made me reconsider Nate—and when I got a look at his keys by suggesting lunch off campus one day, I actually *found* one. A U of O keychain.

Right at the end of his school lanyard.

In an instant, evidence aligned: Nate listening to my Camie stories. That Mom had seemed to recognize him before the bake sale. That it was *him* who suggested we search Camie's room for YOU. What if Nate only did that because he *is* YOU, and knew exactly what to look for, and wanted to take it before I could find it (but not before throwing us off with *Les Misérables*)?

Then we stood in line for burgers and my theory hit a pothole:

A student ahead of us was wearing a Ducks shirt.

Anyone could have Ducks swag, I realized. And if Heather saw the mystery keys last winter, why would Nate have had the lanyard already? He didn't go to school here. He was still living in Eugene.

Answer: He wouldn't have.

Right?

So that idea was shot.

With my You leads exhausted and events to plan at Booster on Thursdays, it's hard to feel I'm doing anything real for my sister anymore—so after break I turn my efforts to a new project: a Camilla collection, inspired by the wall I saw at 8-Ball. I've got a desk drawer full of odds and ends from all the Places She Was I've visited; and because Mom's re-granted access to Cam's room—I think she realized how much she'd lost touch with me when Brand showed up New Year's—I have access to her things again, too.

Now I've got folders of Camie's photos as well as heaps of tokens from places visited: coasters, tickets, brochures, fliers, passes, receipts; broken-down Voodoo and pizza boxes, Dutch Bros stickers, unused chopsticks and boba straws; relics I have pulled from our rooms like album art, stamp cards, sheet music, and old notes passed between us on the road or at cafés. I haul them all to the art studio at school, and Ms. Gilbert lends me the loft again to figure out what to do with them.

I'm laying out some photos on the table there when knuckles rap the door and my favorite voice says, "Special delivery."

I break into a grin. Brand meets me where I stand, pulling me to him by the waist and kissing me on the lips. Brand and I have been seeing each other ever since New Year's—mostly in secret, often here or at his practices. That we're dating isn't a secret per se—obviously his band mates and my parents have some idea—but it *is* still new and exciting, and arguably more of a thrill, to keep our meetings to ourselves.

Our kisses still spin fireworks and raging snow.

"Mm. Fresh from the source."

"Hang on. I think there's a fresher one. Let me check."

He pulls me in and kisses me again, long and deep, until I laugh and say, "Wait, wait! We're crumpling the pictures!"

Reluctantly he allows me to extricate myself and smooth out the images that have folded in my hand.

"Besides," I say, turning away to sort them into their stacks, "I have something for you."

"Oh?" Brand closes the distance between us again. "It wouldn't happen to be in your pockets, would it?" His hands slide down my back in search of the answer. I giggle like one of Rush Hollister's hopeless fan girls.

"No . . ."

He kisses my neck. "Somewhere"—a palm traces lightly back up—"closer to your heart?" I catch his hand and spin to face him and he grins.

"In fact"—I duck out and sashay away from him—"what I have for you isn't here at all."

Brand bites his lip, eyes trailing after me. I fish a flier from my bag.

"You know about the Shaker the GSBC puts on, right?"

He looks over the paper. "You're asking me to the Valentine's dance?"

"Not 'asking.'"

"Ooh," he says, play-huskily. "I love it when you tell me what to do."

I push his chest. "I'm *in* the GSBC, remember? Helping plan the event?"

I watch for comprehension. He still doesn't get it.

"A dance like this . . ." I quirk a brow. "They want live music."

Something crosses his face. "You mean——?"

"I talked to Keegan and booked Muffin Wars a ridiculously well-paid gig next month? Yes. Yes I did. You're welcome."

For a moment Brand just stares at me. Then he says, "God, you're even hotter when you're managing," and prowls forward again.

This time, I let him. We kiss, and Brand cups my cheek and presses a hand low on my back, pinning our hips together. I lean into him and squeeze his torso and he groans and lifts me up onto the table.

"Not the project! Not the project!"

Brand slides me away from my papers and draws back ever so slightly, his lips brushing mine. "Five more minutes."

"Okay, but I'm timing us."

"Liar."

It is definitely more than five minutes before we stop again, and then it's only because a stack of folders—my sorted and unsorted materials—tips over and spills off the far corner of the table.

"Whoops."

Brand helps me down and moves to pick up what has fallen. I straighten the pieces of the groups I'd been working on—a California trip, a Halloween party, a day spent at the Waterfront Blues Fest—while Brand stacks the folders back one by one.

"How *is* the project going?" Brand looks over the table. For weeks now I've been pairing shots of Camie and Bristol to physical souvenirs from both Before and After.

"It's going," I say—which is as much as I can ever say,

without adequate wall space. "I've started trying to put it all in order, but that doesn't work for everything and I still don't know what I'll—"

"What's this?" Brand holds up a page I hadn't meant for him to find: a Venn diagram comparing ANGELA and SPONGE.

Busted.

I make to reclaim the sheet, but Brand holds it out of reach. "'Likes: learning French; poetry; the neon spectrum.' *Juniper.*"

"What?" I lunge and seize the paper back.

"You're not their fairy godmother."

"I didn't say I was."

"If you don't stop messing with other people's business, sooner or later you're gonna get burned."

"They're just observations."

"Whatever." Brand takes out a stick of cinnamon gum and his lighter and sets fire to it, apparently dropping the subject. I hastily pull a drawing board from the shelf and swat the flame out against the table.

"Why are you always destroying things?"

His devious smile. "I'm not destroying them. I'm testing them."

I scoff. "Testing?"

"Yeah. I'm seeing what they're made of. And let's not forget who cleaned up after whose ceramic rampage."

That corks any comeback.

"Look." Brand sighs and pushes a hand through his hair so that the front is freshly rumpled. "I'm sorry. I just . . . I know what it's like to have someone think they're helping you and really, they're just making things worse."

I wonder if I know what he's talking about. "Do you . . . want to talk about it?"

"Not really. But I'd like to make it up to you."

He walks over, smoothes his thumbs over my hands.

"Well, good." My eyes stray to another of the pages he retrieved from the floor. "'Cause I think I know how you can."

"Oh?" He starts to kiss my neck, but I walk us backward.

"You know that . . . scavenger hunt that Booster's doing tomorrow?" Brand's breath on my skin makes it hard to concentrate. I retrieve the page and display it between us. "I was wondering if—"

"If I'd do it with you?"

He pulls back to meet my eye. I push my lips together.

"I'm one of the planners, so I can't participate . . . but I was wondering if you wanted to meet up beforehand to help set up? We're doing breakfast at Pippa's and then splitting up to plant the clues."

"Who's 'we'?"

"Me, the rest of GSBC—and Sponge."

"Sponge?" Brand tilts his chin down.

"Angela invited him."

The tilt steepens.

"What! We all have French together. Sponge heard me and Angela talking about it and said it sounded fun. Can we focus on the matter at hand here?"

Brand studies me. "You want to go together tomorrow. Like—officially."

"Yeah," I say softly. Brand is so close, I could count his eyelashes. "I know Muffin Wars gets more love when the fan girls think you're single, but—" I draw a breath and glance at the floor. "These are my friends we're talking about. Camilla kept her relationship a secret from *everyone,* even those closest to her, and . . ." And it's bred more trouble than I care to tally, and still cuts me to the core. "That's one example I don't want to follow."

Brand's chest inflates.

On the exhale he says, "All right."

"Really?"

He shrugs. "If it means that much to—ow!"

I am squeezing him in my arms, elated. I guess I've never seized Brand with such enthusiasm before, because before I let go he actually winces.

"Thank you!" I cheer, though I try to dial it down a little.

I lace my fingers through his and lean into him. Brand sways with me, hand in my hair, but I can't help noticing he looks winded.

"You okay?" I peel back to search his face. "I didn't just crack a rib or something, did I?"

"With your puny biceps?" He folds me back against his chest. "I don't think so."

I attack a ticklish spot above his hip. Brand yelps and jerks back, then retaliates, then puts an end to the war by pulling me and my lips up to his.

"Sorry I'm late."

Nate pulls up a chair to our double table at Pippa's the next morning. "There was confusion about who was taking what car this morning, and then the usual *Where are you going, What are you doing, Who—*"

He breaks off, belatedly noticing that there are more of us than usual.

"Ahem. New people. Hi—I'm Nate." He holds up a hand in greeting, then inclines his head at Sponge. "Wait a second— don't I know you?"

Sponge actually closes his laptop.

"Lawrence," he offers, hailing back. "But nobody calls me that."

"Sponge, right? We met at the bake sale."

"Yeah." Sponge grins, pleased to be remembered.

"Good to see you, man. And . . ." Nate freezes when he gets to Brand, recognition with a tinge of disgust registering.

"Brand," supplies Brand—not without a cheeky grin of his own.

Nate looks around the table, presumably for some indication of who he is here with, and all eyes gravitate tellingly toward me. Brand smirks and drapes an arm across the back of my seat.

"Right," says Nate, and his throat moves like he's swallowed something hot.

Kody, ever the peacemaker, shuffles things forward by passing Nate a copy of our stop list: the dozen places we'll be visiting and leaving clues before the hunt begins this afternoon. Kody and Angela were officially instated as president and VP after the bake sale, so Fun Fact: The club now has its first full cabinet since 1982. "Okay, guys," she says, picking up where we left off. "So who wants what?"

My eyes move down the list. Our stops are divided into groups, three sets determined by what's close to what and total drive time. The last has only two stops, and one is—

"Cedar Falls," I call, raising a hand. "I mean, the last set—if you guys don't mind." I'm not normally one to call things, but Cedar Falls was one of the first places I thought of to remember Camie. Between the distance, icy roads, and being grounded, I never managed to get to it. But who knows? If she went there with YOU—

Maybe there's still evidence of YOU up there for me to find.

Angela says, "Fine by me. But can I do the second set? That rabbit thing in the other one freaks me out. Ever since *Donnie Darko* I don't do rabbits."

Angela must mean Harvey, the float-sized statue of a rabbit in a captain's coat in the first set—a landmark, oddly enough, for a boat business. With gloved hands and cartoonish blue eyes, he looks a lot like a character who might have been called back, but was ultimately rejected for the roles of both the Trix and the Cap'n Crunch mascots.

"What?" Nate screws up his face. "Harvey looks nothing like the one in *Donnie Darko*."

"Je n'aime pas les lapins," Angela insists.

"Oh hey," I inject, suddenly seeing an opportunity, "the

second set has Maison Leclair. You should go with her, Sponge. That way you guys can pick up some extra credit along the way."

"Ooh!" Angela nods. *"Et macarons."*

Her eyes find Sponge's.

She asks him shyly, "You want to?"

Sponge grins. *"Mais oui."*

Victory jab. I've been looking for unsuspicious circumstances to pair those kids forever.

"Hang on."

Five heads swivel to Brand.

He says to Kody, "I thought you were a Killmaniac."

She frowns. "How'd you know that?"

Brand's eye strays meaningfully to me, and for a long, terrible moment I fear he is going to tell all.

But then he looks at Kody and just shrugs. "Seen your lunchbox." I feel the blood unstick in my veins. "Anyway, don't you wanna do the library thing?" He points to the clue that involves looking up the Latin from Lucy Killman spells there.

Also in Set #2.

"I guess, but . . ." You can tell Kody totally wanted to.

Nate says, "Then you and Angela go, Kody. Sponge and I can face the Great White Rabbit, and afterward he can help me pick out a hat." Hat Museum: second stop in the first set. "What do you say, Sponge?"

Sponge tilts up his hot blue frames and slides out his feet, displaying lime-green Vans. "I *do* have an eye for accessories."

"But—"

My protest is cut short by a shout of "Nate, number

twenty-seven!" Nate gets up to claim his order; by the time he returns the matter is settled, Sponge claiming that he doesn't really need extra credit for French anyway.

Brand nudges me with a smirk. "Guess that means I'm stuck with you."

I fix him with a look and mouth "Date block."

I'm still grumbling when we arrive at Cedar Falls over an hour later: a long bridge high above the ground before an epic waterfall. One of the more popular hikes in the area, Cedar Falls was a place Camie and I used to go to get away. Sometimes, on a warm summer's day, we'd come up with a blanket, spread it out on the grass in the picnic area, and lounge. We'd read. Tan. Drink cream sodas with lemon and blow bubbles. A couple times Cam even brought her guitar.

I haven't been up here since she died, but it occurred to me this morning that it *is* relatively secluded. Nice place for a private outing.

Or to take your secret boyfriend.

"'Thank you, Brand,'" Brand mimics when I shut my door and start up the trail without waiting for him.

"I'm still mad at you," I grouch without turning.

"About Angela and Sponge?" Brand jogs after me, shoes crunching gravel. "Come on."

"But you *knew* I was trying to set them up. You knew, and you still totally date-blocked me."

"*Hey.*"

Brand brushes by and overtakes me, bracing my arms so I'll stop and look at him. When I do, I half expect him to be mad.

But Brand just studies me and breaks into a grin. "Has

anyone ever told you you're incredibly cute when you're angry?"

"*No*, probably because they knew it would be the last thing they ever did."

"Go ahead. Take a shot at me." He holds out his arms in full breadth, a manly invitation to throw a swing at his chest. I glower at him, an exasperated look like I've grown weary of his games, and push aside some bushes to start around him.

Then, when he doesn't expect it, I spin back and aim a fist at his shoulder.

He catches it easily, laughing as I struggle against his muscle.

"I hate you," I tell him to his grinning face.

"You hate it when I'm right," he says, pulling me in.

"I hate it when . . ."

He leans close as he stays my fists, daring me not to meet his lips instead of finishing that thought. I see two options:

A) Let him kiss me and then say, all breathy and defeated, "God damn you, Brand Sayers."

B) Go for the exposed crotch.

I raise a knee to feign B and Brand flinches, swearing.

"I never said I played fair!" I cackle, and sprint off up the hill ahead of him.

"Were you raised by mountain lions?" Brand asks a few minutes later, panting behind me as we reach the top.

I don't answer. I'm already at the bridge.

I take a few deep breaths before eagerly skimming the

messages carved in wood: single words like *Smile!* and *BAS-TARD,* couples' equations, drawings of weird creatures and characters with speech bubbles.

"You're looking for her." Brand has caught up to me, and caught on.

I don't lift my sweeping gaze. "She'd have brought him here. I know it."

He doesn't answer, but I can tell by the way he watches me from the foot of the bridge that Brand pities me. He thinks I'm deluding myself: grasping at straws, groping for traces where there aren't any.

But what he says is, "Want a hand?"

We each take a side. But after several minutes scouring, nothing with YOU or ME or Camie's initials turns up, and with a sinking feeling I realize that I *am* chasing fantasy. There's nothing here. Just another dead end. I was stupid to hope for more.

My chest deflates with a sigh. "I don't know what I even expected to find. 'You' and 'Me'? What would that've told me that I didn't not know already?"

"Uh . . ." says Brand.

"Exactly."

I slouch to the side near the falls and lean over the railing. Brand does the same.

"The guy you're looking for might not be here, Juniper . . ." He inclines into my eye line. "But he's out there somewhere. And knowing you, you're too stubborn not to find him. You'll get him the letter eventually."

I smile a little. One thing I like about Brand Sayers: For all the things he fights me on or annoys me with, sometimes he knows exactly what to say. He also knows when to say nothing, and just let the moment be. Like now, as he rubs my back and doesn't press for an answer.

"C'mon," I say after a while. "We better hurry if we're gonna make Madame's by two."

We kneel to chalk our clue onto the bridge. Then, when I dust my hands and pick up the box to put the stick away—

"Brand!"

He jumps. Frantically I point at where the box was sitting.

On the floor, beside the fresh streaks of pink, are two minute lines inked in black:

i carry Your heart with Me
(i carry it in my heart)

His eyes widen.

"Camilla's letter said almost exactly the same thing," I recall. "'Wherever I am in the unknown ahead, you (in the pocket of my heart) will also be.'" I've read it enough times to know.

"Is it her handwriting?"

I check the cursive again. "No."

"Think it's the guy's?"

"Looks like." I root in my bag for my camera, forgetting the chalk dust. "But I have something at home to compare it to."

"Then what are we waiting for? Let's go!"

I snap a picture of the message, and we start back down the trail for his car.

∞

Our last stop, Madame Viera's, is impossible to miss. It is the only house in the neighborhood buried in ornaments and sculptures. Brand and I pick our way through weird crafts and spinning devices strewn across the lawn and must duck rows of crystals and pipe chimes to get to the door. As he's stooping, Brand brushes and nearly pricks himself on the talons of a metal griffin. He jerks away, catching a whole wall of bells and hanging trinkets with the back of his head.

I laugh as he spins to untangle himself. "You okay?"

He curses at the clanking curtain. "Just ring the bell."

"You know," I say, reaching for the buzzer, "you would *think* a psychic wouldn't need a doorbell. Wouldn't she SEE us coming?"

"Or Jesus, HEAR us?"

The door opens abruptly. Brand and I bite back our barbs just in time to greet the bohemian twentysomething who answers with innocent smiles.

She predicts, airily: "You're here to see Madame."

"Actually"—Brand laugh-coughs behind me—"we just came to drop something off. A clue for our school's scavenger hunt?"

I hold out the envelope we've come to deliver.

"Oh." She drops all mysterious pretense and snatches the package. "Anything else?"

Brand and I exchange glances. We must not conceal our amusement very well, because the girl says, "Have a nice day," and shuts the door in our faces. We stand there, blinking.

I propound, "Not just any psychic has a receptionist, you know."

Brand agrees, "Yeah. Only the really good ones."

We meet each other's eyes and jackknife with laughter.

"Shhhh!" I hiss, shooing him away from the door.

Brand, too busy laughing to pay attention, walks plumb into the chimes and bells again.

"Fucking—" He half swears, half laughs as he sidesteps the jangling forest, at which point there is a very loud *rip* and more cursing than laughter.

"Are you okay?"

"God, I'm *stuck*—"

He pulls at his shirt, currently pinned in the claws of the griffin he'd just missed on the way in. I smother laughter and tears and help him unsnag it.

"Christ," he mutters when the fabric tears free, and darkly eyes the statue before lifting his shirt to inspect the damage. "Don't need to be psychic to see a lawsuit in *some*body's future."

"Did it get—?" I glance at his stomach. "Oh my god, Brand, are you—?"

I reach to touch the exposed skin, alarmed by the purples and greens there.

At the same moment Brand sees what I am seeing and hastily pulls his shirt back down.

I realize that the bruises are too many, too ripe and widespread to be new.

They aren't from the griffin.

Somehow we make it to the car before we start to argue.

"Are you going to tell me how you got those?"

Silence.

"They're from him, aren't they?"

Nothing. Houses blur by out the window.

"When, Brand? Was it a one-time thing, or—"

"It isn't your business."

"Brand. If your dad is hurting you—"

"Stay *out* of it, Juniper."

"*Don't* tell me what to do. I agreed not to tell anyone before, but only because I thought you were safe. You obviously aren't—"

"Jun—"

"—and if you don't do something about your situation, *I will*."

Brand slams the brakes. The car swerves violently over to the curb.

"What?" I dare him when we lurch to a stop, and his fingers clench and unclench around the steering wheel. "What are you going to do?"

He draws a furious breath. His jaw is clenched and he doesn't look at me.

"Out."

I don't move.

"Do you hear yourself? Ignoring the problem won't—"

"OUT."

His face is hard. He releases my seat belt and starts shoving me toward the door.

"Brand—" My eyes prickle with anger or tears, maybe both. "You can't just—"

"Get the FUCK out of my car!"

Face stinging, determined not to cry, I bite my lip in and almost comply when something in me snaps, and I whirl around and shove him in the chest instead. "I'm trying to *help* you, asshat. If you'd just—"

Brand grabs my arm. "I am *not* another problem you can fix to feel better about your sister."

His eyes challenge mine, cold.

Well.

Those last words accomplish what all the shouting, shoving, and cursing could not.

I rip my arm from him, fling the door open, and go. Brand yanks it shut behind me, pulls into the street, and speeds off.

"Brand?" a voice asks two weeks later.

I snap to. Kody lands at the lunch table and nods at the phone in my hand, at the thumb that hovers absently over CALL.

"Yeah . . ."

I put the phone away. She lends a lumpy half smile in sympathy: one of many she has given me since Sunday, a Valentine's Day infinitely worse than last year's. I knew I'd be missing Camie this year; I hadn't expected to fall for a boy and then lose him, too.

I wish I could tell Kody everything. About Brand and why we're fighting; the bruises; New Year's; the time he was hurt so badly he was limping; that the *real* reason he gets himself put in detention is to postpone going home after school. In fact, since the scavenger hunt two weeks ago, I've wanted terribly to tell *all* these things to someone. Not just Kody; an adult. Someone who can do something about them.

But then I remember Brand's warnings; what he's said about interfering with people; how, even if my intentions are good, any action would just mean consequences for him. I talk myself out of it.

"He'll come around."

"I know," I say. But I don't really believe it. Brand is avoiding me for a reason: because he knows, as evinced by the dozen messages I've left him, that I'm not going to drop it.

"What's that?" Kody nods at some papers I laid out before my phone sucked me in.

"Oh, crap." I'd almost forgotten my watercolor washes due next period. I stuff a fry in my mouth and assemble my supplies. "It's for art. We're supposed to make 'grounds' before class today."

"Grounds?"

"Foundations. Like, the base layer."

Kody watches me scramble for something to pour water in. "Cutting it kind of close, aren't you?"

"I didn't mean to. I've just been . . ." My phone stares at me through my backpack.

She understands.

When I nab an empty ketchup cup from the counter, I am on my way. Soon the others arrive, their laughter and lunch trays filling the table: Sponge nabs fries from me and Angela; Angela and Kody argue over what movie to see this weekend; Nate asks Sponge if he's seen any "Cats in Hats" lately, some inside joke they've shared since the scavenger hunt, and all the while I try to paint as Brand weighs on my spirits. I'm so consumed, I can't even muster a smile when Angela snatches up a stack of books Sponge extracts from his backpack: poetry. They've discovered their mutual affection for verse.

I almost don't catch the sticker on one of the volumes when the bell rings and she gathers them up. A familiar sticker.

One from *Fullbrook University Bookstore*.

"Uh, Juniper?"

"What?" I look quickly away from it.

"You're salting your painting."

I glance down at my watercolor. Sure enough, it's now coated in crystals.

"Crap!"

I pick it up and shake it like a grassy towel, but the salt rocks cling like barnacles, and those that *do* come off take bites of color with them.

The result is a sickly looking, blotchy pox in my blues.

So much for that assignment.

When art begins, I have one botched and barely dry wash for a ground. I feel extra foolish when today's lesson turns out to be led by a girl named Emile, a guest speaker from Polaris Experimental Arts. While everyone else tries out the Sharpies and chalk and paint pens she's provided on their grounds, I am left to kick myself and stare at my failure. This wouldn't have happened if I hadn't been drooling over Sponge's Fullbrook sticker, getting my hopes up about YOU again.

I sigh at my ruin, debating whether or not to start a new wash.

"Stuck?"

I look up. Emile is circling around my table.

"Ehh . . ." I suck in air and shamefully push my work into view. "Well, the thing is—this happened."

"Ooh," she pips. "You've discovered salt. Nice! That's one of my favorite ways to add texture."

"It is?" I frown, certain she's just saying that to make me feel better. But then Emile says "One minute," and rounds up some supplies: a clean page, a palette, some water, Q-tips, and a blue bottle of nail polish remover.

"This is another of my favorite methods. May I?" She

takes one of my brushes and works water over the page, adds in soft clouds of purples and reds. Then she dips a Q-tip in remover and pogos it across the surface—and instead of blotches, it leaves footprints, neat little stars in its wake.

The salt and remover weren't corroding the paint, I realize; they were absorbing it.

"See? Like the salt, it's painting with subtraction. But tools like this can give you more control over the shapes the holes make."

I sit up straighter. Did she just say *holes*?

"Wanna try?"

She hands me a Q-tip and the bottle. I imitate what she did and dot a trail in the wet paint: the spots that follow are like freckles or falling snow.

Constellations of negative space.

Emile grins. "*Now* you look like you're having fun. I'll leave you to it."

"Wait." She turns back as I reach for the ground with the salt still on it. I brush off the crystals, revealing more star holes, and ask, "What should I do with this one?"

Emile considers. "You could still try some mediums on top of it. Or . . ." She shrugs. "Maybe it's complete as it is."

In my room that afternoon, I tell Kody about Sponge's Fullbrook sticker.

She cuts me off with a terse "Coincidence."

"But he—" I start to tell her about his love poem, but then recall that that would mean telling her how I found it. "He's still at Fairfield," I finish. "He was in International Club with Camilla. He's in 3 Hall a lot for theater, and he knows his way around poetry. If Sponge *has* a book from Fullbrook, it can only mean—"

"Nothing. There could be a dozen reasons he has that book." Kody shifts on the bed, where we're both sitting, to better face me. "And didn't you say YOU had a Ducks keychain? Do you really think fact-quoting, computer-toting, color-coordinating *Sponge Torres* is our guy?"

I fling myself back into pillows. "No . . ."

But as I stare at the ceiling, I really don't know. There's a reason Camilla kept YOU a secret. Something that made him different from the boyfriends before him. Could it have been age? Social status? An unnatural attachment to his laptop? Who's to say? Maybe YOU isn't Sponge or Nate *or* Brand, or even a boy at all. *May*be YOU is a girl, and I've been looking in all the wrong places from the beginning.

I lay an arm across my eyes and groan.

"Oh, don't be such a drama queen. You'll find YOU eventually."

Always *eventually*.

"And anyway," says Kody when my phone buzzes and I scramble up to check it, but it's only Dad, "I get the feeling that YOU isn't the problem we should be talking about."

I wince. I think I know what is.

"What happened between you guys? I mean, maybe it's none of my business, but you've been miserable ever since the scavenger hunt. Can I ask what's going on?"

"It's . . ." I sigh and drop back again. "Complicated."

I can feel Kody studying me, worrying.

But she just says, "You'll still come to the dance, though, right? I mean—even if you guys are fighting?"

The St. Valentine's Shaker is tomorrow. It makes my chest ache to think that Brand might still be ignoring me then.

"Plenty of people go stag," Kody fills in. "I am. If Angela—"

"I'm not worried about going stag."

"Then what?"

"If Brand and I are still fighting . . ." I stare at my empty hands. "I just . . . I don't know how to handle it. And his band is playing, so if things blow up—"

"Is he avoiding confrontation with you, or are you avoiding it with him?" Kody holds my eye, probing. "'Cause it sounds to *me* like you're making excuses."

I realize, with a start, that she is right.

"But what if I'm afraid?" I whisper.

Kody answers, softly, "Everyone's afraid, Juniper."

The next morning, I call and leave the following voicemail for Brand:

"Hey, it's me." I take a slow breath, allowing the device to record silence. I wonder if he's even listening to my messages, or just deleting them when he sees they're from me. "Look Brand, you don't have to talk to me. But I still care about you, all right? And I won't continue to watch you get hurt. *Even* if that means taking action myself. Okay? I'm here for you, but I mean it. I won't stay silent forever. Call me."

I hang up and slump across my steering wheel. It's late morning and I'm parked across the street from his house, where I don't see his Pontiac. There is, however, another car—a black one I don't recognize—in front of the property. I think maybe it's a loan from Keegan, or whoever Brand is staying with. But then, why not park in the driveway?

I decide to watch the door from my car. I wanted to catch Brand in person today, to talk face-to-face like Kody suggested—to make peace, even if we didn't really fix anything. Not because today is the Shaker; I just *miss* him. And I need to know he's okay. Since today is the dance, I figure he'll at least swing home for a nicer change of clothes at some point.

Assuming he's still playing tonight.

I wait. Fifteen minutes pass. Thirty.

At forty-five I start to worry what the neighbors think, but just as some lady is walking by with her dog and giving me the stink eye, the front door opens.

I sit up. A well-dressed figure emerges, starts down the sunken porch. It's . . .

A woman?

I see the business blazer, the heels clicking on concrete as she reaches the drive, and somehow understand that this is a house visit. But for what? By whom? The woman slips a clipboard into a work bag and comes out with car keys.

The black car is hers.

As she gets in and shuts the door, there's a split in the blinds from the house. I can't see the eyes there, but I feel their heat. They watch the woman start the engine.

Before she can pull away, however, a vehicle in the street slows and pulls into the driveway.

A Pontiac.

The lights go off and the driver's door opens.

"Brand!"

I'm outside my car before I can think about it. But Brand doesn't seem to have heard me; he's gotten out and is busy hefting out duffel bags, his cell phone cradled to an ear with his shoulder. He isn't talking. He looks, I realize, as if he's listening to messages . . .

I start to say his name again—

"Brandon Sayers?"

But the house call woman beats me to it.

Brand looks as surprised as I do. I can't hear what the woman says when she clops over to him, but she must've introduced herself, because she brings out the clipboard again. As she speaks, Brand goes rigid. The stranger indicates the house with a gesture, an invitation almost like the residence were her own, and for a moment I think it is—that this woman is his absent mother. But then I remember the clipboard and know this is wrong, and in the next terrible moment two things happen at once:

1) Brand, who's facing out toward the street, looks up, finally seeing my car and me outside of it, and
2) I realize the woman with the clipboard is a social worker.

His jaw sets and he swallows, hard.

He thinks I did this.

I open my mouth to correct him, to protest, to explain—the words falter and die in my throat. His eyes smolder, lingering on me as he lets the woman guide him to the door, almost too shocked, too hurt to be angry.

Almost.

But not quite.

An hour into the dance, I get a text from Kody:

Brand's here. Muffin Wars is killing it. You should come!

Kody's the only one who knows I'm really home right now because of Brand. I told the others I was feeling sick.

Which, to be fair, is not a total lie.

I peel myself up from my bed and text:

How does he look?

I never got a chance to talk to him, and though I've been trying to reach him all day, his phone just goes straight to voicemail.

Kody answers:

> Intense. But I think that's just his face.

I purse my lips. She adds:

> He's fine. And come on, screw Brand! Dance with ME. I'm pretty freakin' hot in this dress you know.

Angela:

> she totally is. if i were into ladies id be on her like PB on J.

Sponge:

> Okay, but is anyone going to say how great *I* look?

Me:

> Why aren't any of you dancing??

Silence as the troops regroup. Kody says:

> Because you should BE here! Hurry up and get over yourself and stop sucking the fun out of everything. Geez.

I smirk.

Well when you put it THAT way . . .

I'm tempted to fall back on the bed and block out the world with a pillow. Should I go? If I don't, am I just delaying the inevitable?

The next message is from Nate.

> Juniper. We all worked hard on this. You should be here enjoying the fruits of your labor.

When I don't answer, he adds:

> Don't let a boy ruin your fun.

A corner of my mouth quirks.

That's exactly what Camie would say.

I draw a deep breath, sit up despite my turning stomach, and text back:

> Okay. Save me a dance.

The entrance to 3 Hall is open when I arrive, and through it pours the rich, smoky milk of Brand's voice. I follow it in a trance to the gym, and there, in the dark and freckled diamonds, I find him haloed by the lights on stage.

You'd never know, to look at him, the kind of shit that Brand's been through. He utterly lends himself to the music: lips open, eyes closed, left hand working the neck of his guitar while the right one strums in time. He undulates to the beat, feeling the song with his body. When he plays, it's like he's in another world.

I realize I am, too, as an archipelago of drums ends the song, and the crowd dissolves into whooping and screams. I stop and clap with the rest.

"Thank you," he says over the room, a dream that echoes through surrounding speakers. "Thanks."

"There you are."

A hand on my arm brings me back to earth.

"Hey!" I hug Kody in greeting. "God, you weren't kidding. You are *smokin'*!" Her dress is actually two pieces, a black crop top with a green skirt that makes her eyes and red hair pop.

Kody appraises me when we pull apart. "So are you! God, I *love* that dress. Vintage?"

"In a manner of speaking." I fluff the ends of the skater skirt. "It's Camilla's."

I hadn't planned to wear it. But with Camie's door open again, raiding her closet felt second nature. I could almost hear her saying *Go ahead. Take one out for a spin.*

If Kody's weirded out by this, she doesn't show it. She just loops her arm in mine and says, "Well. Good taste must run in the family," and steers us through the crowd as the band takes up a new beat, slower, for swaying. If not for her pulling me along, I'd probably just stand there as the floor emptied out, watching Brand sing into the mike like a lover's ear.

We thread our way to the banquet tables. At a fruit and chocolate platter, Kody splits off for some water. I spy Angela eyeing Sponge in a hot-pink suit that looks *made* to pair with her yellow dress.

"You should ask him to dance."

Angela startles. "Juniper!"

She hugs me, then asks, "Who?" I fold my arms, and soon enough her eyes trail back to the punch bowl, where Sponge and Nate are chatting. "Do you think he likes me?"

"Are you kidding? I think he planned his whole wardrobe around yours."

Angela bites her lip. I turn her toward him by the shoulders.

"Just ask him if he wants to dance with the other best-dressed person here."

She squeals. "Okay. Okayokayokay." Fans herself, calming. "I'm gonna do it."

With a breath, she starts over. I punch another victory jab. Even if Sponge *were* YOU, he'd deserve another shot at happiness.

"Avec toi? Mais oui."

I glance up to see him bow and kiss Angela's hand. From the far end of the table, Nate also watches them go, hands in his pockets.

As Sponge and Angela begin to sway, my gaze wanders back to the stage. That's when I find another set of eyes on the pair: Brand's.

They trace a long, burning line across the dance floor to me. Kody must notice the way they narrow then, 'cause she steps closer and squeezes my arm—a protective gesture. Brand looks away, and doesn't look back again.

When the slow dance ends in a glimmer of cymbals, couples stop swaying to cheer and clap.

"Thank you," Brand says into the mike again. He turns from the applauding crowd, huddling for a moment with his band mates. The bassist nods at something, and then the drummer holds his sticks at the ready. Brand steps back to the mike.

"We're gonna play a little something newer now." Looking pointedly at me: "Something we've never played live before. We're premiering it here, for *you*."

The drummer punctuates this with percussion and the gym resounds with cheers. A countdown, and Muffin Wars blasts into a beat and sexy, foot-pumping electric. There are fan girl screams, and more than one shriek just for Brand (Ugh, was that Morgan Malloy?). All through the intro Brand watches me, even as Nate and Kody pull me into the crowd to rejoin a now bopping and rocking Sponge and Angela.

Why do I have a bad feeling about this?

The intro recedes, and Brand leans into the microphone.

> *"We touched by chance one afternoon*
> *And neither of us was immune:*
> *The spark inflamed to fevered flu 'cause*
> *Boy, I had a crush on you."*

Why does that—?

No.

No.

> *"Your shining eyes, your golden hair*
> *You caught me watching from the stairs*
> *And waltzed right up and said you knew that*
> *Boy, I had a crush on you."*

My gaze drifts helplessly to Sponge.

Sponge has stopped dancing. His face is as blank as a

white sheet of paper. Angela leans in, probably to ask him what's wrong.

He doesn't answer.

> *"We kissed, we danced, the seasons changed*
> *Our hopes and dreams and fears exchanged—"*

Sponge is gone.

Sponge is moving.

Sponge is headed for the sound equipment.

> *"You were my butter, bread, and moon*
> *Oh boy, I had a cru—"*

There's a loud, electric buzzing and the sound cuts. Sponge stands next to the mixer, cord in hand.

The dance floor goes still. Confused faces turn toward the stage, looking to the band for answers. But, with the exception of Brand, Muffin Wars looks as mystified as they do; Derrick, the bassist, even looks angry.

Sponge storms the platform and gets right in his face.

". . . some kind of sick joke?"

The crowd murmurs and gasps as Sponge shoves Derrick in the chest. Keegan and Tyler rush to hold him back, but Derrick holds up a hand and placates them. When he nods at the exit, Sponge stops struggling and throws down his hands, and then the five of them—Sponge and the band—start toward it. Only Brand lingers a moment to hold my eye.

I feel sick to my stomach then because I know what I must do.

I follow them out.

"What the hell is your problem?" Derrick demands out in the corridor. Brand is the last to shed his instrument to intervene.

"You *stole* my *poem!*" Sponge lunges and is restrained. A look enters the bassist's eyes: sorrow. Pity.

"Look, Lawrence." Derrick pinches his forehead as some alarm sounds at the use of Sponge's real name. "Things haven't been easy for me, either, but I'm seeing Phil now, and if you can't handle that—"

"I don't give a shit about *Phil,* Derrick. I'm talking about my *poem.*"

"Poem?" Derrick blinks.

"The one you were just *singing?*"

The bassist's brow creases. He looks around to his band mates for clues. Eyeing Brand I, too, wonder about the poem. How long have they been playing it? Has Brand had this up his sleeve ever since our fight?

Reading Derrick's confusion, Sponge stops struggling. Keegan and Tyler let him go.

"You—" Derrick pales. "But Brand wrote those lyrics. It couldn't—"

"I didn't write them."

All heads turn: Brand stands with folded arms, cool. He says, looking icily at me, "I got them from Juniper."

The heads snap to me as if called by a spotlight. The stares even feel bright and blinding.

Sponge croaks out, "Juniper . . . ?"

Kody, Angela, and Nate choose this moment to pile into the hall behind me. I am paralyzed from head to toe, mouth dry, stuck worse than in those dreams where you get up in front of your class to make a speech and then discover that hey, you never got dressed that morning.

I say, like an idiot, "I can explain."

Sponge says, "But I threw that poem away."

I say, "I found it."

"In the trash?"

At first I can't answer him. Then I mumble something about independent study and found art projects, and Sponge stares and stares at me, incredulous.

Brand says, "And what else have you 'found,' Juniper?"

We lock gazes. Those hooded eyes, those thin lips, those high cheekbones that have become so familiar to me—everything is foreign now. Hard set, the way I always thought of Brand before I knew him. Can this be the same person who offered me tissues and gummy bears? I try to say "Please," but can't manage even that.

Angela touches my arm. "What's going on?"

"Love letters?" Brand offers, venturing toward her but looking pointedly at me. "'Dear Leo'? 'Dear Oscar'?"

Angela's face goes slack.

"Class notes?" He stalks a line from her to Kody. "Index cards? Reading responses scribbled out and annotated with, oh, let's say, a pretty personal footnote?"

Kody stiffens. Her green eyes are sharp, mortified, and when they meet mine I feel as though the breath has been squeezed out of me.

"You found my note?" It comes out a whisper.

What can I tell her?

"Kody . . ."

Her mouth twists. She looks angry, she looks disgusted, she looks like she's about to cry. Whatever Kody is, she is so much of it that her face passes red and goes straight to white.

She says, "*That's* why you started hanging out with me?"

"No! I—"

But I can't finish the sentence. However my motives may have changed, I can't deny that her note was the reason I reached out to her.

When I can't meet her eyes I just nod into my chest. Kody stares at me, just stares, for a grueling eternity.

Then she pushes past and down the hallway for the exit.

Sponge adds, "Unbelievable," and follows.

Brand's band mates, sensing that they've landed in the path of something ugly, exchange glances and silently clear out, returning to the gym. Nate catches my eye like he wants to say something—but then he, too, goes after Kody.

A hand on my shoulder.

Angela.

Angela sighs. "I knew it was you, Juniper—the one who dropped the ticket in my locker. I knew it as soon as I saw you at the museum and Kody said your mom had 'won' tickets, too. I didn't say anything because I thought *you* could use a friend." She pats my arm a couple times, then goes after the others.

At last I am alone with Brand.

Brand says nothing; only looks at me with that grim and hardened countenance. I feel moisture in my eyes, fire climbing my chest.

I shove him. "What the *hell*, Brand?"

"*You* have the nerve to ask *me*?"

The social worker.

"I didn't—"

"*Don't*. Bullshit me." His snarl hits me like a backhand. He closes the space between us and for once, there is nothing romantic about it. "I trusted you."

"But I di—"

"Do you know what's going to happen now?" His eyes gleam, most savage of all. "They're investigating my dad. If he's found unfit to be my guardian—"

"*What?*" I rear back. "Then you won't—"

"Get yanked out of Oregon to go live with my aunt? *Lose the band?*" He prowls away from me and wheels back. "Do you understand what you've done?"

My stomach swims with all the things I want to say and can't. Is this what it feels like to lose someone who's still alive?

"I didn't tell anyone."

Brand's eyes burn in the dim of the hallway.

"Even so," I add softly, wanting suddenly to touch him, but afraid to, "I'm glad somebody did."

Brand pushes back his hair and wipes his face. Instead of looking at me, he shakes his head and goes to pick up his guitar.

This is it, I think. *Now he'll leave me forever.*

But before he does, Brand nods at something down the corridor. He mutters, "Ask *him* about your lost card."

I follow his gaze toward the exit. Outside, beyond the doors, Angela consoles a tearful Kody, and Nate is trying to calm Sponge.

Brand is looking at Nate.

245

Happiness: -10

I have lost everyone (————————————
————————————————————————
————————————————————————
———————————————— x∞).

Just two weeks after the St. Valentine's Shitstorm comes another occasion I was expecting to be hard.

In the late afternoon, after I have forced myself from bed, washed, and mechanically dressed myself, I leave the house and make a stop at the florist's.

Then I drive to Oak Hills Cemetery.

I haven't visited since we buried her. As I shut the door of the car and start up the path through the grass, a wave of guilt crashes over me. I should have come here sooner. I should have come here to see her not because I needed her or because today is a special day, but simply to be with her.

To not be with her.

To remember her.

When I reach the grave I find it already laden with bouquets of flowers, pictures, and trinkets, probably from friends or people Camie worked or volunteered with. It doesn't surprise me at all to see the little notes and charms like you sometimes see at street-side memorials.

I crouch, leveling with the letters cut in stone.

CAMILLA ALEXIS LEMON

"Happy birthday, sis."

I lay the lilies I've brought on the ground and sit on the grass. Clouds wash the landscape in gray, but it isn't raining. Yet.

"I'm sorry it's been so long. I know it might not seem like it, but I miss you. A lot."

I look around. I can't help it; I feel stupid talking to a headstone. But this is where she rests.

This is as close as I'll ever again physically get to her.

"So much has happened since July." Where do I start? "It's a different world without you. Mom and Dad are different. School is different. My friends are—well. I kind of screwed that up." Nate's the only one who seems to still want anything to do with me after the Shaker, but I've been dodging even him; if Brand is right and he found 65, that means he knows my secret, and that fills me with shame. Even if Nate *isn't* YOU, I can't help thinking that I've been his pity project.

I'm beginning to understand just how badly I've hurt Kody.

"I've been screwing up a lot lately."

I look down where the stone meets the ground. A bitter smile twists my lips.

"On the first day of school, like an *idiot,* I lost an Index. THE Index. The ONE card where I wrote what I—" My breath goes short. I can't even say it. "I looked for it, Camie. I *dumpster-dived* for it. DUMPSTER-DIVED. Me. In a way, I guess you'd be proud. You always were telling me to get out of my comfort zone . . ."

It's true. Because of Camilla, I took a lot of risks I would've never taken otherwise: I joined choir. I auditioned for my first solo and musical despite paralyzing stage fright.

I went to a party.

I went to a party and talked to strangers and had a drink and had another and I wondered what it would feel like to be buzzed, tried it, wondered what it would feel like to be drunk, tried it, got very very drunk, blacked out, challenged Brand Sayers to a sing-off, sang and danced and had a drunken blast, belted Queen on the way home and she died.

And just like that I'm crying again.

I'm crying like I never stopped, like the last 245 days haven't happened, like I just woke up in a hospital bed with a cracked throat and a throbbing head and horrible breath and blood-ratted hair and crimson caked under my nails and uttered, "Camie?" into the face of a stranger, and the stranger shook her head and said, "I'm sorry."

"I'm sorry, Camie. I'm so sorry."

I curl into my knees, curl into the ground, curl my fingers into my palms in the grass and sob.

I don't even care anymore. I've lost Camilla. I've lost Mom and Dad. I've lost Brand, who's now staying with Keegan and not speaking to me; I've lost Angela and Kody, who won't even take my calls, let alone return them. What do I care if a stranger sees me wailing at my sister's grave?

After a while—ten minutes, an hour—I feel warmth on the tops of my shoulders and lift my head from the ground. The sun has triumphed through the heavy ranks of gray. Somewhere, a bird sings.

I raise my eyes back to the stone.

I tell her, "I found your letter to YOU. I promised myself I'd find him, I'd deliver it, that I would do it as a final favor to you, but I've looked high and low for the guy and I can't . . . I don't know where else to look. You kept him a secret, you left nothing. All I've got to go by are a couple lines of poetry and freaking *3 Hall*."

Even though I looked up the lines from the falls, found the e. e. cummings poem they belong to, and matched the handwriting on the bridge to the one in the yearbook—what does it mean? (*What are we going to do?*) All I have to go on, as ever, is "You" and "Me."

"Why didn't you tell me, Cam? Even if it *was* someone younger, a girl, I don't care—couldn't you tell *me*? I'm your *sis*ter!" I realize I am wringing fistfuls of grass but I don't let go; I dig tighter, clinging to their physical texture, angry that something so wispy is all I have to hold on to.

I stand and grip my head in my hands, walk away; snarl and pace back and kick at one of the flower arrangements. The vase topples over, taking another two with it.

I accuse, through the tears, "Didn't I keep your secrets? Didn't you trust me? Didn't you know I would love you no matter w—"

That's when I see it: a scrap of paper sticking out from one of the spilled arrangements.

White lilies.

Not the ones that I brought.

I stoop, pick the scrap from a mess of petals and stems, unfold it in a tangle of fingers and read:

C,

I will carry you always.

Love,
Me

Reminders

What matters:

- Camilla and You loved each other. A lot.
- You still cares about her.

What doesn't:

- Not delivering the letter
- My own disappointment at not being able to deliver the letter
- Not knowing who You is
- That I <u>just</u> missed him—again
- That You has been around town, in all likelihood seen my Message horses, and <u>chosen</u> not to contact me
- That I can never be sure

Around noon two days later, I'm walking through 3 Hall for the art studio, where I've been taking refuge during lunches since the Shaker, when I pass Morgan Malloy putting something up on a bulletin board—the same where Nate and I found Cam's memorial notice back in September, and where I have since added a Camilla Was Here print. Morgan's flier, something about Yearbook, is perilously close to the red ink Dala horse I've worked hard to keep visible—so I keep my head down and say nothing, figuring that if she doesn't see me, she can't raise a squawk about it.

But she notices me, anyway.

"Hey," Morgan says once I've passed her. I don't turn around. "This board is for school announcements and activities. You know—things that concern the living?"

There is a loud paper *rip*.

I turn to see the Camilla print in her hand, torn. She didn't even bother to take the tack out—just pulled it off.

"Oh." Morgan frowns in mock pity from me to the split paper. "But if you're worried about honoring your holier-than-thou half, Juni, don't be. Principal Wu wants a line in the yearbook, so I was thinking a nice footnote: in *loving* memory of—"

But that's as far as she gets.

Because that is when I storm back and deck her.

After school, I'm shipped directly from in-school suspension to detention. For once Brand is absent; it's just me, Mrs. Davies, and the Amazing Power Snore.

And at five minutes and seventeen seconds past the time the bell rings, when Mrs. Davies again transforms into a roaring slumberjack, I slip from the room undetected.

I am restless. I'm on edge. I've been pent-up, angry, brooding in chairs since lunch, and now that I am on my feet and prowling the halls I feel unstoppable: both powerful and powerless to stop the chaos crashing through me.

My phone buzzes. Nate again.

I rip the battery out and smother it inside my backpack.

They say grief comes in stages: Denial. Anger. Bargaining. Depression. And lastly, if you follow that model, Acceptance. This has not been my experience at all. Yes, there have been episodes, even periods of each, but the "stages" don't present themselves in any order. They are not chronological like the days of the week; they cannot be quantified and arranged like teaspoons from smallest to largest. For me it's been more like cards, a trick game Camie used to play when we were little: Smoke or Fire. In it, the "dealer" holds up a deck at an unsuspecting player and tells them to call out the suit of each card they display, "smoke" for black and "fire" for red—except, on the first "fire," the dealer launches the deck at them.

Grief is like that: One minute you think you know the rules and it's one card, one emotion at a time; the next, the deck explodes all around you.

Boom.

Now I realize one can't really trash what is, by definition, trash to begin with. But sometimes you just need to destroy things.

So I storm to the dumpsters. And there, without the safety of my gloves or rubber boots, I throw one open and hit OBLITERATE.

I thrash and I tear and I kick and I hurl and I bludgeon. Some of the sacks aren't tied very well and spill their guts across the concrete, spewing food and wrappers and sprays of unidentified liquids. I punt the items that drop out: Good-bye, half-eaten Hot Pocket. So long, fugly poster board. *Au revoir,* shitty crapsack of essays.

Finally, exhausted and bespattered with what I think are ketchup and Mountain Dew, I scream and pound a flurry of punches straight into the dumpster. At first I don't even feel it. Then the backs of my fingers sting. Then they numb again.

When I get home Dad does not ask me "What's the score?" "When's the parade?" or "How many cookies with dinner?" He says, "Your vice principal called."

Me: (freezing guiltily halfway up the stairs) "Uh, what?"

Dad: "I spoke with Mr. Rosen about an hour ago. He tells me you've received both in-school suspension and detention today for attacking another student."

Me: "Does he."

Dad: "Says you gave a senior a bloody nose. That it's the *second* time you've attacked this girl this year."

Me: "Strawberry milk is not—oh. I guess there was some tackling."

Dad: "And that one more outburst like that could result in your suspension for the rest of the semester."

That wipes any cleverness from my face.

Dad says, "You want to tell me what's going on here, Juniper?"

I turn to face him.

It's the first time I've looked Dad full in the face in weeks. I am surprised to see the unkempt state of his hair, how gray it suddenly looks, the white salted in with a few days' stubble. His eyes are strained, foreign somehow.

"Are you mad?"

He considers me a measure. After a few restless, circling paces, he sighs and haggardly sits at the bottom of the stairs. I hesitate, then join him. He gives me a small smile.

"To be honest, Juniper . . ." His tired eyes search mine. "I'm actually a little relieved."

Relieved?

"You've excelled in all of your classes this year, done a tremendous amount of work with Booster, and stayed after school more often than not for those activities. You've been working yourself to the ground."

"So?"

"So your mother and I—Juni, I know we haven't been good at communicating lately, but we're both concerned about you."

I blink at him. "You are?"

He nods. "I know you and Camilla weren't . . . on great terms at the time of the accident. And I admire that you've done so much for those around you since then—I'm proud of your club work and volunteering. But . . . you can't just throw yourself at causes in the hopes that they'll make up for something you can't fix. It isn't fair. If you hold yourself to a standard you can never attain, what can the pressure do but build until you blow a gasket? I'm just glad you didn't hurt yourself or suffer some kind of breakdown."

No need to mention the Ceramic Rampage.

Or my little trashcapade this afternoon.

I bite my lip. "About my long club hours . . ."

"I know, Juniper."

"You do?"

Dad's smile, though worn, is not without warmth. "As textbook as it sounds, and as sick as you probably are of hearing it, we really are all dealing with your sister's death in different ways—and yes, sometimes we butt heads about it, but we're all still adjusting and need to respect one another's needs. I understand if you prefer to spend time away from home right now."

"Dad . . ."

Smoke or fire.

The cards erupt in my chest: gratitude, guilt, remorse. A sense of hope that even though things are broken right now, even though they can never be whole again, maybe they can be okay.

I sink into his arms, find him waiting. Tears fall before I even feel them.

"I'm sorry," I squeeze out.

"You don't have to be."

Dad cradles me, quieting, and when we part he plants a kiss on my forehead.

Then, with a *sniff-sniff* and a double take: "Is that Sriracha in your hair?"

A long shower and a change of clothes later I am back, parking in the gravel lot of Oak Hills Cemetery. I need a place to unwind, to settle, to think. There's nothing I can do about Morgan's dedication—but I guess it won't do any harm to Camie's memory, and it may even do some good. What I need to figure out now is what *I* can still do for Cam.

If anything.

As I'm starting up the path through the headstones, my phone buzzes in my pocket.

Nate.

I push IGNORE and turn my phone off.

When I get to Camilla's grave, I see that the flowers from her birthday are already turning. Some, I realize—a few singles that were left without water—have actually been removed. For some reason, this infuriates me. It's like Camilla's been robbed of something (again). And how devastating, how miserably lonesome is it to think how few days a year, in the years to come, my sister will be visited and graced with any tribute at all. I feel suddenly like a jerk for not bringing something myself today, not even picking any of the wildflowers on my way up for her.

I think, not for the first time: *She didn't deserve this.*

She didn't fucking deserve this.

"Juniper?"

I halt cold. That sounded like—

"Nate?"

I whip around and find him standing on the path behind me. He is holding his hands together, gripping something. Nervous.

He steps toward me. "Your dad said I'd find you here."

His hands come apart.

In one of them is *65*.

∞

My whole body goes leaden.

"Brand said you knew something," I whisper. "I didn't want to believe him."

"Brand was right."

Nate stops in front of me and holds out the card. I reach for it with trembling hands.

"You had it?" Despite my granite body, I feel fainter than a breath of fog.

Nate nods.

"How? When?"

He draws a breath through his nose. "The Club Fair," he says. "When we bumped into each other, we—"

"Switched copies of *Great Expectations*. Oh my god."

I see it again: the mess of books, some of them not mine; "wintergreen" on a box of Tic Tacs; picking it up before I'd finished stacking everything; Brand popping balloons, jeering—

I picked up *the wrong book.*

"You've had this since the beginning of the year?"

Nod.

"You read it?"

Wince.

Of course he did.

"Why . . ." The questions are bubbling up faster than I can ask them. "Why didn't you say anything before?"

Nate inhales sharply. "I *tried*, but—Juniper, it's . . ."

"Try me."

He slips his hands into his pockets.

"I—" With a shaky exhale, he looks away from me. "I wanted you to like me."

My pulse redoubles. All my former theories swarm my

head: that Nate is YOU; that he isn't YOU but has some kind of crush on me; that Nate has withheld and been hiding something all along.

I wait for elaboration.

"I wanted you . . . to forgive me."

I turn my head. This I wasn't expecting.

"Forgive you?" A wave of cold engulfs my stomach. "For what?"

He braces his lips together. A *now or never* kind of look.

"Remember . . . when we were baking at your house?"

Nod.

"Remember . . . how your mom reacted when she heard my name?"

I knew it, I *knew* there was something weird about that.

Nate exhales. "My guess is that she read the obituary."

The numbness spreads to my throat. "What obituary?"

"For Aaron," says Nate. "Chamberlain."

Aaron *Chamb*—

The boy in the baking soda.

The other driver.

Nate hesitates, then adds, "My stepbrother."

My knees waver.

"Stepbrother." My lips feel stupid and blue.

"Yeah."

Nate swallows and watches me. He looks concerned, but afraid to comfort me, like I'm too fragile or might regain myself and strike him across the face.

"Okay." I flex my hands—not in anger, but to ground and steady myself. "Okay," I say again. "You're his stepbrother. But that isn't your fault, Nate—family's not something you can control. I wouldn't hold something like that agains—"

"You don't understand. The night it happened, Juniper . . ." He clenches his jaw. "The night it happened, we were having a party. His dad was gone for the Fourth and Aaron said to come, see old friends.

"Aaron was . . ." Nate looks at the ground. "Could be an animal when it came to parties. He got louder, more animated. Sometimes aggressive. And at this party . . ." A lump moves in his throat.

"I went upstairs at one point to use the bathroom. It was late, almost two thirty. On my way back, I heard something shatter—it sounded like in his room. I went to investigate and—" His brow contorts. "Aaron was standing over this girl, blocking her mouth with his hand. I yelled at him to stop, and he didn't, so I rushed him.

"I was more sober than he was, and after a few swings I pinned him down. The girl grabbed her shirt and ran. I was so furious, I was shaking. I told him to get out, *out,* I'd call the cops myself if I had to, and I guess he decided I wasn't bluffing, 'cause he got in his car, and . . ."

Nate doesn't finish the sentence. He can't. He just stares at her grave, at the hollow letters CAMILLA ALEXIS LEMON.

Slowly he drags his miserable gaze up to me. In it, I see agonies I recognize: the wrench of loss.

Guilt.

He chokes out, almost without sound, "I'm sorry."

My neck goes hot and my hands shake, whitening as they curl into fists.

Camilla is dead because of him.

Because of him.

Because of him.

A second truth rips through me like a hurricane:

And because of me.

I swing.

Nate flinches, but the blow doesn't land—when my fist hits his sternum it is empty, spent, and instead of trying again I fall against him, into his chest.

Nate's arms wrap around me and hold tight.

We both cry.

248

During lunch the next day I go to the art studio. The Secret Board is waiting for me behind the shelf in the loft, an artifact kept safe in its hiding place. I lay it out on the table and look over its pieces: the weathered Life Savers wrapper; Angela's letters to Leo and Oscar; Kody's scribbled-out card; Sponge's poem to Derrick. A hole in the board, a last vacancy waiting for an occupant, stares out at me the way only something unfinished can.

In my hand is the returned 65.

With a brush, I spread glue across its back and affix the Index, a contribution from me and Nate both. And just like that the last gap is patched. I may never have all the cards in my Index again, but for the first time in a long time, I feel like I've completed a thing that means something.

"You wanted to show me something?"

My breath catches. I turn to find Brand in the doorway, one foot in, one out, tentative like he isn't sure he's really welcome. I didn't think he'd come. When I texted yesterday to tell him that I finally talked to Nate, and wanted to show him something up in the studio sometime, he didn't answer.

But here he is.

"Yeah," I finally manage. I gesture at the finished project on the table, and with a wary air, he enters.

"What is this?" He looks the board over. Quickly his eyes fall on the Life Savers wrapper. "Is that—?"

"I took it."

His brow furrows. Instead of demanding why or lashing out, though, Brand just looks over the other pieces, identifying the ones he knows—and then comes to the centerpiece. He might not recognize it, but I can tell by the way his face changes as he reads that he knows it for what it is.

"This?" he asks, pointing. "This is what had you digging through dumpsters?"

I nod.

He looks at 65 again. At me.

His features soften. "She knew you loved her, Juniper."

I know, a part of me answers him, but another demands, *How?*

How can you know that?

When I stare at the floor, he changes the subject. "So you talked to Nate."

I swallow the tightness away. "Yeah."

"And what was his . . ." Brand shifts weight. "What did he say?"

It dawns on me that until just a moment ago, Brand didn't know what 65 said or why Nate kept it, either. That maybe *he* had thought Nate had some kind of crush on me.

I smile a little despite myself.

I tell him what Nate told me: about the party and Aaron; that he felt Camie's blood was on his hands; how, when he found my card, Nate saw a way to atone by helping me grieve for her.

Brand studies me. "You're not—mad at him."

"Mad?"

How could I be mad? I understand perfectly the need to make up for a thing you can never fix. Nate couldn't know what would happen when he told Aaron to get lost. He's only human. And as much as the guilt-worn hole in my heart disagrees, so am I.

"No," I manage.

"Are you . . . mad at me? For not telling you he had it before?" Brand nods at 65. "I saw it in the book you dropped way back at the Club Fair. I didn't know what it was then, but—"

"Wait—you saw Nate pick it up?"

Nod.

"And you never *said anything* until just now?"

His eyes move away.

"Jerkface!"

I shove him, only half in jest. Brand grins a little, apologetically, and I'm not sorry.

I've missed that damn smirk of his.

"Why the hell not?"

The smile vanishes. Brand's lips press in as if concealing a secret.

"What?" I demand.

He makes a pained face. "It's cheesy as fuck."

"Tell me."

"I . . ." With an exhale, Brand roughs up the back of his hair. "I wanted an excuse to talk to you."

"Y—?" Now I feel my face change: screwing up in disbelief.

Did I intimidate Brand Sayers?

"Why?"

"Tell me *you* wouldn't be intrigued by some sexy rebel who climbed up on your stage and outsang you at a gig."

"And you couldn't have asked me out like a normal person."

"Well, when? You're a junior, I'm a senior—it's not like we had classes together. When you said you'd lost your card, I saw an opportunity, and . . ." He lifts his shoulders. "Okay, yeah. I milked it."

"And after? When I wasn't looking?"

"I couldn't tell you after. Then you'd know I'd been holding out on you."

"So?"

"So you'd be pissed! You'd have stopped talking to me."

"Would I? You know, I seem to recall someone lecturing me about assumptions that concern other people. Something like 'You Can't Go Around Assuming—'"

Brand holds up his hands. "All right, all right." He looks behind him, finds the table and sits on it like he's just run a marathon. "You got me."

I watch him exhale and kick his feet in the air. After a moment, I sit down beside him.

"Why *were* you so adamant about me not helping other people? Kody was fine, but then with Angela and Sponge—"

"Sponge is gay," Brand reminds me. "He didn't need your matchmaking services."

I feel my mouth make an O. "You *knew*."

Brand's nostrils flare in defense—but then he just looks down and nods.

"Why didn't you tell me?"

"Same reason I didn't want you matchmaking for Angela: 'cause you were starting to make a habit of 'helping' people when you learned their secrets, and what if

I was next on your radar? I didn't want you 'fixing' my problems. I figured if you saw your efforts crash and burn once—"

"I wouldn't go crying to social services when I saw that your dad had hurt you?"

Brand grimaces. "Yeah."

For a moment we both stare ahead in silence.

"I'm not sorry somebody did," I say quietly.

"I know." I feel Brand look at me, so I cautiously lift my eyes back to his. "And I also know it wasn't you now, so I'm sorry for taking it out on you."

"Who did?"

"Keegan's mom."

"Keegan's mom? Did—aren't you staying with them?"

"Yeah, but it's only temporary." He closes his mouth and shoves his hands in his pockets. "My . . . aunt wants me to live with her in Washington. I'll be moving at the end of spring break."

Even though we haven't been talking, this news guts me like a hook.

"I'm sorry to hear that."

"Me too."

Brand nests his hands more deeply in his jacket, looks around him.

"How is the, uh"—he gestures generally at the walls and clotheslines, both crowded with Camie and Bristol miscellany—"project coming?"

I blow out a sigh. "Same old, same old. I've grouped things and ordered them more, but still no clue what I'll do with it all. Maybe I just like having something to work on."

Especially when some tasks seem forever out of reach.

"I'm guessing you haven't made any progress with YOU," Brand says as though he's read my thoughts.

"No. But . . ." I gaze at 65 and think of Nate, of his anguish at the cemetery. "I think Camie wouldn't've wanted me to torment myself over something beyond my control, either. If I can't find YOU, I can't deliver her letter to him—end of story. She'd understand."

Brand frowns, but he doesn't disagree. "And uh . . ." He licks his lips and raises his pale china eyes to mine. "Are you okay?"

"Am I?"

"Yeah. What I did at the dance." His gaze shies away a moment. "That was pretty fucking douchey. In fact, it was award-winningly, record-settingly douchey."

I raise a brow. "Is this an apology?"

"Would you forgive me if it was?"

Is it wrong that I enjoy seeing him squirm a little?

"Maybe."

Brand stands and pulls me to my feet, leveling with me, and leans in close the way he used to when he wanted to end an argument with a kiss. This time I'm assuming it's to apologize. But what he says is, "I also heard you punched Morgan Malloy in the face."

He grins.

And then, I can't help it—I grin, too. "Three days of ISS and detention."

"If I didn't know any better, I'd almost think I'd been a bad influence on you."

The light in his eyes is contagious.

"Not that I'm complaining," he adds as he leans, but doesn't sit, against the table edge. "But why'd you do it?"

It takes me a moment to remember we are talking about Morgan. When I do, I tell him about her distaste for Camie and her plans for the yearbook dedication.

He shakes his head. "Disgusting. Spiting you in private is one thing, but doing it in public, where *everyone* will see—"

"What?" I interrupt. Brand freezes mid-sentence, startled by my sudden raptness. "What did you just say?"

Everyone will see it.

"I said—"

He stops talking because I am kissing him on the mouth. I feel him go rigid, then reanimate, then kiss back.

When we part he holds my face in his hands.

"What was that for?" he asks, gaze dizzy between my eyes and lips.

I tell him, "I know how to deliver the letter."

The next day I send a group text to Kody, Angela, Brand, Nate, and Sponge. Not everyone is receptive to it, but when Angela joins those who are in the computer lab of the public library that afternoon, I feel lighter than I have in weeks.

I drop what I am working on to embrace her by the door. She lets me, and then even hugs me back.

"I'm so sorry, Angela. I shouldn't have lied to you. It was manipulative, and idiotic, and—"

"In the past." Angela smiles and pats my arm. "Besides, it wasn't all bad. I mean, I met some new people"—Brand, Nate, and Sponge are all here and she waves at them in greeting—"and I *did* get to see the da Vinci exhibit for free."

I laugh. It feels good to laugh with Angela again.

"So what do you need me to do?"

I show her over to our station, the boxes of pictures and Camie's postcards heaped on the tables. A separate folder contains a batch of fresh Camilla Was Here prints.

When everyone is up to speed, we hit the machines, scanning and making copies. I'm pretty pleased with the whole operation, and it fills my heart to the brim to be among friends again, but as the minutes pass and we work our way through album after album, folder after folder, and Sponge jumps on his computer to start preparing the print order, I can't shake the feeling that an essential part is lacking—and might be lost forever.

"Hey." I peer around a scanner bed to question Angela. "Do you know if Kody is coming? She never answered any of my texts."

Angela frowns. "She's been pretty quiet since the Shaker. I'm not sure if—"

But Angela stops talking then.

Because that's when the door of the computer lab creaks open again, and Kody herself passes through it.

She watches me stone-faced, unreadable. I cross the room to meet her slowly, decide it would be pushing my luck to try a hug.

After a long silence, she says, "That was a really shitty thing you did, Juniper."

My eyes find the dusty blue carpet. "I know."

Kody says nothing.

"I . . . I never meant to hurt you, Kody."

"Yeah, well—you did."

The room holds its breath.

"I trusted you. You let me think you were my friend, and all I ever was to you was—was some pity project or good deed."

"Kody, you have to know that isn't—"

"I *believed* in you," she says louder, over me, and I feel like crawling under one of the tables and pulling in the chair. "I believed in the girl who stood up for me and told Morgan off and borrowed my books and sat with me at lunch and told me things about her sister she never told anyone else. And you know what?"

I shut my eyes, waiting for the coup de grâce.

"I want to believe in her again."

I crack a lid open. Kody holds out her hand.

"What do you say we start over?"

I stare at her open palm, at her. Then, because my throat tenses and I can't choke an answer out, I nod and take it. Half frowning, half smiling, Kody says "Aw, screw it," and pulls me into a watery hug.

I squeeze back.

- 254 -

Our library group meets every afternoon for six days, and on Sunday we sneak into the school using one of Brand's keys to set up.

Monday morning, our efforts go live.

"You have to see this."

The first half of the school day is like any other, but at lunch I find Nate and Kody waiting for me.

"Now?" I ask them. "But we have lit next period. Wouldn't it be less conspicuous to wait till then?"

"Trust me," says Kody. "No one will be looking at us."

With a rush, I follow them toward 3 Hall. Did it work? Did YOU see it? Hope against hope—did he return the message somehow??

As we approach, the noise level increases. At first I just think it's the lunch crowd, but the closer we get, the louder the chatter, and when we finally emerge into 3 Hall it is swarming with people.

"Whoa."

I feel myself step back. I knew it would be transformed; my friends and I spent the better part of yesterday wallpapering the wing from floor to ceiling, north end to south, with Camilla Was Here prints, printed pictures, and souvenirs from home or one of countless Places She Was: ticket stubs and fliers and train maps; stamp cards and coffee cups and quarter machine prizes; photo strips and game tokens and art show cards. Sometimes themes crop together: Cam's guitar tabs with album art, pictures of her playing, sheets of lyrics she wrote herself and backstage passes; book jackets with reading lists and makeshift bookmarks; travel trinkets, postcards, shots of Bristol and groups abroad beneath the banner of flags from International Club.

We made my project into a real exhibit:

The Camilla Lemon Gallery.

What I don't expect is the crowd vying for space before the central bulletin board, which we cleared completely to display two things:

1) a row of my post-Camilla observations: People Caught Staring, "Holes," "Falling," the reading response comparing myself to Billy Pilgrim and Miss Havisham, New Units of Time, Instructions for Remembering Your Sister, my Places She Was list, the bullet portraits of Thanksgiving and Christmas, "Reminders," and:

2) the Secret Board—to which we have added Camie's letter to You.

I'm even more speechless to realize that the onlookers aren't just viewing the bulletin board; they're *adding* to it. Post-It notes, index cards, all manner of torn bits of paper.

"What are those?" I ask Kody.

"*Secrets,*" she replies, giddy. "Someone tacked up a pen on a string last period and people have been adding their own ever since!"

My pulse quickens. What if one of those scraps is from YOU?

"Juniper." Nate, who's been standing off to the side, touches my arm. "Isn't that one of your horses?"

I follow his gaze to a photo on the wall. Nate's right: The Dala horse it features isn't Bristol, but one of my many message attempts to reach YOU. I recognize the desk I left it on at the Fairfield Library.

But I don't remember taking the picture . . .

"And this one." He moves another photo.

The keychain at Pippa's.

I walk over to it, too. The picture's held there by a blue strip of craft tape. When I lift it off the wall and check the back, I see the trademark black square of a Polaroid.

But I don't expect the script that says on it, in white:

Camilla, your smile was sweeter than your favorite orange cinnamon roll. We miss you here.

♥ Pippa

I check the library picture. The square on back is covered in neon—signatures along with messages like "I remember when you used to turn in books with thank-you notes to librarians ☺" and "It was such a joy to watch you fly through Harry Potter!"

How is this possible?

"And there's Grimaudi's," Nate continues. "And the music shop. And—"

Suddenly I'm seeing Not Bristols everywhere, photos easily distinguished by blue tape. There must be dozens of them.

I check a third. A fourth. Then three more.

All of them have messages to Camilla.

I raise a hand to my mouth.

"Did you tell them we were doing this?" Nate must mean the community members whose handwriting fills the backs of picture after picture in milk pen.

"No." I sniff and quickly wipe my eyes. "Did you?"

Nate shakes his head. When we look at Kody, she just shrugs.

"Then who—"

That's when I realize:

All of the new pictures are Polaroids.

And the one person I know with a vintage Polaroid camera is—

"Lauren."

Like magic, when I say her name, I see her across the way: by the trophy cases, taping up another photo. She must have cut class all morning to put them up.

When she spots me, Lauren holds up a hand and gives a small, timid smile. I can't help it.

I actually cry.

"Uh-oh. Principal Wu's coming."

A slim, incisive woman in a sharp suit and Nikes is cutting through the crowd like a shark out for blood. She spies a few teachers who've left their rooms to see what all the fuss is about—Ms. Gilbert and Mr. Bodily among them—and powers over to question them. I take a sobby breath and quickly mop my tears so that I can accept my punishment with dignity. It has to be clear, after all, that I'm the one behind this project—and even if it isn't, Ms. Gilbert can link the Secret Board to me. Really, we planned it that way, so that when consequences came, I'd be the one to absorb them.

Knowing the end is near, I move through the crowd (which Wu and some of the teachers are now breaking up at her direction) to scan some of the notes that have been added to the central bulletin board.

Just before I'm close enough to read, a hand falls on my shoulder.

"Juniper?"

It's Mom.

"What's going on? I got a call from—"

But Mom breaks off. Having come through the visitor's entrance, she is only now seeing the walls: the Camie artifacts and Dala horses everywhere. Her mouth opens. She wanders forward in awe, taking everything in.

Her eyes fall on the Secret Board.

"Ms. Lemon."

Mom and I both jump. Principal Wu is stalking up to me, but notices Mom and shifts her focus.

"Excuse me," she says. "Are you Juniper's mother?"

"Yes," Mom returns. But she's still entranced. Her eyes are glued to the bulletin board, and instead of turning to face Principal Wu, Mom pushes closer to it.

She stops in front of 65 and reads.

65

Happiness: 0
A few days before the accident, I told her
I wished she wasn't my sister.
My wish came true.

"I'm glad you're here," Wu is saying. "Now, if you'll follow me to my office, we can discuss the appropriate disciplinary con—"

But Mom isn't listening. She says, "Oh, Juniper," and flings her arms around me with an eagerness, a need, a desperate warmth she hasn't shown me the last two hundred and fifty-four days—and cries into my shoulder.

Things Unsaid

Six nights before the accident, at just past three in the morning, Camie snuck into the house in tears.

I asked her what was wrong. First she said she didn't want to talk about it—then she said she couldn't. <u>Don't want to</u> and <u>can't</u> are two different things, and I was worried. I thought maybe Cam was in trouble.

The next day, I called Melissa and Heather to see if they knew anything. Melissa said Cam'd been scarce for several months now; she didn't know why. Heather said nothing.

But Heather <u>did</u> tell Camie I was asking.

Cam was furious.

"Why would you do that?" she demanded when she cornered me in my room. "I <u>told you</u> I didn't want to talk about it. Why would you go behind my back and embarrass me like that?"

"Like you've been going behind mine? Behind <u>everybody's</u>?"

Camie said her private life was none of my concern.

I said it was if it hurt her.

She said, <u>Juni,</u> some pains are beyond your power to spare.

I said, Oh yeah?

I told Mom and Dad about her secret outing. Mom and Dad took her keys away. I thought I was protecting Cam from something, or that whatever had happened, this would push her to get the help she needed. But all it really encouraged her to do was lash out at me.

And I lashed back.

"Nosy!"

"Evasive."

"Sneak!"

"Hypocrite."

She said to me, You don't know anything.

I shot back, And whose fault is that?

Wasn't I her sister? What couldn't she tell me? I told her everything.

Oh-ho, she said. So that's what this is about. You just need me to need you and you're sore because I don't.

I <u>was</u> wounded she'd keep a huge secret from me. Secrecy was half the issue. But I also felt insulted, and I wasn't about to concede the point.

What kind of sister are you? I asked her. Sisters don't make each other feel this way.

Then I told her I wished she wasn't my sister.

Then neither of us said anything at all.

* * *

I didn't approach her the next day.

Or the next day.

Or the next.

In fact, for the last several days of her life, I was bitter and petty and prideful toward Camie: I slammed things; I stormed from the room whenever she came in; I got Mom and Dad to ask her to pass the asparagus at dinner.

I waited for <u>her</u> to apologize.

Camie acted in kind—until, after five days of fighting, she offered to take me to Shawn's Fourth of July party (contingent on Mom and Dad's approval, of course). I thought it was a peace offering. We all did. That's why Mom and Dad ungrounded her for the occasion; why I accepted.

I never suspected she had an ulterior motive.

Was our sudden truce July Fourth just a ploy? A way for Cam to see You again, or else to give some messenger her final decision? I'm not sure why the letter wasn't delivered; did he never show? Did she just say it instead? Was Cam actually having so much fun chaperoning me that she forgot? (Wishful thinking.)

I may never know.

I <u>do</u> know that I never said I'm sorry. That I never took it back.

That now, I never can.

* * *

Camie never told a soul her secret. But with the 3 Hall Project and owning up to Mom, I've finally said mine. It isn't the "I'm sorry," "I didn't mean it," or "I love you" I wish it could be—but whether or not Brand was right, and Camie knew those things, they're true.

Maybe that's enough.

When I get home from school that Friday, I head straight for the freezer. It's been five full days since 3 Hall and there's *still* been no word from YOU. I should know; I've scoured the 1,001 secrets people have added to the Board religiously. Every day I check, and I hope, and I'm disappointed.

So to hell with hoping.

I want a Fudgsicle.

I'm rummaging past some frozen broccoli for one when Mom appears in the kitchen.

"Hey, you."

"Mom." I turn, surprised. "You're home early."

"I have my first session with Dr. Prasad today." She holds up her purse as evidence. I shut the freezer empty-handed.

"Nervous?"

"A little," she admits. "But it's time to talk about it."

I nod. "I'm glad you are."

"Me too. I'm glad—*we* are."

Perhaps the greatest reward of 3 Hall: Mom and I are talking again.

"Juniper . . ." Mom sets down her purse and crosses the kitchen to lean against the counter beside me. "I know I haven't really been there for you in a while, but I'm going to work on that. And I want you to know that you can *always* talk to me. About anything."

I know without her saying that she's thinking of Camie and her letter. It was hard to miss her other daughter's handwriting beside 65, after all; I could see on Mom's face how much it hurt to learn what Cam had been keeping from her.

"That goes both ways." My eyes stray to the pantry where the baking soda used to be. Mom reads this and nods with a shaky breath.

"Good."

She smiles at me softly. Then she checks her wristwatch and returns to her purse. She almost picks it up, but then stops and turns around again.

"How was school today, Juniper?"

My heart staggers a beat. It still gets me when she asks. But I recover:

"You mean ISS?" As penalty for 3 Hall, I was given a week of in-school suspension. But I haven't minded too much; no one's taken down the display yet—that will be part of my punishment later—and today, "It was interesting, now that you mention it. A guy from Polaris came and gave me his card."

"Polaris?" Mom takes the card I produce from my pocket.

"It's an experimental arts school. The guy who gave me that teaches there. Ms. Gilbert mentioned 3 Hall to him and he dropped by to see it, and I guess he was impressed, 'cause he came and found me and introduced himself. He said they have a special summer program, and if I'm interested, to give him a call—he'd be glad to arrange a tour or put my name in for a scholarship."

Mom's eyes go wide. "That's great, honey!" She bites her lip, then adds, "Your sister would be so proud."

That makes me flush with pride.

"Why don't you look into it? You can tell us more about it over dinner."

"I will. That sounds good."

"Okay, honey. See you."

Mom smiles, and this time actually grabs her purse and keys and starts for the door. But just when she steps out, she ducks back in and yells, "Oh, Juni! I almost forgot. You got mail today—it's on the table."

"Thanks!"

She heads off with a wave. I watch her pull out of the driveway and wave back, then turn my attention to a manila mailer on the table.

MS. JUNIPER LEMON

it says, in plain block letters in marker.

Suspiciously plain block letters.

I snatch the parcel up and turn it over. No return address. But there's a bulge at the bottom.

Yanking scissors from a drawer, I turn it seal-side up and slash the end. Whatever's inside is so small and deeply wedged in a bubbled corner that I have to turn the package over and shake to get it out.

Then it falls in my palm: a small wooden horse, cadmium red with painted white reins and a colored saddle. A golden star glints on its belly.

My jaw drops open.

Bristol.

I rip the rest of the package apart, this time revealing a small white envelope. Inside it is a photograph—Camilla throwing up her arms to the colors and lights of Times Square. YOU is in her smile, her shining eyes.

With shaking hands, I turn it over.

Thank you.

says the back in YOU's thin cursive.

From both of us.

At the coast eight days later, six bottles rise, their dark shapes glinting with firelight against the night.

"To us," I prompt. "Go Team 3 Hall!"

"Team 3 Hall!"

Bottles clink and Brand, Kody, Angela, Nate, and Sponge and I all drink from our vanilla cream sodas.

Today is March 26: the end of spring break, Brand's last day in Oregon, and the first in two hundred and sixty-six that I have purposefully not filled out an Index card. After dismantling 3 Hall by myself the last few days, I'm not so sure I need to anymore.

"Wow," says Kody, smacking her lips as she lowers her bottle. "The lemon really gives it a zing."

"You should try it with some of these." Brand holds up an open sack of gummy bears. "Well?" he prompts when she does.

Kody tips her bottle down quickly. "It's, um." She clears her throat, not quite concealing a laugh. "Fruity."

"Told you, gummy bears," I tease.

"NO REGRETS." Brand loads gummies into his own as if to prove the point. "Anyway," he says, "I'm guessing you didn't ask us here to settle the best way to drink a soda."

"No." The fire, wind, and rush of waves in the distance

all press closer as the group quiets and turns to me. "I didn't."

With a breath, I reach for a paper grocery sack beside the cooler.

"What's that?" asks Angela.

"A couple of things. First—" I reach in and withdraw a collection of papers: rectangles and scraps, some torn, some creased, all weathered and stiff with old glue. I gather them up like a pile of leaves and stand, setting the bag in the sand. "Some returns."

I think I see recognition alight on a few faces.

"Kody." I cross the circle to where she sits on a sun-bleached log and hand over her scribbled-out index card. Her eyes widen. For a moment I fear it brings bad memories, but then she crumples it in her palm and pulls me into a hug.

After Kody, "Angela." I remove the letters to Leo and Oscar and press them into her hands. Angela smiles, then squeezes mine in hers.

"Sponge."

Sponge lifts up his frames as I hand him the folded sheet with his poem, then raises a bag of Reese's Pieces to me in thanks. The deal he struck for his lines with Muffin Wars, not to mention the street cred he gained as a poet after the Shaker, may or may not have had something to do with his quickness to forgive me.

"Nate."

Beside Sponge, Nate blinks up at me. What could I have for him?

"Nate . . . you understand me in ways I think maybe nobody else ever will." I take his hand, and in it, I plant 65.

Nate looks for a moment like he might fight me on this—on accepting what he'd so long kept from me, on accepting my forgiveness and his own—that it wasn't his fault. But then he just looks down at the sand, and nods.

Lastly, I turn to Brand.

"Brand . . ." I turn up his palm, place the Life Savers wrapper in it, and clasp my other hand on top. "You foxy nuisance."

Amused indignation. "How come I'm the only one who gets called a name?"

I kiss him on the lips, earning several hoots and a *bow chicka WOW wow*!, mostly from Angela and Kody.

Brand says, "Apology accepted."

"And now," I continue, ignoring him, "I want to show you all a secret of mine."

I return to the sack and lift out one of two things left in it: a narrow shoebox.

"Is that—?" asks Nate.

I remove the top, displaying the stash of perfectly fitted cards, and file back to the one that would have been today's. "See the number on top?"

Everyone cranes closer. You can just make out

266

in the firelight.

"That's how many days since Camilla died. I've kept track, a card a day, every day. It used to be something I did to acknowledge the good things—something Camie suggested, actually." I exchange looks with Nate. The fire crackles and a log snaps in two. "I've tried to honor that since she's been gone, but it's been . . . really hard to live with her more positive outlook. My Index has been kind of a lifeline to that. To her.

"But then, when I was taking down 3 Hall and looking over some of the things we put up—" I take a breath. Brand touches my back. "I realized that I *have* been. Retaining her influence. The Dala horse prints were from the art class she suggested; my 'portraits' frame the holidays in good memories; when I thought I'd never find You, I made a list of what mattered instead. Even 3 Hall itself was a pretty Camie move."

There's a wet spot on my cheek before I even feel tears in my eyes. I smile apologetically and wipe at them.

"All this time, I'd been afraid I was losing Camie, but now—" Breath. "I realize I can find her anywhere: in places, in the memories that belong to them . . ." I catch Nate's eye again. "In people and situations . . ." Brand's ability to feel a song. "In fact I think, directly or indirectly, Camilla's the reason I've gotten to know each of you."

Everything ties back to her: If I hadn't found her letter, I would've filled out 65 on time. I wouldn't have taken it to school with me and lost it. Nate wouldn't have read it and wanted to help me grieve; I wouldn't have struck up a haphazard friendship with Brand, found Kody's notecard, Angela's love letters, Sponge's poem.

"So . . . tonight I'm letting go. Not of my sister, but of the fear that I won't remember her. Because . . ." I exhale. "Because I know she is with me."

Said the poet: *i carry [her] heart with me(i carry it in my heart)*.

I lift my bottle of vanilla cream. "To Camilla."

"Camilla!"

The bottles chime, everyone drinks, and I throw the Index—all 266 numbered cards, plus the originals, still in the box—into the fire. The flames lick slowly up the sides, devouring it from the bottom like a gnarled log. In my pocket, I clutch the first card. I've long since memorized its contents in Cam's loop cursive:

February 14

1. *orange sweet roll*
2. *that I get to spend time with loved ones*
3. *that I am here right now with a sister who makes me smile and laugh and keeps me grounded*

—but her words mean too much to me to burn, so I'm keeping them.

"Me too." Brand follows suit and crushes the old Life Savers wrapper, lobs it into flames.

After him, Kody creases her lined card and lays it on; Angela crumples the notebook love letters into balls and shoots in two baskets.

Sponge, eyeing his poem, asks Brand: "I burn the original, I still get royalties, right?"

Brand nods.

Sponge dispatches the poem.

Nate, staring at 65, reads its shameful words a final time. Then, with a breath and a last glance at me, he tosses it on.

I wait a beat, letting the flames do their work. When the moment is right, I reach into the paper Lauer's sack for the third and final time.

Kody's eyes go wide. "Is that what I think it is?"

The paper is thick in my fingers. I grip it in both hands. "Camie's letter."

The circle is silent. I feel a sudden squeeze in my chest and I'm not sure if it's because I'm remembering You's answer, or because this is really it. Brand reaches for my hand and it's more than I need; I close my eyes, press his once, and let go.

Then I hold the letter out against the fire.

For a while no one says anything. Once the letter has caught I drop it into the pit and we all just watch the secrets burn, our own and Camilla's, now browning, now shrinking, now crackling in a shower of sparks. I know among them is July 4, the night of the accident, and as the Index is swallowed and bits of ash begin to flake into the night, I can't stop a hitched sigh from escaping. Brand puts his arm around me and I lean into him.

Kody and Angela look on in silence. Nate and Sponge hold hands.

"Told you," Brand whispers in my ear.

"Told you," says Angela, nudging Kody.

After s'mores, Brand pulls me aside for a walk.

Down by the shoreline, where the waves gush and grate back, we fall into pace side by side.

"How'd your coffee with Lauren go?" he asks me.

"Good."

Another perk of taking down 3 Hall by myself: I got to see and consider, in my own laugh- and tear-bespattered time, every last Polaroid and memory Lauren collected from the community. I counted 49 in all, each with notes to Camie on the back; she must've spent the whole week taking more and putting them up. I also discovered some of her own pictures: Han & Lemon sisters shenanigans like pajama parties and snow forts and day trips to Portland.

When I finally reached out to Lauren a few days ago, she actually answered on the first ring.

"It was still a bit awkward, but . . ." I smile and shrug. "I think we're gonna try to start over."

Brand smiles back. "That's great, Juniper."

The wet sand sucks at our shoes. Feeling light, on the high of a special occasion and knowing it's something Camie would do, I steel myself and kick off my sneakers, allowing the muck to rush between my toes. The sand is cool: a balm, unexpectedly smooth. Brand, not one to be out-machoed, does the same.

"Cold!" he gripes.

I toe a few sinking steps in front of him, smirking.

"What?" he asks.

"Nothing. Just—making a memory. This is your last day here, so I need something to laugh at when you're gone."

"Shut up." He play-shoves me toward the water. I yelp and barely dodge a reaching wave.

"But seriously," I say from his other side, guarded against further attempts. "This is it: your last night in Oregon."

"And this is how I spend it."

Now I shove him. Brand laughs and stumbles away, grinning until he trips on a deposit of seaweed and face-plants. This is hilarious until he lunges and pulls me down, and we both roll shrieking and wrestling through the sodden pulp.

When we finally roll out of it and prop ourselves up, there is sand and a slimy frond of kelp in my hair. Brand cups my face and pulls it out.

When it's gone, he leaves his hand right where it is.

"Hey," I say quietly.

"Hey," he says.

"I'm really going to miss you."

"Quit stealing my lines."

He leans closer, lashes fluttering up and down—and then a renegade tide breaks against us, bowling us over. We clamber up, laughing and screaming, and splash back to dry sand.

"Ugh," Brand concludes when we drop onto a washed-up log. Sand clings to our wet skin, coats our calves and ankles and feet. Our dripping clothes make the wind that much sharper, but at least it's warm out for this time of year.

I watch Brand shake his bangs and empty water from his shoes.

"What are you thinking about?"

"You. The band. You." He chucks the shoes into the sand and turns to face me.

"You'll still see us both." We've already looked up the drive: just over two hours. Easily managed weekends.

"Not nearly enough."

Brand eyes me like a man condemned, and I know which of the two he is thinking of.

But I ask him, "Will Muffin Wars be okay?"

A half frown, then a nod. "The drive'll make practice harder, but we'll make up for it when we go on tour this summer. Oh, and speaking of: We're going on tour this summer! You should come."

"I might . . . if I'm not busy with that program at Polaris."

Brand's brows go up. "You're gonna do it?"

I smile. "Haven't decided yet, but I scheduled a visit. I

- 336 -

got the impression that if I liked what I saw, I'd be in."

"Well, if *you're* busy, there're always the dozens of fan girls who'd be eager to take your place . . ."

"In what, a sweaty band van ripe with fast food and Axe musk? Let 'em."

"C'mere."

He pulls me to him. I murmur and fold him closer like a blanket. For a long time we just sit like that, my head against his neck, his arms around me, both watching the waves crash and roll flat, suck back. I find the motion like breath: in/out, push/pull, a living constant. The night feels eternal, and even though I hear laughter, shouting, and Angela and Kody bickering over something in the distance (Reese's Pieces vs. gummy bear s'mores, it sounds like), this moment might as well be forever.

"Okay, you have a point about the band van," Brand observes, at last ending the silence. "But you were wrong about another thing."

I turn in the cradle of his shoulder. "What's that?"

"It wasn't your sister who brought everyone together." He combs the hair back from my face. "It was you."

I smile, kiss his wind-blasted cheek, and nestle back.

"Speaking of *You*," he says, the thought suddenly occurring. "That was a pretty big move back there."

I smile again, this time to myself. "It wasn't so hard after the thank-you note he sent."

"The *what*?" Brand's spine straightens. He turns me by the shoulders to meet my eye. "You wrote to you? Who was it? What did he say?"

I fight the urge to laugh as my smile grows coy. "A wise man once told me," I say, extricating myself from his grasp and standing, "to keep my nose out of other people's business."

His jaw falls. "You're not gonna tell me?"

I ease backward, smirking.

He says, "There are ways of *making* you talk . . ."

I say nothing, daring him to try. Brand leaps to his feet and charges. I squeal and turn from him, running wild, barefoot through the sand, the wind streaking free through my hair. When he catches me, and we roll on our backs toward the star-filled sky, I do not see the diamonds, the glittering shards that have shone there for billions of years, but the blue-black canopy between them. I see it and think of my watercolors, of carving Bristol from linoleum, of Polaris— with a twang, of Camie's hand in them all, of the thousand ways she'll never see her touch unfold—and somehow recognize it is this very darkness, the cutouts, the envelope of holes that makes the stars so sharp and beautiful. All that absence isn't negative space.

It's the gum that holds the universe together.

ACKNOWLEDGMENTS

The book at the end of 526 files on one's computer (don't worry, they're not all drafts) does not go from spark to finished product without a lot of help. These are just a few of the many to whom I owe thanks:

Kathy Dawson and Natalie Doherty, my incredible editor duo. Kathy, thank you for being the first to say Yes and taking Juniper on in the US; Natalie, thank you for picking it up in the UK and creating the very lucky scenario of having *two* brilliant minds to guide edits! Thank you both for giving Juniper a home, and for the insights that reached deep into the core of the story and drew out its best elements. You knew just where to dig and to carve and to polish, and your wisdom has brought this book to life in ways I might have never accomplished otherwise.

Susan Hawk, my fairy bookmother and agent extraordinaire. Thank you for loving Juniper. Thank you for seeing the glint in the rock when it was less than refined. Thank you for being my champion, my industry support, and—in the immortal words of Hall & Oates—for making my dreams come true!

My first readers: Aubrey Cann, Laekan Zea Kemp, Kelsey Jordan, and Stefanie Israel. Special thanks to Kelsey, who read more than once, and to Aubrey, who read so many variations, I lost count.

Aubrey, you get your own paragraph. This book would not be where it is without you. Your generosity deserves medals and drinks and desserts named in your honor, and I thank you for supporting Juniper from first draft to final— and for supporting me as a friend along the way.

Mom and Dad. Thank you. I could express my gratitude a new way each day for decades and it would never be enough, never truly repay the gifts of support and encouragement and possibility you have given me. Although I'm sure you could think of a few (Yes, I'll make truffles every once in a while; no, I don't think I'll be able to introduce you to Stephen King). Thank you for believing in me.

My sisters, Darina and Stefanie. Whether the first draft or just test lines ("Gummy bears?"), thanks for letting me pilot new material on you. More importantly, thank you for your confidence and antics and love, which kept me going.

A special hug and thanks to Grandma ("Gramma") Israel, who's always nurtured my addiction to words—and who supplied the little red Dala horse that wandered into this story.

Natasha Rauf, my creative oasis. Thank you for being there for me as a writer, as a fellow artist, as a friend. Making art with you restores me, our laughter could power a town, you are an inspiration of kindness and talent and taste. Our shenaniganza shall go down in history.

To friends dear and far who had faith in me: Kathryn Tanquary, Saori Den, Peter O'Duffy. Thank you.

To the many at Kathy Dawson Books and Penguin Random House Children's UK who have helped Juniper behind the scenes: Claire Evans, Emma Jones, Harriet Venn, Tash

Collie, and Rachel Khoo, among others. You have my eternal gratitude.

To Liveright Publishing Corporation for gracious permission to reproduce lines from E. E. Cummings. Thank You! I have also drawn inspiration from Queen's "Bicycle Race" and "Bohemian Rhapsody," both written by Freddie Mercury.

To You, dear reader. All 526 files, the efforts of everyone I have named, and likely those of many I have not (please forgive me if I've missed you; I am no less grateful to you!), have led to this moment and the story you now hold in your hands. Thank you for picking it up and bringing it to life.

With hugs to my sisters.
Stef, Darina, if you're reading this—YOU MADE IT!
Fame by association!